Christmas 1986

To Mrs. D. Nairn,

From Leuha & Bales.

with best wishes.

Best Short Stories 1986

EDITED BY GILES GORDON AND DAVID HUGHES

HEINEMANN : LONDON

William Heinemann Ltd
10 Upper Grosvenor Street, London W1X 9PA

LONDON   MELBOURNE
JOHANNESBURG   AUCKLAND

This collection first published in Great Britain 1986
This collection, together with the introduction and notes, is
copyright © Giles Gordon and David Hughes 1986

ISBN 0 434 35419 8

Printed and bound in Great Britain by
Biddles Ltd, Guildford and King's Lynn

Contents

INTRODUCTION

THIS VOLUME HAS been put together with affection for the most exigent and elegant of prose forms, and with far more work than either of us anticipated at the outset. We are both addicts of the short story – that well-rounded finish to the day, that glimpse of bedtime revelation or new world – who have never altogether subscribed to the received idea that its more ambitious authors are not numerous and, in any case, lack outlets.

Yet when we decided to work together on an annual volume of the best stories the previous twelve months had to offer, whether published in magazine, periodical or newspaper or heard on the air, we did not fully anticipate either the vigour or the size of the output. Although it was decided to exclude American writers – they have their own annual volumes – we imagined it would be possible to read at leisure every story published. When that ideal turned out to be a task that would cost us both a year's work, we sought help from editors and literary agents by asking them to select their personal favourites for submission. So it is their taste and time, in generously suggesting scores of stories between them, that underlie these pages. In our final choice, we doubt if we have missed a masterpiece. But there are plenty of stories left over that would honour a book twice this size.

We determined that every genre – including mystery, historical romance, SF – could be represented; the example chosen just had to be the best of its kind. That is why the range of publications in which these twenty pieces first appeared is wide. If no fewer than four come from the *London Magazine* and two from *Stand*, both edited for decades with commitment to the best of the art by Alan Ross and Jon Silkin respectively, we were delighted to find that the women's magazines, once considered receptacles of trash, are now regularly providing their readers with fiction of high quality. *Cosmopolitan* and *Woman's Own* are both represented; our regret in not including this year a story from *Woman's Journal* is a tribute to that magazine's devotion to the craft of the well-turned tale.

Our contributors come from, and cast light upon, all four countries of the British Isles. India, South Africa and Australia are present too. In kind, the stories swing from the traditional beginning, middle and end to the more demanding stops and starts of the avant-garde. Without exception they meet the classic challenge of the form, to display individuals in moments of stress or illumination, sometimes at a point of crisis in their lives which, thanks to the skill of the telling, reflects their whole existence; and something ours. Varying in tone from light to dark, they are often both.

No reader will relish every story equally. But most of us will recognize in all of them a touch of this or that truth. Some of the writers are among our best-known, others at the launch of their literary lives. For those interested to read further in particular authors, we have provided notes on our contributors.

Giles Gordon
David Hughes
June 1986

Best Short Stories 1986

Answers to a Questionnaire

J. G. BALLARD

1) Yes.
2) Male (?)
3) c/o Terminal 3, London Airport, Heathrow.
4) 27.
5) Unknown.
6) Dr Barnardo's Primary, Kingston-on-Thames; HM Borstal, Send, Sussex; Brunel University Computer Sciences Department.
7) Floor cleaner, Mecca Amusement Arcades, Leicester Square.
8) If I can avoid it.
9) System Analyst, Sperry-Univac, 1979–83.
10) Manchester Crown Court, 1984.
11) Credit card and computer fraud.
12) Guilty.
13) Two years, HM Prisons, Parkhurst.
14) Stockhausen, De Kooning, Jack Kerouac.
15) Whenever possible.
16) Twice a day.
17) NUS, herpes, gonorrhoea.
18) Husbands.
19) My greatest amibition is to turn into a TV programme.

20) I first saw the deceased on 17 February 1986, in the chapel at London Airport. He was praying in the front pew.

21) At the time I was living in an out-of-order cubicle in the air traffic controllers' washroom in Terminal 3.

22) Approx. 5 ft 7 in, aged 33, slim build, albino skin and thin black beard, some kind of crash injuries to both hands. At first I thought he was a Palestinian terrorist.

23) He was wearing the stolen uniform trousers of an El Al flight engineer.

24) With my last money I bought him a prawnburger in the mezzanine cafeteria. He thanked me and, although not carrying a bank-card, extracted £100 from a service till on the main concourse.

25) Already I was convinced that I was in the presence of a messianic figure who would help me to penetrate the Nat West deposit account computer codes.

26) No sexual activity occurred.

27) I took him to Richmond Ice Rink where he immediately performed six triple salchows. I urged him to take up ice-dancing with an eye to the European Championships and eventual gold at Seoul, but he began to trace out huge double spirals on the ice. I tried to convince him that these did not feature in the compulsory figures, but he told me that the spirals represented a model of synthetic DNA.

28) No.

29) He gave me to understand that he had important connections at the highest levels of government.

30) Suite 17B, London Penta Hotel. I slept on the floor in the bathroom.

31) Service tills in Oxford Street, Knightsbridge and Earls Court.

32) Approx. £275,000 in three weeks.

33) Porno videos. He took a particular interest in Kamera Klimax and Electric Blue.

34) Almost every day.

35) When he was drunk. He claimed that he brought the gift of eternal life.

36) At the Penta Hotel I tried to introduce him to Torvill and

Dean. He was interested in meeting only members of the Stock Exchange and Fellows of the Royal Society.

37) Females of all ages.

38) Group sex.

39) Marie Drummond, 22, sales assistant, HMV Records; Denise Attwell, research supervisor, Geigy Pharmaceuticals; Florence Burgess, 55, deaconess, Bible Society Bookshop; Angelina Gomez, 23, air hostess, Iberian Airways; Phoebe Adams, 43, cruise protestor, Camp Orange, Greenham Common.

40) Sometimes, at his suggestion.

41) Unsatisfactory.

42) Premature ejaculation; impotence.

43) He urged me to have a sex-change operation.

44) National Gallery, Wallace Collection, British Museum. He was much intrigued by representations of Jesus, Zoroaster and the Gautama Buddha, and commented on the likenesses.

45) With the permission of the manager, NE District, British Telecom.

46) We erected the antenna on the roof of the Post Office Tower.

47) 2500 KHz.

48) Towards the constellation Orion.

49) I heard his voice, apparently transmitted from the star Betelgeuse 2000 years ago.

50) Interference to TV reception all over London and the South-East.

51) No. 1 in the Jictar Ratings, exceeding the combined audiences for Coronation Street, Dallas and Dynasty.

52) Regular visitors included Princess Diana, Prince Charles and Dr Billy Graham.

53) He hired the Wembley Conference Centre.

54) 'Immortality in the Service of Mankind'.

55) Guests were drawn from the worlds of science and politics, the church, armed forces and the Inland Revenue.

56) Generous fees.

57) Service tills in Mayfair and Regent Street.

58) He had a keen appreciation of money, but was not impressed when I told him of Torvill and Dean's earnings.

59) He was obsessed by the nature of the chemical bond.

60) Sitting beside him at the top table were: (1) The Leader of Her Majesty's Opposition, (2) The President of the Royal Society, (3) The Archbishop of Canterbury, (4) The Chief Rabbi, (5) The Chairman of the Diners Club, (6) The Chairman of the Bank of England, (7) The General Secretary of the Inland Revenue Staff Federation, (8) The President of Hertz Rent-a-Car, (9) The President of IBM, (10) The Chief of the General Staff, (11) Mr Henry Kissinger, (12) Myself.

61) He stated that synthetic DNA introduced into the human germ plasm would arrest the process of ageing and extend human life almost indefinitely.

62) Perhaps 1 million years.

63) He announced that Princess Diana was immortal.

64) Astonishment/disbelief.

65) He advised the audience to invest heavily in leisure industries.

66) The value of the pound sterling rose to $8.75.

67) American TV networks, *Time Magazine*, *Newsweek*.

68) The Second Coming.

69) He expressed strong disappointment at the negative attitude of the Third World.

70) The Kremlin.

71) He wanted me to become the warhead of a cruise missile.

72) My growing disenchantment.

73) Sexual malaise.

74) He complained that I was spending too much time at Richmond Ice Rink.

75) The Royal Proclamation.

76) The pound sterling rose to $75.50.

77) Prince Andrew. Repeatedly.

78) Injection into the testicles.

79) The side-effects were permanent impotence and sterility. However, as immortality was ensured, no further offspring would be needed and the procreative urge would atrophy.

80) I seriously considered a sex-change operation.

81) Government White Paper on Immortality.

82) Compulsory injection into the testicles of the entire male population over 11 years.

83) Smith & Wesson short-barrel 38.

84) Entirely my own idea.

85) Many hours at Richmond Ice Rink trying unsuccessfully to erase the patterns of DNA.

86) Westminster Hall.

87) Premeditated. I questioned his real motives.

88) Assassination.

89) I was neither paid nor incited by agents of a foreign power.

90) Despair. I wish to go back to my cubicle at London Airport.

91) Between Princess Diana and the Governor of Nevada.

92) At the climax of Thus Spake Zarathustra.

93) 7 feet.

94) Three shots.

95) Blood Group O.

96) I did not wish to spend the rest of eternity in my own company.

97) I was visited in the death cell by Mr Terry Waite, special envoy of the Archbishop of Canterbury.

98) That I had killed the Son of God.

99) He walked with a slight limp. He told me that, as a condemned prisoner, I alone had been spared the sterilising injections, and that the restoration of the national birthrate was now my sole duty.

100) Yes.

The Last Island Boy

GEORGE MACKAY BROWN

'CHRISTMAS!' SAID THE man. 'What do we want with Christmas? What's Christmas to us? All I know is, it's winter. The worst storms are still to come. Will we last through the winter? That's what I'd like to know.'

The woman said nothing. She put a few pieces of salt fish into the pot and began to peel potatoes.

Outside, it was another grey cold day. Sometimes the greyness outside would darken, as if another shadow or cloud had been mixed into it. Then sleet would blatter on the window for a while, a bleak cold sound.

'We should never have come here in the first place,' said the man. 'It hasn't worked. But if I hadn't come – if I hadn't left that office in Leeds and come, I would be tormenting myself still with the dream – the island of innocence and peace in the north, face to face with the elements. That, I thought in my ignorance, was how people should live . . .'

The boy had just been ferried across from the bigger island that had the school on it. From the few lights on the pier he had been ferried, the sole passenger, to the lamp in the solitary island croft.

'It's just that they're having a Christmas party in the school,' he said.

The woman broke another peat into the range and stirred the ribs till a new flame appeared.

'Come over and warm yourself,' she said.

The next day was Saturday. The boy lay warm in the nest of his bed till nine o'clock.

When he got up and went into the kitchen the lamp was still lit. The woman was baking at the table. Her face was flushed. It seemed to be a different baking from the usual Saturday morning oatcakes and floury bannocks. There were three stone jars on the table. She was intent on a cookery book. The whole stove seemed to throb with the red glow of the peat.

'There's tea in the pot,' said the woman. 'The porridge is a bit cold.'

'Where is he?' said the boy.

'He's out in the boat,' said the woman. 'There's a storm forecast. He wants to get a few fish if he can.'

It was a much better morning. The night wind had swept the sky clear of the last rag of cloud. The sky was a delicate blue, like china. The sun was low in the south-east, making silver undulations on the rise and fall of the sea.

'Goodness!' cried the woman, 'the sun's out . . .' She screwed down the wick and blew out the lamp flame with a small spurt of breath.

The boy wandered outside, among a quick welcome and dispersal of hens (because they saw he had no food for them).

He had the whole morning to himself. He wondered if it would be possible, before dinner-time, to visit every ruined croft in the island. . . . No, it wouldn't be possible. The midwinter sun would be down before he had half completed his round, and he might not find his way home again.

Still, he would manage six or seven.

The first croft, Smert, wasn't far away, across two fields and a wet ditch. It was still in passable shape, Smert. An island family had lived there till two years before, then suddenly they had sold up and gone to live in the town. The croft had been advertised for sale. Nobody had wanted it. (Who would want to live and work in a dying island?)

But for his dark resolute father, there were no crofters in the island now.

The boy peered through the window of Smert. There was a table and two chairs inside, a box bed, a rusted range; a picture of the Channel Fleet on one wall. But the place breathed dampness and decay.

The boy left Smert and ran towards the next croft. It was an utter ruin. He did not know what its name was. Naked rafters showed through the few roofing flags that remained. Door and windows were vacant rectangles. Long and low the croft lay on the first slope of the hill, as if it had sailed forever on that green wave, from the foundation stone to the first sag of the roof: ten generations maybe. Beyond the living-quarters lay the remnants of byre and barn; the floor a confusion of stones.

And yet, thought the boy, there was a freshness and cleanness about it, like a bone in the wind and rain, now that the last rags and shards of life were no longer there.

The nameless place must have been deserted for half a century, at least.

From the top of the low island hill the boy could see seven or eight other islands. His own island was spread beneath him like a drab brown cloth, pitted with ruins and half-ruins, and a few mounds from the very ancient past.

The winter sun had reached its zenith and in another three hours, would go, a cold bright diamond, into the Atlantic.

Ah, there was the boat, under the cliff, with the man in it! He was leaning over and looking deep into the sea, one oar upraised.

And there she was, the woman, outside the door, throwing cold porridge and breadcrumbs and oats to the hens.

(Since the time of the poor harvest, they had stopped using names. 'The man', 'the woman', 'the boy' – that's how they referred to each other.)

He drifted down, slowly, to the biggest house in the island, the laird's Hall. The tall house was stubborn in its fight against time. The great door still stood, and the shutters, though the paint had long since peeled from them and they were beginning to warp. But the stonework – it could outface centuries, so firmly the masonry had been dressed and set. The walls of the great garden, too, showed not a breach or a fissure, though the garden itself – once plotted into a formal Italian style by two gardeners from the south – was a jungle of weeds and nettles.

The tall octagonal sundial intrigued the boy. Last summer the indicator had thrown the sun's shadow on precisely the right mark. The wet autumn had corroded it, and time fell a blank on the stone's intricate angles.

Here, in the great drawing-room, there would have been winter balls a hundred years ago, rustling of silk gowns, music of violin and piano, old formal courtesies of invitation and acceptance, smells of Havana cigars, hot punch, trout, grouse.

Standing on tiptoe outside the tall window, the boy felt a desolation he had not known before. Where was it now, all that wealth and beauty? When had the roses and butterflies left the garden?

He ran, squelching through a wet field to the shore. Well, he had heard all about this ruin and its former tenant. It had been called 'Jamaica', and Captain Haraldson had lived there between his retirement from the sea until he went his last voyage to the hospital, and soon into the deeper waters of death.

The islanders said he hadn't been a skipper at all; an ordinary seaman all his career, at best maybe bosun. And the left forearm he said had been taken by a shark – that, said the last islanders, had been the result of a wild punch-up in Amsterdam in his youth. 'That shark,' the skipper had said, 'he had my arm, but I had his life – I ripped him open from fin to tail!' And the wives he had had, in the Gilbert Islands and San Francisco and St John's, and the horde of children, scattered world-wide . . . 'It's a funny thing,' old Widow Wilson had said, 'whenever he came on leave, not a lass would look at him, in this island or that.'

The ruin of the skipper's house stood right on the edge of the sea-banks. Erosion was eating so fast into this part of the shore, that a cornerstone of the house was actually overhanging the edge of the shallow cliff. It would not be very long, thought the boy, till all those stones would be mingled with the shore stones and the sea.

He wondered where the old sailor had sat and told his stories. Over there it must be, in a chair beside that blackened stone, the hearth. He stooped and turned a stone. The sun through the broken west wall took a dull gleam from a coin! The boy picked it up. It had strange devices on either side, and foreign lettering. Was it – could it conceivably be – gold? It was yellow and untarnished. Had the skipper hidden it away for some purpose? Had it fallen out of his coin-box one night and rolled into an interstice of the flagstone floor?

Whatever had happened, it was a marvellous thing to have found! He would carry it home. Perhaps it would save them from ruin that the man said was staring them in the face . . .

The thought that next year the island might be utterly empty put a shiver of fear over him.

He stowed the coin carefully in his pocket.

Across the Sound he could see the island where he went to school five mornings a week. He looked. Yes, there it was, the big building at the back of the village, between the church and the shop. As he looked, the declining sun flashed from the school window, suddenly, intolerable brightness, as if the interior was a mass of cold silver flames.

He walked along the shore, eastwards. A few skeletons of fishing boats rotted among the stones. He could just make out the name of one boat: *Star*.

Going up the shore path to the road above, he passed the green mound with its few underground dwellings where the archaeologists from England had worked all last summer. There, in stone hollows not so very different from the crofts of recent times, had lived the first islanders of all, with their fish-oil lamps and clay pots of grain and milk. But were they really the first? The boy's mind moved back through time to a still earlier folk. Ah, how cruel it must have been for them in winter, clad in sealskin and otter skin, with only a few shreds of beach-growth to put in their mouths! And yet they had endured till the light's return. How wonderful it must have been to those shadowy folk, the sun of early summer, the springing grass, larksong, the silver legions of fish . . .

Right on the ness stood the ruins of a little medieval monastery.

The boy thought he might just get there before the sun went down. Then he could find his way home well enough in the sunset afterglow.

How tired he was! Here and there, the chapel walls were almost at ground level, but the apse and stone floor of the nave were still there, and a single arch in the south.

About a dozen monks had lived there, the teacher had told him, and the brothers had farmed, fished, kept bees, and recited or sung the 'office' that was appropriate to each season of the turning year.

As the boy sat against a grey-lichened wall near the ruined floor, he heard them singing. The separate voices, high and low, grave yet full of joy, interwove, mingled, blended. There issued from the invisible choir a texture of peace deeper than any natural silence. The hymn was in a foreign language – Norwegian? Gaelic? – and yet the boy seemed to grasp a meaning at once.

> *Benedictus es, qui ambulas*
> *super pennas ventorum, super*
> *undas maris. Et laudabilis,*
> *et gloriosus in secula . . .*

The sun was down. The first wind of night began to stir, and it shifted a thin wash of sea over the shore stones below, again and again.

The voices in the choir mingled with the wind and the sea and were lost . . .

Ah, there was the lamp in the window!

The boy ran up the last slope to the door.

A rich spicy smell met him at the threshold. The woman – his mother – had baked a large cake.

There it stood on the table, cooling on a wire tray.

The man – his father – was not long in from the sea. A basket of haddocks stood at the door. The fisherman was testing the edge of a knife on his thumb.

'I'm glad you're home,' said the woman. 'There's going to be another storm.'

The wind was beginning to make songs in the chimney.

The boy could hear, through the open door, the noise of the breakers against the stones.

The cow lowed from the byre.

Dealing in Fictions

CHRISTOPHER BURNS

I

(a)

LIFE ALWAYS LEAVES you unfinished.

The love affair that is over and cannot die, the major work that becomes increasingly more complex and expansive but will not stop, the problems of living from day to day that may be remoulded but remain beyond solution – all these resist an end. Their existence continues. Art can be written off, disposed of, forgotten. In life the blade never truly falls.

So Peter felt as the wife he had deserted moved beneath him.

They made love with the intensity of those who have something to prove to the other, and it left them gasping. It lifted them and it dumped them. As their hearts and lungs eased they began again to hear the city noises coming in through the open window – traffic, faraway radios, construction work on high buildings. The curtains let in the sun and moved in the roof-high breeze.

Ruth's book lay beside the bed. Its pages turned.

The breeze paused, the pages rested, and Peter looked at paired images that after a few seconds he realized belonged to a diptych. That geometrical burst of discolouration at the inner edge of each image, like a stylized explosion or star, was the hinge. A glowing Christ, his face suffused by joy and his forehead bloody with thorns, terrified and humbled an everyday family with his splendour. Elsewhere lovers entered their earthly bliss unaware that a skeleton enclosed them with its scythe. At the opposite side a saint ascended to heaven carried by angels with the wings of swans but the faces of children. Beneath them, in the sulphurous caverns of hell, devils tortured the sinful forever under the eyes of extravagant beasts.

The breeze lifted again.

Such blends of the erotic and the macabre, of real worlds and the fantastic, gave Peter little insight or pleasure. The wind blurred the pages. They toppled with a whirr like passing wings. Ruth reached over him and closed it.

He must have dozed off for about ten minutes, because the next thing was that he was in bed on his own and a voice was coming from the other room.

She had switched on the radio cassette and was recording a talk by a man with exact tones who used long words and jargon like *post-structuralism*, *ontology* and *genre differentiation*. 'Heavy stuff,' Peter said, sitting down.

'I'm interested,' she said.

'I know.'

'He died a couple of days ago. The man he's talking about.'

'Who?'

'Zurawski. He was a Polish literary critic and . . . well, cultural analyst, I suppose you'd call him.'

'You always amazed me with the amount you knew,' he said softly.

'You always said it was misplaced knowledge,' she said.

Later there was music. They sat and drank coffee. An ambulance careered down the road outside with its horn high and penetrating.

'Still given up smoking?' she said.

'I try. Twenty a day?'

She shook her head. 'Rather more. My luxury. Or my vice.'

'A common enough symptom, I suppose.'

It was as if she had something to launch from. 'Ah,' she said, 'we have symptoms now. Marriage break-up as a medical condition. With symptoms, progression and, by inference, cure. I think of it much more destructively. Like an execution or an

explosion. Someone just cuts your life in half. Like the condemned prisoner I was eating hearty breakfasts to the last.'

'I didn't mean you to take me so literally. In fact I didn't even
want you to start talking about it.'

'We can hardly ignore it.'

'We ignored it just now. When we were together.'

'I didn't mean that to happen.'

'You think I planned it?' He had, of course, planned it. 'Some
things just happen.'

'That's a slick, glib way of avoiding responsibility.'

Peter got up and looked out of the window. London stretched
away on all sides, modulating towards colourlessness with distance. The streets below were coloured stone, cement, rooftiles.
And it was difficult to believe that all those people down there
had nothing in common but accidents of location.

That his marriage to Ruth and his subsequent affair were the
result of chance encounters, nothing more.

'All right,' he said, and stopped. Despite himself, and despite
all of Ruth's alterations to it, the flat was beginning to be familiar
again. The furniture, the poster in the kitchen, the shelf of ageing
paperbacks in the corner, the worn carpet – they were all his. He
belonged with them.

'I can't stop thinking of this as my home,' he said weakly.
Ruth pursed her lips.

'Well?'

'Well what?'

'Can't you say anything? Anything at all?'

'I can probably say lots of things very badly. I haven't been
able to sharpen my phraseology for a while now. Unlike you.'

'That's *over* with, for Christ's sake. How many more times do
I have to say it?'

'Oh, I could practise some telling phrases on Louisa, but she
is a little young. I don't think she'd appreciate it. It would
probably make her very disturbed.'

'You always knew how to rub salt into a wound.'

They each said nothing for a while.

'I didn't come round here planning for us to go to bed, or
anything like that,' Peter said.

He sat and fixed his eyes on something. It was a painting Louisa must have brought home from school. She would be there now running round the yard with all the other kids, giggling and enjoying the sunshine. He supposed that her teacher had asked them all to paint their families. He was gratified and guilty that he was on it. At least he supposed that; there were three bulbous heads with great wounds of paint for the features. He was sure one would be him.

'Something happened that forced us apart,' he said wearily. 'It was all my fault. I admit that. I was stupid and immature and all that sort of stuff. Just think of me as being ill for a while. That's all.'

She was silent, then asked quietly, 'Does this feel like home?'

He nodded.

'Sorry,' he said, paused, and asked, 'And you?'

'I don't know my own thoughts,' she said.

'Give it a try, go on.'

She put her forehead against the back of her wrist. 'One day I want you back. I think I feel that way now. It's easy to believe that my natural position in life is as your wife and Louisa's mother. Fixed in place, with all the possessions, all the assumptions and benefits that go with it. There's a certain comfort in that. But the next day I'm happy with myself as I am now. I enjoy sleeping on my own. Doing what I want to do. Looking after Louisa without having to discuss what I'm going to do or how she feels and having you disagree about it. It just seems to be an opportunity I should make the most of while I can.'

'I know what you mean.'

'Do you?'

'Don't think you have a prerogative on uncertainty.'

'We were certain once. Or pretended we were.'

He sighed. 'Ah,' he said, 'pretence. Which of us knows the other?'

'That's it, you see. You make a slight joke out of it all. Say *Ah, pretence* in that rather stagey way and hope to defuse the problem.'

Peter swept the floor with an exaggerated bow. She looked at him as a teacher looks at a foolish child. He coloured slightly.

'I don't know,' she said, resigned, 'maybe it's something to do with leaving one's youth behind. Only when you're young it is possible to believe in an ideal with an intensity and a grasp that changes your whole life. You can believe in politics so much that you think the millennium is just around the corner, out in the street, through the window. You can fall in love so deeply that you realize how grand the senses are. You realize exactly what the poets say, exactly what all the songs mean. And then as you grow and mature you think how absurd it all was, how green and trusting you were. And you vow you'll never let it happen again. And it's not that you won't let it. You've moved on. It's impossible now. It *can't* happen again.'

'I really didn't want things to get this heavy, Ruth,' he said, but she had entered the broad stream of confession and was carried along by it.

She told him now she had always had doubts. Well, since Louisa was born. How their arguments, their periods of sullen silence and their apparent need to destroy each other had at last forced her to think of a life without any other permanent relationship. How she had believed as a girl that what she felt for Peter was a transcendence available to all lovers.

'It happens to us all,' he said, trying to comfort her. 'We just have to get ahead with compromise, defeat, adjustments, rejections. We learn to get on with people we swore we'd like to kill. We live with each other when —'

'But there's nothing to hang on to,' she said. 'Nothing to fix the sights on. It's not like this table. I can measure this table. I know what it's used for. I can describe it in terms of shape, height, colour, style. It has an objective, verifiable existence, not only for me but for you. We know it's *there*.' She slapped it with the flat of her hand and the sudden noise sounded like a pistol shot in the close confines of the flat. Peter winced.

'With us it's different, Peter. We're not sure what we ourselves feel. Every time I make a statement I believe to be true a little doubt creeps in. I begin to qualify it in my mind. How can I expect to give you anything fixed, objective, dependable? How can you know I'm not just stringing you along, or acting up to what I think are your preconceptions, or lying to myself? The

19

possibilities are endless. There are no certainties. There is no great unifying understanding, no common ground of belief. We deal in fictions.'

He listened to the street noise.

'But that's all we have to go on,' he said.

'Even my feelings towards Louisa are . . . ambivalent. Does that shock you? I don't know if she shackles me or frees me.'

She talked about their daughter. They remembered her as a baby, how she learned to walk, her first words, the sleepless nights they had shared. Peter began to feel the sharp but sick experience of guilt. It was confirmation that he was needed no matter how often he was told that he wasn't. The things they had in common were stronger and more important than that which divided them.

'Things pass,' he said, 'but nothing ever ends. It's true. There should be some law of existence that states that. Nothing is ever really finished.'

'I don't –'

He held his hand up to silence her and was surprised when she obeyed. 'It's the opposite side of the coin,' he said. 'So we can't live with the intensity you're talking about, but on the other hand no one crosses us off forever.' Suddenly inspired into a dangerous act, he got down on his knees and spread his arms like a priest inviting God. 'After we're dead we'll still be here. Everytime someone sings the songs we used to sing, every time this flat is occupied, every moment of Louisa's life and the lives of Louisa's children –'

She put a finger on his lips. 'Enough,' she said. She had enough to worry about without a wash of romantic mysticism.

And it was true that as he walked back through the sunshine he began to think that he had flirted outrageously with the realities of their lives. Ruth had been right.

And yet he also thought that maybe they'd be given another chance. Some deity had seen the pattern and arranged for it to be symmetrical.

The more he considered this the less certain he was about it.

He didn't want to think about it.

The leaves were new on the trees, the girls were out in their summer dresses; it was a good day. He stopped in a park to hear a military band play the familiar largo from *New World* and, as usual, it made him feel that mankind really was a whole. After they'd finished he followed them into a nearby pub. The pub was dark and cool, the wood was polished and the carpet clean. On the way in he almost fell over a Labrador dog which had stretched out beside the bar, its owner apologized, and he and Peter began a casually pleasant discussion about sport.

He had taken about two drinks from his pint. The man was not reckoning much to Liverpool's chances this year when Peter was distracted. The pub was normal. Then he looked down and saw, standing beside him, a child who smiled up at him.

Something was wrong. He knew it.

The room exploded.

Peter was one of the three civilians who were killed in the blast along with five bandsmen. A six-inch nail hit the side of his head with the force of a crossbow bolt. He was hurled sideways out of the window and on to the pavement outside.

If Tony had been there he would not have been horrified. If God had allowed him to walk unscathed through the blast, to study its effects with a casually divine presence, he would have felt neither sickened nor guilty. If he could have studied it in slow motion like an analyst can study a film frame by frame he would have found a panoply of effects. A kind of balletic beauty. Justice.

Of course he couldn't be there. He'd planted the bomb and had to be away, although even at the distance of a couple of streets the explosion stopped everything.

But he'd rehearsed the effect of the bomb in his mind. In his imagination he watched the casing rupture in incandescent flame, the windows shatter away from the blast in shards and flying crystalline powder, the chairs and bottles and soldiers blow apart, the building collapse.

He went miles out of his way. When he got back to the flat Mary was already waiting for him. 'Thank Christ you're back,' she said.

'Trouble?'

She shook her head.

'Nor me. It was like falling off a log.'

She was watching television for the news flashes and had the remote control unit in her hand. She flicked from channel to channel. He sat down beside her and she squeezed his hand.

'A few dead,' she said, 'several injured. They don't know how many yet. We just blew the place to bits.'

They watched the coverage as the images lurched and closed in on rubble, ambulances, stretchers with bodies covered in blankets. If they opened the window of the flat they could hear the sirens wail.

Absentmindedly he played with a strand of her hair as they watched. 'Jesus,' he said after a while, 'we've hit the bastards hard.'

'You smell,' she said.

'As soon as I got away I started sweating like a pig. I was all right until then. When we were doing it I was calm.' He looked appealingly at her. 'You would testify to that, wouldn't you? You'd swear to it?'

'Of course I would.'

She bathed him. His body looked thin and spare in the wide bath, and the damp made his beard wispy and his hair bedraggled. She was struck again at how white his body was, how small the hands were. When he closed his eyes drops of water lay on the lids and he looked ascetic, almost dead.

'It was perfect,' she said.

'They all thought things had gone quiet,' he said, with almost a chortle. The bathroom made his voice echo like a ghost's. 'Ambulances, police cars, fire engines – they don't know what to do. We've disrupted the lot.'

She put her hand through his wet hair. She could feel the skull beneath the skin. He tilted his head back and looked at her. His eyes were innnocent blue. She kissed him.

'Time you were out. The water's getting cold. It'll do you no good.'

'You're just like an Irish mother.'

'You're just like a fucking English aristocrat.'

He laughed and got out of the bath, trailing around the flat with a large towel and drying himself on it. His hair, dried but uncombed, stuck out in all directions.

'It was all so *easy*,' Tony said, 'that's what I can't get over.'

'The next one will be more difficult.'

'We'll handle the next one as easy as we handled this one. No – better. We'll be more experienced.'

'Time for a drink.'

'Christ, yes.'

She came in from the kitchen with two glasses and a bottle. He tapped the bottle lightly with a fingernail. 'Symbol of bourgeois decadence,' he said.

She clung to him as he poured the champagne. 'It's too good for them,' she said.

They clinked glasses.

The champagne made them warm and expansive. Tony stretched and yawned. He was close to rapture.

'I kept thinking,' Mary said, 'what if . . .'

'There are no *what ifs*. It had to be done. We did it. If it hadn't been us it would have been someone else.'

'I sometimes think of them as your people.'

'In your moments of weakness? For God's sake, you know how you've changed me.'

She smiled, they grinned, giggled, and before long, triggered by the absurd success of their mission and the sense of euphoric freedom they enjoyed, they were almost hysterical with laughter, hanging on to each other and gasping. The television continued to show rubble and carnage. They took a couple of minutes to calm down.

'You know what this makes me feel?' Mary asked.

When they made love it was with a ferocious harmony. When they had finished they did not know what time it was so they wandered back to the television. All the familiar programmes had vanished, displaced by the urgency of today's news. They had spent weeks watching anything and everything from children's programmes to the Open University. Occasionally they tired of the set and read magazines instead. Tony had tried to interest Mary in the breakdown of feudalism but she had remained obstinately concerned with the practical and con-temporary. Without her they could never have done it.

When a policeman came on the screen and remarked that the

bombers must be barbarians she said, 'No, surgeons' softly to herself.

'Jesus,' he said. 'I love you.'

During the night they awoke to hear the sound of huge beating wings compressing and relaxing the air, but they hung on to each other knowing it was a dream.

The next day they made sorties outside to buy the Sunday papers. Back inside the flat they examined all they could on the effects of the bomb and the speculation as to who they were and what were their motives. And they read about everything else that had happened that day, that week. They wanted to remember their time in all its local and international perspectives. They read details, not only about the bombing, but about everything else that had happened that day. Thus they read not only about Peter (an unimportant person, they thought, without any place in the grand scheme of things), but about suggested changes in government monetary policy, a royal visit, a tug-of-love child, the problems caused by poorly fitting shoes, and the death in Lodz of an obscure Polish literary critic and historian called Zurawski.

They did not know they were already being watched.

Once the central framework is constructed the idea can be extended in any direction. Additions can be made, qualifications entered, further examples detailed. Perhaps this is why the work remains incomplete. Over the years the author saw it grow like coral encrusting his basic idea. Each seemingly disparate article, each textual exegesis or notation was to become part of the great scheme. And whatever the weight of evidence the main crux of his argument would still be seen.

The table faces a large sash window which lets in sunlight and fresh air. My working papers are spread across the desk. There are sheets of lined A4 paper covered in balloons and squiggles and boxes that show provisional translations and those that I'm happier with.

Three books also lie on the desk. One is a thesaurus, one a Polish–English dictionary. The third is Zurawski's book.

He called it *A Theory of Genre Structures*. I wanted to retitle it, but my publisher will have none of it. He favours such weighty titles.

I'm on schedule, more or less. I can allow myself some time off to read the papers or watch the small portable TV I've installed in the corner of the room. In the opposite corner there is a bed. Sometimes R comes round and we make love. I find this less satisfying than our discussion about culture and the contribution to it of sustained intelligence.

Zurawski's Plan was to divide the book into two parts. The first is called *Fiction As History*. In this part he examines narrative structures, testing them for comprehensiveness, symbolism, exclusion, naturalism and realism. Possibly he meant to extend the list further, but those he dealt with are –

the intersecting biographies scheme

the work of individual growth and development, or *bildungsroman*

the family saga, or conflict between generations

the thriller, or work of pursuit – or revenge – and detection

the comedy, or grotesque, or farce

the fantasy, or science fiction, or modern satire

magic realism, or, in Zurawski's phrase, surreal naturalism

the love story or romance

R believes that Zurawski oversimplifies things, that his scheme has the feel of something imposed rather than organic. I reply that this misses the point. In providing us with a grid and references, Zurawski has enabled us to take sightings on the processes of evaluation and change.

For Zurawski is not interested in individual psychology or fate, but in a kind of total history, or historic totality. All these genres and sub-genres are approaches, tangents, slices into a totality which any given work (or body of work) can only approximate. We read a completeness into it just as we read the complete body from a biopsy.

The amount of approaches is, of course, infinite. Like some Platonic ideal, the totality always lies outside the grasp. All we can deal with are approximations.

The corollary to all this massive effort of tabulation, codification and analysis was to be Part Two of his work. But he never wrote it. Perhaps he died just before he was about to begin. His potential was suddenly and pointlessly expunged.

All we have is the title, *History as Fiction*, and a few subject headings – *ideology and development, morality and outlook, terrorism and justice*.

Sometimes R and I play guessing games as to how this second part would have been constructed. 'I think' I say to her, 'that he would have used abstractions as the baseline for his arguments. Turned the argument of the first part on its head, so to speak.'

'What, and moved from generalizations to the particular?'

'I think so. He wanted to show how the only way in which the world can be interpreted is in a fictional sense. That one's beliefs, religion, politics are no more *real* than, say Leopold Bloom, or Hamlet, or Tarzan. That there is, in the world, no such thing as the verifiable – not when you're talking about life, and how to live your life, and what people think are great universal truths.'

'But how can you say that? If there is no evidence to enable us to grasp any truth, if all we have to go on are approximations, then aren't you providing your own great truth from the limited evidence of what he left behind him? Isn't such a thing in itself a fiction?'

I consider this.

'Yes,' I say, 'I suppose so. But it's the only way I can get to the whole. Art always tends towards completeness, no matter how limited it may appear. There's no such thing, in art, as a completely pointless death. Everything has a purpose.'

'Ah, that's the distinction. In art, meaning stalks everything.'

'Just as we make it stalk the parts of our lives that surround us. They may be random, accidental, the results of chance alone. But we lead meaning sniffing around them like a pet Labrador, hoping it'll find the pattern.'

I sit and brood about the impossibility of the task. The wind stirs my papers, turning them, making leaf topple over on to leaf. They whirr with a steady beat, like passing wings.

I cannot decide if, hidden within Zurawski's work, there is the idea of a solution.

(b)

It was Ruth who identified Peter. She felt that nothing in her life had prepared her for this. The Warwickshire childhood, the years at university, her first unhappy affair – nothing had made her expect this.

He was stored in a pullout freezer cabinet with a tight white bandage wrapped round his head and chin. He looked not dead but drugged, as if he was awaiting an operation rather than cremation. But he was dead all right. The temperature of the skin jolted her like a shock.

The bomb was there by careful design. Peter's presence was an accident, a freak of location. That was all.

Even though she kept thinking *if only*, she knew she could not live her life in a thicket of possibilities that never happened. She determined to live it in as positive a way as she could.

She succeeded.

Many years later, the owner of her own small business, the mother of a teenage daughter, the wife of a dapper administrator in the arts, she was to attend an exhibition of the work of Belfast children. The paintings showed soldiers, armoured cars, gunmen, barricades. In one a man and woman fled from a stylized explosion which tossed arms, legs, bodies into the air. The bodies were featureless but the bombers had the flat, placid faces of icons.

(c)

If this spanned generations, then a part of it, a few chapters perhaps, would tell how one of the family sons rebelled. How his parents, themselves the product of toil and secret business deals and social climbing and affairs, cut him off as he disappeared into a seedy world of bedsits, arms deals, revolutionary plots. How he turned his back on wealth, and society parties, and the Range Rover set, and entered the underground.

He met a girl from a family of poor Irish farmers drawn into the rundown terraces of the big cities. Her zeal, her fervour had a grandeur about them. Her family were sympathetic, but too cautious for action. She heard tales from her grandfather, a boy soldier who'd killed a Black-and-Tan with a pistol. Her parents begged her not to be so rash; things would sort themselves out in time.

After they died, the families continued. There were other sons, other daughters, another generation. Life carried on.

(d)

Our detective must be honest. Compromised, less than successful, but incorruptible. He'll have a sharp wife with whom he maintains a dull marriage. She'll be a *cordon bleu* cook or a terribly bad one, I haven't decided yet. But she'll know she is secondary to his job.

Since he is British, he cannot afford to have a sharp, romantic and toughly-American name. His will be an idiosyncratic name, the name of a rundown seaside town or a shabby piece of clothing.

The breaks, when they come his way, will be part intuition and part sheer, unrelenting, footslogging work.

And he'll fail insofar as they'll plant the bomb just a few days before he can get at them.

As regards the terrorists the thriller must maintain a factual exactness. Their beliefs will be underpinned by theoretical and historical references. The careful reader will draw correspondences between these and the detective's confused but morally superior liberalism.

Most of all it must be exact to the point of treason on the mechanics of a terror campaign, the black market in weapons, the economic support for terrorist groups. It will even tell you how to make a bomb.

The detective will not want them dead, but they will be killed. Shot down in cold blood on orders from above. When he argues furiously against his superiors, he finds a nest of compromise, appeasement, and moral weakness.

He alone does not have ambition.

(e)

Ruth never confessed she had a lover with whom she indulged

in active bouts of sex. They yelped and rolled across floors, more like animals than humans, knocking their heads against chairlegs. They covered up their affair with ludicrously convoluted arrangements and alibis which Peter was too dim to see through.

The Labrador in the pub was disembowelled by the blast. Its body came to rest upside-down, legs apart, on top of the video game in the corner.

When she identified Peter she smelt a clinging, fetid odour that she thought must be something to do with bodily preservation or decay. It was, in fact, the mortuary attendant. He'd been unable to resist breaking wind just before she walked in. Now, almost doubled up, with pained expressions flitting across his face, he teetered on tiptoe at the edge of her vision, filled up the explosive gases and holding them in by a supreme effort of the sphincter.

The final raid was a chaos of misheard instructions, mistaken identities, wrong conclusions. Policemen tripped over each other in a silent Keystone flurry of limbs.

What other cliché would you like? A stoned-drunk customer, bottle in hand, to stand among the wreckage and say, 'My God, that was strong stuff'? A selfish, boorish and violent man, who had just denied the existence of God, to have his hands fixed by nails to the wall like Christ?

(f)

Peter was transported to an alternative universe where he fought dark creatures of the imagination, monsters from the id, with scales of fur and tongues of fire. His only help was a trusty Labrador dog, transported with him to the same mad world.

Or, alternatively –

Peter was transported to a parallel world where, history having taken a different course, he became a Gulliver in a distorted, fragmented, mirror-image of the world he had left.

He could go into a multiplicity of universes, and in some of these the explosion would never have happened. Because it had no cause to happen.

(g)

He stood in the pub with a drink in his hand. Heard a noise and turned to one side. Standing beside him a child with its face bathed in light. Around him the room blows slowly away, ripping away like burned paper torn by wind, streaming outwards, disintegrating. But the child stands there. The child does not move.

Some days later Tony and Mary eat their last breakfast and leave the flat. As they walk through the door they stop.

'What are they?' he asked, but she doesn't know.

Round the door are lights, yellow, white, blue. Music plays, distant like music from across the park or over rooftops. They recognize the tune as their own.

The lights were shattered as the bullets hit them. Afterwards no broken bulbs could be found, but the smashed fragments of the tune littered the floor beside their bodies.

(h)

No one had ever felt this way before. They knew it. Only in fiction were there realistic parallels for what they felt. If they could have chosen how to die, they would have chosen to die as they did, in each other's arms.

After their death the disaffected young took them to their hearts, sang their song, adopted their names. They lived again in teeshirts, banners, posters, slogans aerosolled on walls. Their love was absolute – conceived in ideological purity, forged in political action, destroyed by the forces of repression, made eternal by myth.

He was buried in England, she in Ireland. Her photograph was carried on her coffin in an image like that of Christ. At her graveside six black-hooded men fired pistol salutes.

His family took his body back. Some time later the grave was desecrated, and for ever afterwards a rumour circulated that his heart had been removed and buried beside her.

II

Processions with banners scattered beneath sharp fire. Priests, crouched, waving handkerchiefs, led men carrying the wounded and dying. Girls were found lashed to lamp-posts, their hair shorn, their heads glistening with black tar. Children hurled half-bricks, cobbles, petrol bombs, or played among derelict buildings and burned-out buses. Slogans glared from walls. Prisoners starved themselves in cells daubed with shit. Bombs, grenades, mortar bombs burst in shops, cars, garages, a bandstand.

Cars are fired on at roadblocks. Kidnap victims lie on beds at gun-point. Men testify against their fellows. Bombs knock out windows in quiet streets. A teacher is shot in front of the class, a policeman is killed on crossing patrol, bodies lie under blankets in alleys with their shoes and hands stuck out from beneath the cloth.

A bomb in a London pub kills several soldiers, a handful of civilians, a Labrador dog.

Turn the page.

A Present for Christmas 1816

BARBARA CARTLAND

'I FIND CHRISTMAS damned expensive!' a buck said speaking from a comfortable leather arm-chair in the coffee-room at White's Club.

'I agree with you,' a young peer replied, 'and unless I can find somebody to give me a loan, a pretty "Cyprian" is going to be very disappointed.'

With a cynical expression on his face, the Marquis of Lynche rose from the chair in which he had been sitting and walked towards the door.

He knew only too well that because he was so wealthy it was only a question of time before he was 'touched' by one of his friends, and he had already spent a great deal more than he had intended on Christmas presents.

There were not only his relations, who always approached him with open hands and 'pockets to let', but there was also Lady Irene Standish with whom he was having a fiery *affaire de coeur*.

She had set her heart on an ermine cloak which had seemed to him inordinately expensive.

He suspected that a muff was included and that she thought he would pay without being aware of it.

There was also Lulu, his current mistress, who had an insatiable appetite for diamonds and who had unfortunately seen a necklace in Bond Street which had taken her fancy.

He had bought it, but at the same time, he resented the greediness of her request, simply because he was a rich man.

He reached the hall and as the porter gave him his hat and gloves he saw that his carriage was waiting outside in St James's Street.

He walked down the steps, moving carefully because they were slippery, feeling the cold wind sharp on his handsome face after the heat of the coffee-room.

Then as his footman sprang down from the box to open the carriage door with his coat-of-arms emblazoned on it he heard a soft voice.

'Please . . . Sir . . . please buy a present for Christmas!'

It was a very beguiling voice and when he would have brushed the pedlar away impatiently he realised it was also a cultured one.

He hesitated and the woman holding the basket over her arm said:

'A bag of lavender . . . I beg of you . . . Sir, to buy one, and help . . . a child who is . . . sick.'

The pleading in the woman's voice was somehow moving and the Marquis turned his head above his high, exquisitely tied cravat to look at her.

She was wrapped in a thick woollen shawl and her plain bonnet was pulled low over her forehead.

Yet, in the dying light he had the impression of two, very large eyes which seemed to fill a small, heart-shaped face.

Then as she looked at him she made a little exclamation and would have turned away.

'Wait!' he said sharply, and it was an order.

She hesitated. He knew she wanted to run, but reluctantly she looked round at him.

'Selina!' he exclaimed. 'It cannot be!'

'I . . . did not realise it was . . . you!' she faltered.

'But – what has happened? Why are you here?'

He looked down as he spoke at the basket filled with little bags and her hands covered with woollen mittens.

'My brother is . . . ill,' she murmured, 'and . . . we have no . . . money.'

'I cannot believe it!' the Marquis exclaimed.

Making up his mind in a way that was characteristic he said, 'Get into the carriage! I will drive you home.'

'There is . . . no need . . .' she began to say, but with his hand under her arm, he helped her in.

Then as the footman put a fur rug over their knees he asked, 'Where are you living?'

'It is . . . in Chelsea . . . near the Hospital . . . Broom Road.'

The Marquis gave the address, the door was closed and the carriage drove off.

Then he turned to look at her.

It seemed incredible that Lady Selina Warde, whom he had known when she was a very pretty, happy child, should be peddling wares in St James's Street.

Because he was so much older she had followed him around adoringly, carrying out eagerly what orders he condescended to give her.

He remembered now hearing that her father, the 4th Earl of Chetwarde who had always been a gambler, had been killed in a duel some nine months ago.

By the light of the candle-lantern he stared at Lady Selina incredulously.

'What has happened to you?' he asked, knowing the answer.

'Papa's . . . debts were so . . . astronomical,' she answered, 'that . . . everything was . . . taken by . . . the Duns.'

'But your house?' the Marquis questioned. 'Surely, it was entailed?'

'It is let . . . but the monies go . . . towards what Papa . . . still . . . owes.'

The Marquis realised that she was answering him reluctantly and he knew that she was shy and ashamed.

Then he said quietly:

'But, surely your relations . . .'

'They were furious at the way Papa behaved,' she interrupted, 'and I thought I could . . . look after Jamie on my own . . . but he is ill . . .'

She made a helpless little gesture with her hands as she spoke and the Marquis could see her fingers were blue with cold, and a prominent bone in her wrist told him she was starving.

He was silent until the horses drew up outside a tall, gaunt building with cracked window-panes and a dirty front door.

'Thank you . . . for bringing me . . . home,' Lady Selina said.

The Marquis merely helped her out of the carriage saying, 'I am coming in with you.'

'We are . . . in the . . . attic,' she protested, 'and it is . . . quite unnecessary.'

He paid no attention, and turning to his footman who had opened the carriage door he said, 'Follow us!'

They went up three flights of rickety, uncarpeted stairs and Selina opened an attic door.

It was a room without a carpet or curtains, with two dilapidated iron bedsteads, and lying on one of them was a small boy.

Selina hurried to his side, bending over him anxiously and pulling the threadbare blankets closer up to his chin.

In a tone of authority the Marquis gave his orders.

The footman wrapped the blankets around the boy and started to carry him carefully from the room and down the stairs.

Selina looked at the Marquis in astonishment.

'What . . . are you doing? Where are you . . . taking us?'

'Anywhere is better than this hell-hole!' the Marquis answered. 'How can you have let yourself get into this situation?'

'I . . . I tried . . . I really tried,' Selina replied, 'but we have . . . nothing left to sell . . . except for the little bags I made . . . as Christmas presents.'

'Then there is nothing you want in here!' he said firmly.

She was unable to meet his eyes as she said in a frightened voice:

'We . . . owe a lot of money to the . . . landlady for our rent.'

'How much?'

'Nearly . . . two pounds!'

The Marquis put three sovereigns down on a chest-of-drawers with a broken leg, then they went slowly down the stairs because it was difficult to see.

The footman had already put the 5th Earl of Chetwarde on the back seat of the carriage.

Having given an address to the coachman, the Marquis and Selina seated themselves opposite the sick child.

As they drove away Selina said, 'H-how can . . . you be so . . . kind? But . . . I have no . . . wish for us to be an . . . encumbrance on you.'

'Tomorrow,' the Marquis answered, 'I will send you to one of my houses in the country where you will be properly chaperoned. Tonight you will stay in a house I own a few streets from here, and at least you will have something to eat.'

He saw a blush creep over her cheeks as if he embarrassed her and they drove in silence until they arrived at a house in Royal Avenue.

The Marquis had purchased it for an attractive little ballet-dancer from Covent Garden, but a month ago, finding she no longer amused him, he had paid her off.

The footman knocked loudly and after a short wait the door was opened by a middle-aged woman with a kindly face who exclaimed when she saw the Marquis, 'I weren't expectin' you, M'lord!'

'I know that, Abigail, but I have brought someone who needs your attention and food as quickly as you can produce it!'

The footman carried the sleeping Earl up the stairs to a room on the first floor.

He laid the child down on the bed, taking away the threadbare blankets as he did so.

Selina, pulling off her bonnet and shawl, went to her brother's side, tucking him in and bending over him anxiously.

The Marquis, watching, realised she had not noticed the somewhat flamboyant pink silk curtains which fell from a golden corola, or the profusion of mirrors there were in the room.

Instead, her thoughts were concentrated only on her brother.

The Marquis thought as she bent over him that she looked like one of the masterpieces painted over the centuries portraying the Virgin Mary tending the Infant Jesus.

Then he was aware that Abigail was awaiting her orders at the bedroom door.

'The child is hungry,' he said, 'give him warm soup and prepare something more substantial for Her Ladyship. She too is hungry.'

He could see beneath the threadbare gown that had once been an expensive garment that Selina was pathetically thin and the bones of her chin were sharp against her long neck.

She smoothed back the hair from her brother's forehead and, as he did not wake, came across the room to the Marquis, and he could see the tears in her eyes.

'How can I ... ever thank ... you?' she asked in a voice that broke on the words.

Their eyes met, and somehow it was impossible to look away.

'What do you want for Christmas?' the Marquis asked unexpectedly.

There was silence. Then in a voice little above a whisper, she answered: 'Could you ... kiss me ... just once ... so that I shall have ... something ... to remember?'

For a moment the Marquis felt he could not have heard her aright. Then he put his arms around her and gently drew her against him.

Her lips were very soft, sweet and innocent, and he knew that this kiss was different from any he had ever given before.

He felt the blood throbbing in his temples, but as he drew her closer still he knew he wanted to protect her and look after her so that she need never be hungry or unhappy again.

He kissed her until they were both breathless and when he raised his head he thought that no woman could look more radiant or more spiritually beautiful.

'Is that what you wanted?' he asked, and his voice was unsteady.

'Th-thank ... you.'

There was a rapt note in her voice and after a moment he said, 'Now you must give *me* a present.'

Her eyes widened, and he knew she was thinking she had nothing to give him.

'I want your heart!'

Her eye-lashes fluttered and he knew she was shy, then in a whisper he could hardly hear she said, 'It has ... always been yours . . . ever since we were . . . children together.'

'Then I am greedy, for I want not only your heart – but you.'

He realised she did not understand and he said gently. 'I am asking you to marry me, Selina!'

He felt her body stiffen and and as she looked up at him in astonishment her eyes filled her thin face.

Her drew her closer and his lips were very near to hers as she murmured:

'I . . . I am dreaming . . . I know I am . . . dreaming!'

'Then, my darling, I am dreaming, too!' the Marquis said.

He knew as he kissed her again, this time insistently and demandingly, but with an inexpressible tenderness, that they were both carried up into a starlit sky and were no longer on earth.

As the Marquis's kiss became more possessive, as if he was afraid she might vanish and he would lose her, he knew he had found what all men seek but are often disappointed.

It was the pure, unspoilt love which is both human and Divine, and is in fact a present from God.

The Assassination of Indira Gandhi

UPAMANYU CHATTERJEE

BUNNY THREW HIS glass meditatively at the wall. It tinkled into large ugly pieces. One fell on Randeep's head. 'We'd better look out,' he said, 'Cut Surd's getting violent.'

Bunny took off his goggles. His eyes were very red. 'Give me a glass.' Shashi did. Bunny finished it and threw it slowly up at the ceiling fan. Ramnath caught it. 'Stop it, Cut Surd.'

'Stop calling me Cut Surd.'

Mirza fixed Bunny another drink. 'These bloody Hindus yaar Surd.' Everyone laughed drunkenly.

'I'm feeling sick.' Bunny put on his goggles. 'Not pukey, just sick.'

'Throw up in the bathroom. Not here.' said Ramnath.

'Why didn't we get women? I'm sick of just men. I want some sex.'

Shashi said, 'Rum before sundown, that's the problem. I kept saying let's get beer.'

Bunny got up slowly from the floor. He tucked in his teeshirt. He kicked Ramnath. 'I'm going out. I'm getting myself a ticket home.' He felt his pockets. 'Where are the keys? I'll leave the bike with you. Don't kill it.'

Outside, a very loud motorcycle went by. Bunny drew back the curtain and opened the window. The late-afternoon late-

October light bounded in, along with the noises of horns and accelerating cars. He spoke to the traffic. 'I'm sick to my balls of Delhi. A dog of a city. It's almost like Chandigarh.' Bunny looked around the room and looked out again. 'Sick.' His knees and right ankle ached faintly.

'No, Surd, this is just a bad trip. Get some ganja and some sleep, you'll be fine.'

'No, I'm just sick, Dog city.' He liked the phrase. He scratched his beard. 'Next June I'll be apprenticed in Chandigarh, horny and alone.' Drink made Bunny articulate. 'The hep Surds call Chandigarh Chandy. Just red brick and empty spaces.' He moved around the room, leaned against the bathroom door and watched Shashi urinate. 'Your piss is yellow like mustard oil. Maybe you have jaundice.' At the table he slowly poured himself a large rum. 'These days I ejaculate too quickly. It's like school, those jerk-off competitions.'

'Fix me one Surd, thanks.'

Bunny took off his goggles and sat them carefully on the knob of the cupboard door. 'Randeep, just fix my attendance with Kapila. I'll be back maybe in a month or something. 'Bye everybody.' He put on his goggles and left.

An orange October sun, but Bunny was only faintly conscious of it. He was drunk, but not uncontrollably. He was depressed too, but he did not know it. Bunny was twenty-three, and in-articulate and silent when sober. He put on his crash helmet and left the straps loose. He rode off at frightening speed.

He stopped on the peak of a flyover to watch, in the mild light, the traffic and the teenagers around the ice-cream man. He said to himself, if there's a queue at the ticket counter, even a line of three bastards, I'm not going home. He rode away. But there was only one. So he bought a seat on the night bus to Mussoorie. From the bus station, he went for a haircut.

At traffic lights, at other places where he had to slow down or stop, Bunny felt quite ill. He attributed his weakness to his ennui, the drink, the inadequate sleep, Delhi's fickle October weather, his vague distaste for the way he lived his life. But self-examination was not his practice. He lived unthinkingly and encouraged in himself random impulses.

At the saloon, while waiting, he flipped blindly through a film magazine. At saloons, he always remembered his first haircut, in Darjeeling, about eight years ago, the barber's smiles and enthusiasm. He had written to his parents about it. He never wrote letters, for he found expression tiresome, but his parents had had to be forewarned before his return home. They had disapproved vastly. Even now his father, when really angry, called him a bastard Sikh.

Abruptly he felt queasy. He skipped the haircut and rode back to the hostel with a headache. He woke up Yudhvir, a friend. 'This is no time to sleep.'

'What time is it?' Red drugged eyes and porcupine hair, but Yudhvir never got angry.

'Sixish. I've got myself a ticket on the night bus home. You take care of the bike.'

'Okay.'

'And fix Kapila about attendance. I'm going to sleep too. I'll wake you up later to drop me to the bus.'

Bunny liked night bus journeys. The seats were quite comfortable, and he could sleep anywhere. The jolts even lulled him, but during the journey, when he woke up, his knees were stiff and aching.

He wasn't particularly fond of his parents. They bored him. Home was not an exciting place, but he could unwind there, sleep in the sun and eat really well. His mother opened the door. She was not surprised to see him. He always came home unexpectedly. She said, 'You look awful. Are you ill?'

'I just feel exhausted. Must be the journey.'

He went to his room with his bag. His father grunted as he passed his parents' room. Bunny mumbled a reply. His mother came in with two blankets. It was six in the morning. Bunny slept uneasily till nine, and got out of bed after ten.

His father was in the garden, in a white cane chair. 'What, Law Faculty again on strike?'

'Yes.' An easy lie, for at any time, Bunny would have found it difficult to tell his father that he had just *felt* like coming home. He sat down. The small lawn was an odd triangle in shape, the wooden fence a bright white. Beyond the fence, the hill tumbled down to the narrow road, the tea stalls, the shacks selling wooden Taj Mahals and walking-sticks, the Tibetans in bright quilted jackets. Then the hill lurched further down the main road. Behind it lay the vast valley, surrounded by curve after curve of denuded hill. On a clear day, one could see in the valley the dots and dashes of the houses of Dehradun. Above this was an immense pale sky. At ten in the morning it still waited for the sun.

Bunny's mother emerged, in a salwar-kameez and a grey sweater. 'Come, breakfast is ready.'

Bunny didn't want to move or eat. 'Later.'

'What, shall I bring your food here?'

'No, I don't want to eat just now.'

His mother came up. Bunny looked at her defensively and noticed again his own face in hers. 'Are you feeling all right?' She put her hand on his shoulder. He cringed a little.

'You look horrible,' Mr Kairon said, staring steadily at Bunny over his reading glasses. *A History of the Sikhs* dropped on to the table. With a pencil he pushed stray hair into his turban. 'You've lost weight and colour. You don't *look* healthy.'

'Shall we call a doctor?'

'No. I think I'll be okay in a day or two.'

'But do you *feel* ill?' His mother half-bent down and examined Bunny's face.

Then Bunny's resistance collapsed. 'Yes. Maybe we should call Malviya.' He felt a little better. Just the admission of illness eased him, allowing him deeper breaths.

His mother left. His father said, 'What's wrong? Any symptoms?'

'Weakness. No appetite. That's all.' He forgot the faint pain in his knees, and now occasionally, his back.

Mr Kairon pushed his lips up and out till the upper lip touched his nose and breathed heavily into his moustache. He was a cliché of a man, once a brigadier, tall, with an inflexible back, now horribly active after retirement. He used his leisure for his garden and for long walks on the hill roads, and for educative books. He wasn't scholarly or even contemplative, but with the years he had been increasingly assailed by a conviction of his ignorance. One mild heart attack had even made him religious, and now his daily ritual included the Granth Saheb.

Bunny went in and returned with a camp cot. Dragging it tired him incredibly. He lay down. The weakness encouraged only unpleasant thoughts, it only allowed for images of depression, of Chandigarh and some lawyer's chambers, of law tomes and loneliness, of professional inadequacy and dislocation in a dead town.

'Fever?'

'No.'

'Stomach all right?'

'Oh yes.'

Then the sun broke through and warmed them. Somewhere in the house, Bunny could hear his mother giving the maid-servant hell. His mother had a pleasant rich voice. To avoid his father's questions, Bunny pretended to doze.

Mr Kairon was proud of his son's good looks, but Bunny had often disappointed him. For one, he had not joined the Army. And though Mr Kairon admitted that short hair suited Bunny, he had been outraged that Bunny had not asked him *before* the haircut. Now he watched him sleeping in the sun and said, 'I hope your illness is not serious.'

They heard the gate and Dr Malviya appeared, clean, pink and busy. Bunny disliked doctors because they made him insecure. Standing over Bunny, Dr Malviya announced immediately, 'This is jaundice, Kaironji. What, Bunny boy, you've been drinking a lot?' He checked his eyes, spleen and liver, questioned him about his whisky and his urine, ordered blood tests, a special diet and lots of rest and left.

Jaundice. Bunny wondered if it could have been worse and almost immediately told himself yes. The blue of the sky was gathering richer tones. Light cottonwool clouds just above him, long flat strips of grey on the horizon, tiny white waves of cloud, ribbed like desert sand, on the left, and the warm sun. When his father wasn't going on and on about his dissipation and abysmal lack of care, Bunny could hear different birds, on the lawn, and in the distant trees. He knew nothing about them, but they sounded nice.

Out on the lawn time passed easily. Bunny ate a little and drank some juice. Mr Kairon, perhaps regretting his earlier sharpness, asked him if he felt better. Bunny said yes. The telephone rang. Mrs Kairon picked it up, then shrieked through the large white windows, 'from New York!'

'Rajwant,' muttered Mr Kairon. He rushed inside and pushed his hand out peremptorily for the 'phone. 'Here.'

Bunny turned on his side and observed them. He didn't think his sister worth the effort of leaving the camp cot. Older by nine years his sister, like the rest of the family, was distant. He saw his father's back jerk with surprise and heard a loud incredulous 'What!' Bunny turned back to the sky. His mother hurried out a few moments later and blurted out, 'Indira Gandhi has been shot dead. By two of her guards, both Sikhs. In her house in Delhi.' Mrs Kairon looked around uncertainly.

The news was unnerving. 'What else did Rajju say?'

'She wanted details from us, imagine. We didn't know anything, she said it's all over American news, even BBC and Radio Australia. She was taken to hospital but she died quickly. It happened in the morning at about nine-thirty.' Mrs Kairon gulped and sat down.

Just my luck, thought Bunny, to leave the dog city just when something exciting happened. His father returned to his chair, eyes agleam, intently twirling the knobs of a transistor.

'Will Rajju telephone again?' asked Mrs Kairon.

'Yes. As soon as she hears more news.'

All the radio stations played the same mournful song. 'She can't be dead. If she was dead, there'd be no voices and no drums and dholaks.'

'But something *has* happened, all the stations are playing the same music.'

'But this is terrible,' said Mr Kairon, looking out over the valley.

No one spoke, Bunny turned over, now warming his right arm and shoulder. Mr Kairon said, 'In New York the Sikhs are out on the roads, celebrating and distributing mithai. Rajju didn't say so, but even Manjeet seems to be celebrating.' Manjeet was the son-in-law. On the faces of Mr and Mrs Kairon could be discerned a daze, an initial shock, and an inchoate ethnic guilt.

Bunny watched the green and dull-brown ground, a few weeds among the grass. The news thrilled him, momentarily distracted him from himself. Against the white fence and footrule-strips of sky, Bunny visualized the blood dyeing the sari and the collapsing, crumpling female form. Maybe she had even said something to her assassins or to someone nearby. Mr Kairon got up, said, 'I'm telephoning Duggal,' and went inside. The songs from the transistor continued.

Mr Kairon returned, more composed. 'Duggal says AIR is still saying she was shot, but BBC announced her death long ago. The killers are Sikhs, no doubt about that.'

Mrs Kairon said, 'For shame.'

Lunch was dreary and silent. Duggal arrived soon after. Bunny did not move to acknowledge him. 'Hallo, Balwinder,' Duggal said, 'when did you come?' Bunny disliked Duggal because he called him Balwinder and because Duggal disliked Bunny for his good looks, his haircut, his jeans and teeshirts. Duggal was uninterested in Bunny's illness. He sipped his tea noisily and said, 'This is going to cause many problems.'

'A shameful death. This is no way for a person of her stature to go,' said Mrs Kairon.

'But it's no surprise. She had it coming to her.'

Bunny eyed Duggal with amusement and contempt. What a stupid perspective, he thought. In the black and white of Duggal's mind, pain and annihilation, even jaundice probably, were merely retributive. As one sows, so one reaps, even when the harvest was a spray of unexpected bullets, or a debilitating illness. Bunny thought of his own past but could hunt out no redeeming image to refute Duggal's argument. Oh well. His parents and Duggal continued to talk. Bunny dozed off to a constraint in the air and to polite, firm disagreement.

In the late afternoon Mr Kairon and Duggal walked out to get Bunny's blood reports. They sensed, or imagined they sensed, a difference in the narrow lanes of Mussoorie. To them, the honeymooners looked sombre, there were lesser aimless throngs of tourists, an unusually large number of shops was shut, there were fewer lights. The blood reports confirmed acute jaundice. After seeing Duggal off to his dental clinic, Mr Kairon stopped for bread and soap. The grocer said, very gravely, 'Kairon Saab, your people ought not to have done this,' and overcharged him just a little. Mr Kairon could think of nothing in reply.

When Bunny woke up, the pain in his knees and ankles had increased. Must be the weakness, he thought. He found it a little difficult to move back into the house. With each step even the soles of his feet hurt. Bunny was suddenly not sure that he could rely on his body for even the simplest acts. 'Tomorrow morning I'll ring up Pammi,' announced his father over tea. 'Find out what's happening in Delhi.' In the lanes Mr Kairon had sensed a tension, an antagonism. So father and son had lost their different confidences together. At six, TV finally said that Indira Gandhi was dead. Mr Kairon was outraged at the delay in the announcement. 'We first heard the news,' he snorted, 'through a call from New York, what rubbish.' Bunny walked carefully to the telephone, not wanting to exhibit his pain. 'Hallo, may I speak to Dr Malviya? . . . Hallo, this is Bunny here . . . Now my knees and ankles are paining quite a lot . . . I don't know, for about a week I think.' Dr Malviya asked Bunny not to worry, and not to take any painkiller. He attributed the pain to Bunny's exhaustion and weakness. 'You must've slept in some odd position during the day. And perhaps you're not used to the Mussoorie chill, having come up from Delhi.' 'Where things are hotting up,' said Bunny. Dr Malviya's laugh was forced and embarrassed.

'What's this pain?' asked Mr Kairon suspiciously, turning away for a moment from the TV.

'Oh, nothing.'

His mother watched Bunny walk slowly to his room. She wished that he would communicate more. She had placed a heater in his room. Through the window the fading sun depressed him. The room was small, with a single bed. The bedspread was a present from Rajwant on her last visit. On it, on a yellow background, there romped one large red dragon. Bunny looked out at the sun and said to himself, No, I'm not weak. He closed the door and got down slowly on to the floor to exercise. At his third push-up the floor rushed up and hit him. He lost consciousness for a moment or two. When he came to, the cold cement against his left cheek was quite comfortable. An ant hurried by two inches from his right eye. He got into bed slowly, pulled the quilt right up and waited for the warmth. He felt defeated, empty, and now the twilight seemed soothing, like a dying glow. Moments passed and he breathed deeply. He tried momentarily to divert himself with a thought for Indira Gandhi but, like the rest of the world, she was remote and cold. They had in common only a numbness. Under the quilt Bunny felt his knees and tried to rotate his ankles. That pain was his only distraction from that nothingness. Outside he could hear his parents, the TV and the foreign stations on the radio. All three were going on and on about Indira Gandhi.

After some time his mother pushed the door open. 'Sleeping?' 'No.'

'What did Malviya say about the pain?'

Bunny answered, but wondered why his mother wanted to know. One's own pain was one's own, secret and unshareable, even incommunicable. Someone else's pain must be tedium, the cause of boredom and irritation. The ill were always alone, hugging their illness.

'You'd better have a hot-water bottle.'

'Okay.'

Bunny's father locked up early, at about seven. He then checked his Service revolver. From the lawn, the hills and the valley were a black menacing mass, shrouded by mist and topped by a clouded night sky. The quiet of Mussoorie normally gladdened him, but now it made him irascible and uneasy. No intermittent laughter from the teastalls below them, no wink of light from a neighbouring hill. Just the evening chill, the opaque mist, behind it the dark, and an underwater silence. Mr Kairon felt nervy, irrationally remembering the riots of Partition and the wars of '65 and '71. Indoors, the tension was alleviated only by the depression at Bunny's illness. Dinner was short. Bunny nibbled something in bed. His mother asked him to leave his door open and to call whenever necessary.

That night Bunny entered a private, nightmare world. His ankles and knees turned red and doubled in size. His skin

burned with fever. Very very slowly he struggled to sit up in
bed. He touched his left knee and the pain stunned him. He just
looked at his legs and could not believe the horror. Then Bunny
heard the telephone ring and ring, loud and frightening. At last
his father picked it up. 'Oh, Pammi, hallo . . . what, I hope . . .
oh no . . . God . . . no . . .' From his father, Bunny heard only
exclamations. Mrs Kairon joined him, 'What, what's happened?'

Bunny carefully put his two pillows beneath his knees. He
couldn't scream because he was not used to expressing pain or
to pleading for help. His fear and his helplessness drew tears out
of his eyes. His face crumpled. But he cried without sound.
Jerking his head from side to side, his fists squeezing the pliant
quilt, he decided to fight his battles silently and alone.

'Riots in Delhi.' Mr Kairon walked around helplessly. 'Sikhs
pulled out of buses and killed. Some've been burnt. Bonfires of
turbans. Houses attacked and looted. Hundreds dead already.'
Mr Kairon's slippers made the only sound. 'And Pammi?' asked
Mrs Kairon.

'No problem in his area yet.'

Mrs Kairon's eyes followed Mr Kairon. 'And Punjab?'

'No news. There's a news ban there.'

To Bunny in his delirious state, it seemed that the world's chaos
merely mirrored his own. He again tried to move. The pain rushed
up to his hip and back. He sat motionless for what seemed ages.
Bunny eventually began to realize for the first time, what he was
later to get used to, that pain cannot be acute forever. After a time
it turns monotonous, even becomes boring. So, sitting up in bed,
he dozed a little, till some inadvertent movement wrenched him
out of sleep. Awake, he would suffer, grow bored, and doze till the
next wrench. Then, finally, through the window behind him, he
heard the chirrup of the birds and sensed the new dawn.

Thus Bunny provided his parents with something other than
Indira Gandhi to think about. Dr Malviya checked Bunny's heart
and said, avoiding Mr Kairon's eyes, that apart from jaundice,
Bunny probably also had rheumatic arthritis. Dr Malviya called
for more blood tests and even an ECG. Rheumatic arthritis
stunned and later scared and disgusted Mr Kairon. It was *not* an
illness for a young, strong, good-looking Sikh. When the sun

came up he dragged his son out on to the lawn.

In the sunny cottage that he had bought for a song, Mr Kairon now felt helpless and isolated. He was cut off, lost in an idyllic location, while epochal events were taking place elsewhere. He looked at Bunny, lying there with arms folded and eyes closed, with bewilderment.

Out under the sun, Bunny was less scared. He sensed the security of the house, aloof and removed. He was living with people who meant well, who would never do him harm. Home. Though home didn't mean that for everybody, I mean, he chuckled to himself, seeing the orange of the sun under his eyelids, look at Indira Gandhi.

Mrs Kairon brought out the portable black and white TV, another present from Rajwant. They watched Mrs Gandhi lying in state. Initially, they all felt solemn. Bunny said, 'She still looks dignified.' Later he looked down at his torso and then up at her aquiline nose in that grey face surrounded by flowers, and thought, just an old woman. Mrs Kairon murmured obscure expressions of sorrow every time Mrs Gandhi was shown. But Bunny soon wearied of this and returned to the infinite variety of the sky. Malviya's pills were good. If he lay still he could even forget the pain for a while. The weeping women on TV distracted and disgusted him. He watched them beat their breasts and wail on shoulders. But surely tears were more valuable than that, thought Bunny, remembering only his own. The TV continued to spew out words of grief and immediately to deprive them of meaning.

Duggal came again that afternoon and was quite happy to hear of Bunny's new illness. He and Bunny's parents talked interminably, about the assassins, the riots, Punjab, the Anandpur Saheb Resolution, Khalistan, Trilokpuri. 'A communal carnage,' said Mr Kairon, picking up the jargon of the newspapers from Delhi that had just come in. 'The riots are also against the financial dominance of the Sikhs in Delhi.' 'They'll announce the elections soon and this killing will win it.' 'Some young Sikhs are cutting their hair, turning out like Bunny.'

Bunny loved the discussion as background and the stray sentences that registered with him. He idly wondered what Khali-

stan would be like. He was a little surprised at the fervour of
the elders. To him religion was alien. But he liked his state,
without roots or history. With his ugly past and ugly future,
nothing could claim him.

Dr Malviya came again. 'The fever will return. The swelling
will subside in three weeks or so. Later you will need a physio-
therapist.' Over the next few days he visited regularly. 'We
must be careful, Bunny. We must not allow the pain to move
into your wrists and fingers, or up your backbone. No ex-
ertion, complete rest.' 'You'll have to forget alcohol forever,
or almost forever. The jaundice will pass, but the arthritis is
going to stay.' Sometimes Dr Malviya turned quite philoso-
phical. 'You will have to learn to live with pain, with limi-
tations. Learning to live, that can be quite rewarding, Bunny.
Don't think of it too much, and don't talk about it with others.
They'll all have stupid theories. Don't you have hobbies, or
something like that to occupy you?' Bunny said no. He never
read, he had no ear for music, he collected nothing. He wasn't
even used to thought.

As Dr Malviya had prophesied, the fever returned, fitfully.
Then when his mother asked every hour if he felt better, he
couldn't even snap at her because he felt so dulled. Sometimes
he would press his hand to his heart, hard, and say, you are
strong. Sometimes he would giggle when he recalled that earlier,
in Delhi, he had thought that he had problems, and now. Sometimes he would glaze his eyes and not recognize his mother
when she bent over him because he found her concern irritating.
Sometimes he played a game of exaggerating the pain, for the
pain was boring and needed to be embellished.

On 2 and 3 November 1984, Indira Gandhi lay in state and
Delhi, as the newspapers said, was in flames. On the 4th she was
cremated. On the 11th her ashes were flung all over Gangotri, a
cold dead place. The 19th was her birthday. Thus the days passed
for Bunny, and every day the same images of her on TV.

Surprisingly Randeep wrote him a letter. 'My dear Bunny,
where do I begin? I can't believe that I really saw what I am
about to describe to you . . .' I can't read this rubbish, said Bunny
to himself, and crumpled up and threw away the letter. Hours of

introspection had made him love and long only for his own self. His mother sensed this as she watched him spend his hours examining the sky. 'I wish there were more people of your age here, Bunny.' Randeep's letter had broken Bunny's cocoon and the world had rushed in. He thought of his friends and his Delhi life with distaste. He couldn't return there. Bunny hated his past, it had given him his illness, and he distrusted his future, it would bring no respite.

Bunny bathed after the first few days, using an aluminium chair. The skin on his feet was thin and wrinkled. His toes looked like pieces of ginger. He thought, I had once been innocent, when I had assumed I could sprint a hundred yards with ease.

Then Mr Kairon asked once, on a bright morning, again over tea on the lawn, 'Bunny, will you grow your hair? And wear a turban? For my sake?' Mr Kairon did not know what rôle to assume, that of a liberal Sikh, a nationalist Sikh, or what Duggal called a true Sikh. 'And for Chandigarh, when you're a lawyer.' Bunny said yes immediately. He would have said yes to any request, it was not important. There were still months before Chandigarh, and the disease and the assassination had made it clear that the world was a wonderfully unstable place, where anything could happen. The two events ratified Bunny's inaction. One had to wait for the mad event, that was all. Where were the certainties? In the sky and sun? To the questions, there were not solutions; there was only a life, and only one life. Ambition was an absurdity; so-much-to-do-and-so-little-time-to-do-it-in, how pointless an outlook, here, look at Indira Gandhi, Bunny used to think, and often smile at the recollection.

Fulfilment

ÉILÍS NÍ DHUIBHNE

KILLINEY IS THE anglicization of *Cill Inion Léinin*, the chapel of
the daughter of Leinin. Who she was I do not know. Perhaps a
saint, like Gobnait of Kilgobnet. Or a princess, like Isolde of
Chapelizod. Perhaps she was just the daughter of a butcher, born
in the Coombe, moving out to Killiney to demonstrate her
upward social mobility, like many of these who live there. It is a
fashionable address. An inconvenient, overcrowded, unplanned
jumble of estates, possessing, nevertheless, a certain social cachet.
It was that which drew me to it, first.

Some people think I came for the scenery. My house is prac-
tically on the beach. From the front room I can gaze at Bray
Head, spectacular for a suburban view. The strand itself unwinds
in a silver ribbon from the bathroom-window. It is long and
composed of coarse grains of sand which cut your feet if you
walk barefoot thereon. I never do. There is no reason to do so
unless you want to swim. And swimming from Killiney Strand
is an activity which loses much of its appeal as soon as the
hulking grey monster lurking half-way along the stretch of
golden shingle is recognized for what it is: an ineffectual sewage
treatment plant. Shit from Shankill, nuclear waste from Wind-
scale, can have a dissuasive effect. On me, at least. Many people
revel in it, however, and emerge from the sea, not deformed,

but rarely quite the same as they were before they ventured in. Necks swell, pimples speckle peaches and cream, nipples invert and toes turn inward. And worse.

Killiney means much to me. I have lived there for thirteen years and would never forsake it. Not because I cherish any affection for the locality. The roads meandering drunkenly up and down the hill, the opulent villas perched like puffins on the edge of the cliff, the mean houses marshalled in regiments across the flatlands: these, in their essential lack of harmony, disturb my sense of the symmetrical, which is acute. Neither do I cling to Killiney because it provides me with congenial companions. I live in near isolation, enjoying little or no contact with my neighbours, apart from the occasional unavoidable shoulder rub with the post- or milkman. Some stalwart of the local residents' association drops the community newsletter, KRAM, though my letterbox every month. It often contains persuasive advertisements urging the reader to come to a social in the parish hall, or to join in a treasure-hunt on the hill, or to demonstrate community spirit by participating in a litter drive on the strand, all such notices carefully stressing that these events will provide excellent opportunities for neighbours to meet and increase their acquaintanceship. Such temptations I have always resisted with little difficulty. It has never been my idea of fun to spear crisp bags or rack my brain in the solution of improbable clues with a stranger who coincidentally has elected to live within a mile or so of my abode. I am not a neighbourly being, not in that sense.

Killiney means everything to me, nevertheless, for one reason, and that alone. It was in Killiney that I discovered my *métier*. My vocation. What I was born to do.

I am a dog-killer.

I did not choose this way of life deliberately. When I was of an age to select a career, I was too indecisive a character to be able to deliberately single out anything, even a biscuit from a plate containing three different kinds (I used to close my eyes and trust to luck, usually with disastrous results). I was, as the technical term has it, a drifter. I drifted from job to job, from activity to activity, a scrap of flotsam on the sea of life. If you could call the confined noisy hopeless office world of Dublin a sea, or life. First I worked for the corporation, which was a bit like working for the Russian civil service before the Revolution (or perhaps even after, but one doesn't know that experience so intimately). My duties consisted, for the most part, in writing addresses on envelopes, for the least, in dealing with telephone queries from a mystified but cantankerous public. After a destructive eighteen months, I sacrificed my security and pension and studied electronics for a year, at a Tech. Then I worked with a computer company for six months, until I was made redundant. Then I washed dishes in a German café in Capel Street, where, incidentally, I picked up a great deal of my employers' language as well as much other information which I have since found very useful. Then, at long last I got what I considered my great break. I was given a job as a folklore collector by a museum in Dublin. I was supplied with a tape-recorder and camera, and every day I walked around the city and environs ferreting out likely informants. When I had tracked them down, I interviewed them, interrogating them on a wide variety of topics loosely related to traditional belief and practice, with the aid of an easy to follow guide book. It was a fascinating and rewarding task, entirely suited to my skills and disposition. It cultivated in me a taste for adventure, exploration and, above all, absolute freedom to order my days without deference to the will of an authoritative, pettifogging bureaucracy. These tastes, once realized, developed in strength and persistence, so that liberty soon became an imperative for survival as far as I was concerned. When my collecting job finished, as it did inevitably and all too soon, I was left nursing the burden of the knowledge that I could never again return to the slavery of a nine to five position, which indignity I had endured for seven long years before my break.

The question was, what should I do instead? Killiney gave me the answer. I had officially been resident there for two years before my collecting job collapsed. My enthusiasm for my work had been such, however, that I had hitherto paid little attention to my surroundings, frequently, indeed, not returning home at night, but bedding down in the flat of a colleague, or in the home of one of the friendly folk who provided me with the stuff of my occupation. But, even in that state of almost total apathy to environmental hazards, it had often struck me that Killiney suffered from unusually severe infestation by the canine species in all its varieties, too numerous to mention and in any case not known to me by name, except for some of the more common forms, such as golden labrador or cocker spaniel. I had once been bitten by a lean and hungry Alsatian belonging to some itinerants who camped, with my full approval (not that they asked for it, or required it) on an undeveloped site at the end of my lane. I had had to go to St Michael's for a tetanus injection, which had been administered by an aggressive nurse wearing steel-rimmed spectacles. On another occasion, a minute pekinese, a breed which I particularly distrust, scraped the skin off the heel of an expensive shoe I had just purchased. Apart from these extreme incidents, every night I spent in Killiney was filled with the mournful howling of dogs. Any walk taken in the neighbourhood was spoiled by the effort of fighting my fear of being bitten, of planning, futilely, itineraries which would take me out of the beasts' range, or of physically chasing off the ever-encroaching packs of curs.

When I had finished collecting folklore and had begun to live in Killiney almost constantly, it soon became apparent to me that the dog problem was rendering life unbearable: not only my life, but everyone else's as well.

My work as a folklore collector had not only awoken in me a healthy desire to master my own experience. It had imbued me with what can best be described as an altruistic streak. I wanted to improve the existence of others, too. In short, I was burning with ambition to be of service to mankind.

Killiney showed me the way.

My first dog-killing was fortuitous. I was walking home from the station one evening, having spent a particularly wearisome day, trying to get a week's supply of food for four pounds, followed by an attempt to obtain an admission card to the National Library, where I had hoped to improve my mind with some classical reading while I considered my future. Both efforts had been fruitless. Lightly laden with two sliced pans, two tins of baked beans and a pound of liver, I had meandered up Kildare

Street, the consciousness of impending starvation slowing my footsteps. My entrance to the library was first blocked by a stern official in a blue suit, who accused me of trying to force entry without a reader's ticket, and thoroughly investigated the contents of my plastic bag. He suspected it of containing a bomb, he explained afterwards. He then directed me to the office of an even sterner official with startling red hair who informed me in no uncertain terms that the National Library had no accommodation to spare for the likes of me. My pleas lasted the best part of an hour, but were all in vain. The more I reasoned, the stronger grew his opposition. Finally I left, strolling through the reading room on my way out. The porter in the hall did not check my bag, which I found convenient, since I had tucked into it the second volume of Plummer's *Lives of the Saints*, a work now exceedingly difficult to procure honestly but a handsome set of which adorned the library's open-access shelves. I resolved to return at my earliest opportunity to steal the remaining volumes, with the intention of making them available to an antiquarian bookseller just around the corner of Kildare Street.

I refreshed myself after the ordeal with a glass of lager in a nearby hotel, and then used my last fifty pence in the purchase of a ticket to Killiney Station. I was obliged to endure the journey in a vertical position, since I had stupidly elected to travel on the five-fifteen, the most crowded train in Ireland. My state of mind was, therefore, far from tranquil or positive when, halfway down Station Road, a dog, something like a collie but with a terrier's nose, dashed across my path and attempted to grab my raincoat in his mawful of bad teeth. I lowered my umbrella before you could say Jack Robinson and hammered him on the skull. To my intense relief he immediately released his vice-like grip and lay, subdued, at my toes. I stared at his immobile body for a moment or two, enjoying a vigorous sensation of triumph. I waited, patiently, for the beast to struggle to his paws and slink furtively away, tail demurely tucked between legs, aware of who was master. A minute passed and he did not stir. The smile which had played on my lips receded. Thirty more seconds elapsed. He continued to lie prostrate on the concerete path. Not a whimper passed his lips. I bent down and touched his hairy back, somewhat gingerly. It was warm to my fingers, but I felt uneasy. There was an unearthly stillness in the texture of the fur. I turned his head over and his eyes bored into mine. Round and lifeless, rolling in their sockets. Aghast, I sprang to my feet. The cooling lump of dog meat on the path was dead, and I had killed it! Never until that moment had I murdered a fly.

Fortunately, my keen instinct for survival warned me that there was no time to be lost in foolish lamenting over spilt milk. The immediate necessity was to dispose of the dog with maximum haste and secrecy. Observing that all was quiet on the road, not a soul in sight. I emptied my plastic bag of its contents and hid them under a bush. In their place I put the deceased animal, intending to carry him home and give him a decent funeral: I could simply not run the risk of being asked to financially compensate some distraught pet-owner. The dog appeared to be a valueless mongrel but you never know. Sometimes it is precisely the ugliest specimens who turn out to have pedigrees as long as your arm. I knew of a charming spot near the sewage-plant where my victim would rest in eternal peace, since no one, human or canine, ever ventured there, for obvious reasons.

I walked home from what I preferred to regard as the scene of the accident, and placed the victim on the kitchen floor. Then I returned to the black spot to collect my groceries. They, however, were not to be found. Some cruel villain had stolen them. 'There goes dindins for five days,' I thought, glumly. How could I survive without food until dole day, a whole week off? Hunger reared its ugly head, not for the first time during my spell of unemployment.

Strolling homewards, I noticed torn slices of bread, scraps of bloodied butcher's paper, in short, the debris of my groceries, scattered at intervals along the road. About a hundred yards from where the tragedy had occurred a large ugly dog relaxed in the shadow of a tree, langorously devouring the last of the liver. 'Horrible brute!' I thought, wishing I had my umbrella with me, in order to give him a well-deserved whack. But it had stopped raining and my weapon was in its teak-stand in my little hall.

Back in the cottage, I sat in the living room and stared vacantly at Bray Head. It was black and awe-inspiring against the grey evening sky, but it afforded me no refreshment. My stomach rumbled, a dead dog lay on my kitchen floor awaiting burial, and, once again, rain bucketed forth from the heavens, preventing all action. I hadn't a single penny in my purse. After a dreary hour of staring, I went to bed supping a drink of water, the quality of which was far from high.

Morning dawned bright and sunny, lifting my spirits momentarily. My breakfast of stale oats and cold water effected a deterioration of mood, restoring me to a realisation of my undesirable predicament. The eyes of the dog, clear blue, were wide open and seemed to follow every move I made. If I'd had two pennies I would have placed them on those Mona Lisa orbs and shut them for once and for all (it was a trick traditionally used in the preparation of the dead for burial, as my old friends in the Liberties had often told me). As I rinsed my bowl in the earthenware sink, it occurred to me, suddenly, like a bolt out of the sky, that I was not, after all, going to cart the heavy dog all the way down to the sewage-plant, nervously avoiding encounters with morning strollers. I was not going to cart him anywhere at all. I was going to eat him.

In my work as a folklore-collector, I had spent two months investigating a particular genre of tale known professionally as the modern legend. Modern legends are stories which concern strange or horrifying or hilariously amusing events, and circulate as the truth in contemporary society. An example is the story of the theatre tickets. A man finds that his car is missing from its usual parking place. He reports the theft to the police, but a day later the car has been returned. Pinned to the windscreen is a note of apology, and two tickets for a theatre show that night, as a token of amendment. The car-owner and his wife use the tickets, and return at midnight to find that their house has been burgled. Another example is 'The Surprise Birthday Party'. A man wakes on his birthday to find that he has received no cards or greetings whatsoever. He goes to work and, at lunchtime, his secretary invites him to accompany her to her flat for lunch. He accepts the invitation with alacrity, and they proceed to her apart-

ment. She leaves him in the living room and entering the bedroom, says she will be back in a minute. He uses the opportunity
to undress, and is sitting on the sofa, completely naked, when
the bedroom door bursts open and his wife, children, neighbours
and colleagues leap into the room singing 'Happy Birthday to
You'. In the course of my wanderings in Dublin I had learned
that the best-known legend, amounting really to little more than
a belief, reported the use of dog as food in Chinese restaurants.
Alsatian Kung Fu. Sweet and Sour Terrier. Collie Curry, were
familiar names to me. It had taken only a trifle of investigation
to discover that it was untrue that the Chinese served dog in
their Irish outlets, but that in China and other parts of Asia, dog
was consumed as a normal part of the diet.

I got out my carving-knife (my mother had given it to me as
a house-warming present when I moved to the cottage: it is a
long sharp knife with a bone handle, an antique, she told me) and
flayed the animal. It was not easy, but neither was it as difficult
as it may sound. In a matter of an hour or so the soft brown
skin, dripping, it must be admitted, with soft wet blood, lay on
a wad of newspaper on the floor. Then I sliced meat off the
trunk of the dog: its legs were fragile and skinny and would be
food for nothing but stock. Within half an hour, I had removed
all edible flesh from the carcass (I had long ceased to think of it
as a corpse). I carried the remains out to the yard and pondered
how best to dispose of them. First I considered burning, but
decided that the smell of roasting flesh might carry to my unknown neighbours and arouse anxiety among them. I secondly
contemplated dumping them into the adjacent ocean. This
thought developed rapidly into a better plan. I would walk to
the sewage-plant where I had first considered burying the total
animal, and throw what remained of him into the cess-pool,
which was open to the public. The body would be processed
with the effluent from Shankill and whatever else went into the
stinking hole, and leave no trace to be discovered, now or ever.
The plan seemed so foolproof that I immediately felt happier
than I had at any stage of my life since my terrible encounter
with the keepers of the national literature some twenty hours
earlier.

It worked like a dream. No one observed me as I plodded along the uncomfortable shingle towards the plant. No one observed me climb to the edge of the cess-pool, and no one observed me tip the sack of bones into it. Coming home, sauntering along the tide line, now and then running out to avoid a brazen wave, I met a man leading a red setter, and bade him a cheery 'Good morning'. He smiled genially in response. No trace of knowledge or malice marked his weather-beaten countenance. I had been undetected.

I made a curry of the meat for Saturday's dinner: I had some spices in my cupboard, relics from more affluent days, as well as a cup of brown rice, which I prefer to the white: it is so much better for the digestion. The meal was superb: aromatic, tender, of a delicacy which I had never sampled before in the take-aways of Blackrock, Dun Laoghaire or even China, which I had visited as a student on a package trip. I had some left-over curry for Sunday's lunch (it tasted even better then) and two hefty cutlets for tea on the Sabbath. I had not eaten so well in several months.

The skin of the dog lay in my yard over the weekend. The blood dried off and the pelt seemed to be curing itself naturally. I cut off the straggly corners where the legs and tail protruded. I always hate those bits on animal skins, even on sheepskins. They seem so ostentatious. As if one were giving proof that the skin were real and not spun-nylon. I laid my genuine pelt in front of the fireplace. It looked shaggy, warm and inviting. I decided that I would refer to it in future conversations, even those which were conducted exclusively in my own company (which accounted for most) as my antelope, received from a friend who hunted in Gambia, where, I vaguely recalled, antelope still survived in sufficient numbers to be hunted. My friend visited Africa every spring, I'd decided, when the antelope were small.

One thing led to another. My natural antipathy to the canine species, my diagnosis of Killiney's main problem as the dog problem, my urgent need for lucrative entrepreneurial employment, all conspired to persuade me that dog-killing would be my next job. I plunged into it with my whole heart. It was so easy, after all, to find prey. Indeed, it usually found me, snapping and yelping my at fect whenever I ventured out of the house. It was a simple matter to remember to carry my large umbrella, bought, in any case, as a weapon, and to batter any nosy beast on the head, on the right spot just above the temple (death was invariably instant and painless). I always carried a big shopping bag on my hunting expeditions, and suffered few setbacks in transporting carcasses from strand, street or railway to my home.

My methods of disposing of the products of my enterprise varied and expanded in variety as time passed. Initially basing my plans on the knowledge I had acquired as a folklore-collector, I offered the flesh, neatly packaged in plastic cling-foil, to restaurants, at prices which were attractively but not suspiciously low. I did not, of course, approach Chinese or Indonesian restaurants. The owners would have immediately recognized my wares for what they were, and who knows what their reactions would be. Never trust a foreigner. No, I circulated the more exclusive native establishments, the cosy wee bistros with which the southern coastline of Dublin is so liberally peppered. I had, on the rare occasions when I had treated myself to a repast at The Spotted Dog or The Pavlovian Rat, to name a couple of the better establishments, noted that they served food which was spiced and sauced to such a degree that its basic ingredients, no doubt of the best quality, were totally unrecognizable. They might as well have served *Rat á la Provençale*, or *Cat Bourguignonne*, for all the evidence of veal or beef one could detect in either. The inhabitants of South Dublin, reared for the most part in primitive Ireland (i.e. not South Dublin) know nothing about food. All through their formative years they are fed on the Irish housekeeping tradition, and nothing else. Their mothers, bursting with pride about their home cooking, can concoct at best soda bread (the most tasteless, unhealthy bread imaginable), mixed grills, and boiled chicken. The natural reaction after such a diet is to crave the most elaborate messes of marjoram, tarragon, garlic, cream cheese, tomatoes, wine, ginger, and turmeric, all rolled into one cosmopolitan topping for pork masquerading as veal or monkfish doing duty for prawns. This taste is well catered for in every suburban village, if they can be called villages, those outcrops of shops and pubs and chapels which stud the concrete jungle from Bray to Booterstown. The northern Dubliner, at least while he stays on his own side of the river, probably still relies on his native cuisine, that is, coddle. I knew a man in the Corporation from Finglas West who always cooked coddle for lunch. He put it on at eleven o'clock at his tea-break and took it off at one, when it was done to a turn. He gave me a saucerful once.

The reception I received at first from the proprietors and chefs of my local *trattoria* was not enthusiastic. It was on the whole suspicious. Where had I got the meat? Did I have identification? And so on.

It was not hard to procure an identity card. What is identification, after all? Just a card stating that you are who you claim to be. Having to create cards, however, prompted me to use several aliases, something which would never have occurred to me had I not been asked for identification in the first place.

As to explaining the provenance of the meat, I had, prior to my very first visit to the manager of a cosy kitchen in Dalkey, fabricated my story. The meat, I had decided, was not antelope, but wild goat, imported from the North, where wild goats abound in the hills of Antrim and Tyrone. I had a partner in Crossmaglen who procured the meat for me from local lads, target practising in the mountainy regions. It was tasty and healthy, perfect for Cordon Bleu cookery. Indeed, I added, Swiss chefs prized goats above any other viand. The belief that it was stringy and tough was ill-founded. I would give the *restauranteur* a sample batch, free, for testing.

This tale, in conjunction with the identity card, worked. It was the bit about the North which added the final touch of plausibility to my explanation. Anything could happen in the North, in the view of Dublin burghers. They had heard of smuggled TV's and refrigerators, smuggled pigs and cattle. Why not smuggled goat?

Within six months I was regularly supplying twenty restaurants with dog meat and making a tidy profit. I continued to dump the denuded carcasses in the cess-pool, but found that I was having a problem with the increasing heap of skins in my back yard: yellow, black, brown and red, they lay there in a multi-coloured pile. I had carpeted my living-room with them, and very fine it looked, but I did not want my whole house covered with the remainder of my trade, and, even had I wanted it, I would have encountered a problem sooner or later.

After much deliberation I decided to shave the dog skins and keep the hairs. The left-over skin I would, perhaps, at some future stage, sew into handbags, belts and other fancy leather goods. For the present, I contented myself with the purchase of forty yards of yellow cotton, and proceeded to make bean-bags and cushions which I stuffed with dog-hair. I opened a stall in a street market in town where I would not be recognized as the goat importer, and most Saturdays and Sundays I could be found there vending my wares to a receptive public: my products were cheaper, softer and more hard-wearing than anyone else's.

Time went on, as it does, and I became more and more comfortable financially, and more and more fulfilled as a human being. I developed my hunting technique, advancing from the simple umbrella to the more complicated sling, which, of course, had the advantage of being able to kill from a distance, and on to the even more complex pop-gun. I began to travel the length and breadth of Dublin, realizing that if I depleted the canine population of Killiney too much and too quickly someone would become anxious and interfere. As luck would have it, nobody at all seemed to notice what was happening, although the community benefited in no uncertain measure.

Good fortune is never limitless, and, like all the most professional criminals, I was caught at last. It happened as I strolled along Dollymount Strand, popgun in pocket, car parked nearby, stalking a large English sheepdog. Normally I did not touch English sheepdogs or other expensive models with a ten-foot pole, but this one seemed to be very much alone. It had an abandoned look in its shaggy fringes and the lope of its melancholy feet spoke of endless deprivation. I felt it would be a kindness to take the animal out of its misery, and took a shot from a distance of fifty yards. The beast toppled and fell. Immediately, a man grabbed my shoulders. He was young, over six feet tall, and broad-shouldered. I did not struggle.

'I saw what you just did,' he said. He had an American accent and whined. 'You just shot my dawg!'

'Why, yes, I did,' I said.

'You can even stand there and admit it to my face!'

'Of course I can admit it. Why shouldn't I admit it? It was a complete mistake! Please accept my heartfelt apologies.'

'Aw! Sure it was a mistake! I saw you. You took aim and fired at him. My dawg!'

'I was trying to shoot that buoy over there,' I said, pointing at one of those plastery-looking life-savers in a wooden box which was, luckily enough, situated close to where the dog had fallen.

'I'm taking you to the police. Tell them your story if you like.'

He ushered me along the beach towards a Renault 12, red in colour. Then he drove rapidly down to the Bull Wall, across the bridge and to Clontarf barracks.

'You won't believe what I'm going to tell you,' he said to the sergeant, who was sitting beside a gas fire reading the *News of the World*.

'Well?' said the sergeant, with a great show of patience. His name, I noticed from a sign on the desk, was Sergeant Byrne. An unusual name for a Dublin guard.

'This broad here' – he indicated me with a flick of his shoulder – 'shot my dawg.'

'What?' Sergeant Byrne looked up from his paper in some surprise.

'She shot my dawg. With a shotgun.'

'What is your name?' Sergeant Byrne asked me. I handed him one of my identity cards. *Imelda Byrne, 10 Dundela Park, Sandycove*, it stated.

'Do you have a gun licence?'

'No. It's a toy gun.'

'Let me see it.'

I showed him my popgun. It is a toy gun. It shoots wooden pellets. The trick is to aim at the temple.

'Well, well,' said the sergeant, 'and why did you shoot this man's dog?'

'It was a mistake. I was target practising. I play golf, you see, and someone told me it would be good training for the eye to shoot at targets with a popgun.'

'I saw her aim at my dawg.'

'Yes, yes, well,' said the sergeant, 'we'll hold her for questioning. You can press charges, if you like. Fill in this and post it to us as soon as possible.' He handed the American a form.

The American departed, muttering under his breath. The sergeant sat, reopened his paper and looked at me quizzically.

'Target practising is an odd sport for a young lady to carry out on a Sunday afternoon. Can't you find a healthier way of passing the time?'

'I usually play golf.'

'Oh, yes, yes. Where do you play?'

'Newlands.'

'Oh, yes, yes. Hard to get into these days, isn't it? I play a bit of golf myself, you know. Up at Howth, usually. Very hard to get into a good club.'

'Yes.'

'Hm. So you shot this dog, did you? Haha! Well, to tell you the truth, the more dogs get shot, the better life will be in this neighbourhood. I'm moidhered with them and with people's complaints about them. What can I do? I'm only human. Now, be off with you.'

I collected my car from the beach and drove home. It was a great relief to me to know that what my heart has always told me was true: right and might were on my side. I was fighting the good fight.

After my ordeal on Bull Island, I decided to relax for at least one evening. Normally my Sunday nights were absorbed in account-keeping, doing the books, as the phrase has it, for the week. But on this particular Sunday I lit a fire in the drawing room and settled down to watch a video: I had a complete set of Bergman movies that I had not watched before. I adore Bergman. The film I selected was *Face to Face*, a slow-moving study of a psychiatrist and her relationship with her daughter, patients, husband, lovers, and others. I was just getting involved in it when my door-knocker sounded. A rare, almost unique, occurrence. I smelt danger immediately but had no option but to open it, since the blue glow of my living room would have indicated to anyone that I was in, glued to the box. At the door were two policemen, who asked me if I were Jane O'Toole. Shocked, I admitted that I was. They produced a warrant for my arrest.

I got six months. The judge said it was as much as he could impose although he heartily wished he could condemn me to a life of hard labour. My offence, he said, in a long tedious monologue at the end of my three-day trial, was the most heinous he had encountered in his life. I had been responsible, he said, for the killing of at least a thousand dogs (in fact, twice that). Responsible dogs. The beloved pets of the citizens of Dublin.

Now I am sitting in Mountjoy in the female wing, engaged in writing an autobiographical novel. Public sympathy for my crusade against the dogs is expressed by a flood of letters from people who have, in one way or another, been molested by them. Even the warders, a tough and unemotional crew, express concern for the fact that several hundred dogs roam the area within half a mile radius of the prison and threaten them every time they leave for a walk or to go home.

I am comfortable in prison and happy with the degree of freedom which I am allowed. I do not have to work and the only constraints are physical: I am not allowed outside the high walls which surround the penitentiary. Inside, I may do as I wish. I am not as happy as I was when enjoying my career as a dog-killer, but I am happier than I have been in many of my other jobs. I find fulfilment of a kind in writing down my life's experiences and struggle for freedom. More than one publisher has expressed interest in my project, which has already received considerable publicity in the media. According to some agents, I stand to score a huge success with the book. It will, they explain, be a matter of 'hype', and already it has been hyped to a much greater extent that any author would wish, and all for free. I could, taking into account the possibilities of film rights, translations, and so on, make at least a hundred thousand. And it will, like all my previous profits, be tax-free.

Needlework

DOUGLAS DUNN

MRS ESMÉE BOYD-PORTEOUS had been sending donations for over a decade to the orphanage run by the Catholic convent of St Justina's. When she finally managed to visit the convent, during one of her rare shopping trips to Glasgow, she asked if there was anything more she could do. She was told that the benefactors of St Justina's sometimes took a girl for the summer.

'Oh, but I'm so extremely sorry!' she cried. 'That never crossed my mind. Yes, of *course!*'

'You should have brought the Morris,' Mrs Boyd-Porteous said now to her husband as they waited in the car outside the station at Dumfries. Her impatience had led them to be early. 'The Bentley's much too ostentatious. This enormous car will do nothing but harm to her state of mind.'

'I doubt it,' her husband said. 'A ride in a Bentley ought to be a treat for any girl.'

'She isn't coming to us to be initiated into your crass notion of "treats",' she said.

'I wish you'd calm down, Esmée. Don't get so excited.'

'Is it to be held against me,' she said, 'if I'm looking forward to young company at Mickleyaird?'

A protective feeling toward his wife, and a high regard for his

67

peace and quiet now that he was living in semi-retirement, prevented Ronald Boyd-Porteous from taking his grumbling too far. The pair often had words together that brought them to the brink of bitterness, but he halted any conversation with his wife in which dissent threatened to expose what he suspected was his failure as a husband. More and more, he felt it was his selfishness that had stunted their marriage. 'Well,' he said, with a dry realism that Mrs Boyd-Porteous did not appreciate, 'I imagine she's hoping for a spectacular boost to her standard of living. That's what *I'd* be hoping for.'

'Your answer to everything is always money.'

It was a familiar criticism. 'Now, now, Esmée, that's enough of that,' he said lightly. He tapped the clock on the luxurious dashboard. 'The train might be a few minutes early,' he said, and reached for the car door.

At one time, Ronald Boyd-Porteous had been among the youngest professors of civil engineering in the country. Profitable consultancies had enticed him from the academic life and into business. It was during one of his many absences from home that Mrs Boyd-Porteous announced, in a transatlantic telephone call, that she had become a Catholic. Whatever had hitherto crossed his mind as a possible explanation for his wife's polite and considerate listlessness, it was not a crisis of faith that was to build up to a wholehearted religious conversion. It took him a year to get over seeing it as more than an eccentricity. On subsequent trips away from home, he pictured his wife sitting at her desk writing letters of support to deserving in-stitutions dedicated to the relief of misfortune, each with an enclosed cheque. He smiled with affection at the image, but it troubled him, too. He could tell himself that his wife now had plenty to do while he was abroad and preoccupied with the design and construction of projects costing millions, or absorb-ed in tiresome negotiations with governments and international agencies. Still, something was missing. He knew what it was but decided that the time had long passed to do anything about it. Instead of bringing up children of their own, his wife was a distant, anonymous supporter of young victims of famine, war, and loss.

'I hope you won't overdo it,' he told her when they reached the station platform.

'Overdo what?'

The train pulled in from the north and passengers began to get off. People were being met by friends or relatives. It was a small crowd, but brisk and intent.

'I think that might be our Miss O'Hagen,' Mr Boyd-Porteous said, drawing his wife's attention to a girl of seventeen. She carried a coat over one arm and a suitcase in her other hand.

Mrs Boyd-Porteous waved and caught the girl's eye as if it were she who had discovered her among the flow of approaching passengers. 'Olive! My goodness, the train looks so *busy*! Did you have a good journey?'

The girl put down her poor luggage and shook Mrs Boyd-Porteous's hand. She was tall; her hair was dark; her eyes were lively with curiosity, and flickered with a temporary shyness. Her straightforward good looks were poorly set off by the old-fashioned floral print of the dress she wore. She could have been taken for a daughter from the sort of farm or village where people seldom travel beyond the nearest small town – or, Mr Boyd-Porteous thought, for a girl brought up in an orphanage.

'I had to sit among the smokers,' Olive O'Hagen said cheerfully, as if this inconvenience had been interesting, if deplorable.

'Ronald,' Mrs Boyd-Porteous said, looking about distractedly, but her husband was already walking toward the ticket barrier with Olive's suitcase.

'I don't suppose you've been in a car like this before,' Mr Boyd-Porteous said to Olive as they drove off. He half turned toward her in the back seat, his voice rising pleasantly. 'It's my pride and joy. I'm very fond of cars. Ever since I was your age and old enough to learn how to drive. You could say it's one of my hobbies.'

'Ronald, please.' Mrs Boyd-Porteous often seemed to detect a note of condescension that he could swear was not there. 'I hardly imagine that Olive's very interested in cars.'

'Oh, but I like cars,' Olive said. 'My mother used to say I should've been a boy.'

'Do you have any brothers or sisters?' Mrs Boyd-Porteous asked.

'No, just me. I was six when she died,' the girl said.

'I do so much look forward to getting to know you, my dear,' Mrs Boyd-Porteous said, with that open and enthusiastic sincerity which her husband found both laudable and irritating. 'And I do understand how you must be wondering what *we* are like. So if we seem to be doing the wrong thing, then you must tell us. We're not used to children at Mickleyaird. Oh, but you're not a child, are you? No, of course not! St Justina's told us hardly anything about you. Your name, your age, and the time of the train from Glasgow Central, and that's about it. There's so much to do here. So much to see and do, my dear. I intend that you should have a wonderful time.'

'"Mickleyaird" means "the big place". Is that right?' Olive said.

'Fortunately for us, the house is a bit smaller than its name implies,' Mr Boyd-Porteous said, with a laugh that his wife found disagreeable.

'I've been hardly anywhere. It was really exciting, being on a train, and going somewhere,' Olive said. Her voice lilted on the thrill of her day. 'I've been trying to imagine what your house is like, but I'm sure it's going to be a surprise.'

Mrs Boyd-Porteous was relieved at Olive's good-mannered confidence, and impressed: the girl seemed unsubdued by an encounter with a well-to-do couple in their fifties, to whom she was beholden even if, as yet, she had no grounds for gratitude.

Second thoughts about the wisdom of taking a girl from St Justina's had been introduced to Mrs Boyd-Porteous's mind only a few days before. Mrs Buchanan, of Forgallan House, was a co-religionist whom Mrs Boyd-Porteous seldom saw, but the two women had talked at a fund-raising sale for the benefit of a medical mission in Uganda. At one time, Mrs Buchanan told her, she herself had taken in girls from St Justina's. 'One felt tempted to use the place as a sort of employment agency – staff on approval, so to speak. I prefer to think that my motives were more disinterested. That, I suspect, was my big mistake.' A girl had tried to run off with a selection of the more portable treasures of Forgallen House. 'Honestly, it was so obvious – she might as well have written "swag" on her disgusting little suitcase.' Another, given the chance, would have run off with Mr Buchanan, she said. It crossed Mrs Boyd-Porteous's mind that the fault probably lay with Mrs Buchanan's husband, a well-known flirt, since deceased. 'Decency forbids me to go into what one of them did with my gardener's assistant. There was no end of a fuss. One has heard of holiday romances, which are all very well, but really, in one's own home! No, Esmée. Surly, ill-mannered, and ungrateful little madams. You might find yourself having to cope with an amateur femme fatale or a juvenile pilferer. If I were you, I should call it off while there's still time.'

'Well, yes,' Mrs Boyd-Porteous thought, as her husband turned into the long drive that led to Mickleyaird. 'Girls might behave like that in *your* house, but it is unlikely to happen in *mine*.' She felt her benevolent eagerness rise again, although she was less than fully confident of the weeks that lay ahead of her.

Gertrude Naismith had been the housekeeper at Mickleyaird for many years. She was a Presbyterian, and she resented her employer's conversion to what she called 'the Church of Rome'.

'You should be ashamed of yourself,' she had said to Mr Boyd-Porteous on several occasions. 'Your wife keeps bringing her Papist junk into this house, and what's worse is that I'm the one who has to dust her wee statues and wipe the glass on her holy pictures. I should get a rise in wages for having to wipe dirt off craven images,' she complained.

'Graven, with a "g", isn't it?' he answered mildly.

'"Graven", "craven", who cares how it's spelt? It's me who has to clean them!'

Exchanges of that kind were commonplace between Mr Boyd-Porteous and Mrs Naismith. 'And now it's to be convent girls, eh? What do you say to that? She's gone too far this time. I'm sure you must think so yourself.'

'As you very well know, Gertrude, I'm an agnostic. I haven't been to church willingly in years. We've had priests in the house often enough, and although you whinge at the prospect, you're perfectly civil to them when it comes to serving them lunch or tea or whatever. I think you're the sort of person who'd kowtow to *any* man of the cloth. Either that or you're a hypocrite.'

'A hypocrite? Me? Listen to who's talking! Who's the moneybags who never goes to the kirk but who aye coughs up when its roof needs mending, or last year when woodworm got at the pews?' Mrs Naismith said, with self-righteous triumph.

'You can hang your things in the wardrobe,' the housekeeper told Olive as she showed her around her bedroom. 'It's yours as long as you're here. And there's that chest of drawers and the dressing table. You've your own bathroom.' She opened the door to it.

'My own bathroom!'

'I don't suppose I have to teach you how to run a tap?'

Olive smiled at what she took to be a joke. 'Do you live here, too, Mrs Naismith?'

'Well, I don't live on the moon. Most days I'm here by eight-thirty, and I'm away at the back of six – later if they've got visitors. I live down there by the main road.'

The housekeeper had expected someone less winning, or a girl hardened by orphan's sorrow and institutional conformity. Had there been a mean, urban toughness to Olive's manner, Mrs Naismith would not have been surprised. Instead, Olive seemed to behave with a natural candour before the opulence and love-liness of Mickleyaird.

'It's beautiful,' the girl said, feeling the bedspread but giving no impression that it was too good for her. The comfort and prettiness of the room clearly animated the girl, but Mrs Naismith had to admit there was nothing vulgar in the way she appreciated its spaciousness, the elegance of its furnishings, or the wide view of gardens and woodland from the bedroom window.

'Mrs Boyd-Porteous is a kind woman,' Mrs Naismith said sternly. 'Too kind for her own good, if you ask me.' The house-keeper felt obliged to deliver her warning, even if Olive's manner had already suggested that it might be unnecessary. 'To a stranger, she's bound to look like an easy touch – a bit too generous, you might say. And with her having no children of her own, a person might just get it into her mind to take advantage. If that's your type, Miss, then I advise you to forget it.'

Olive's face darkened with an expression that Mrs Naismith decided was genuine hurt.

'Where's our church?' Olive asked.

'*Yours* is in Drumotter, six miles down the road. You won't find many Catholics here in Ferlie.' It was a statement of fact, but Mrs Naismith said it with pride. 'Don't worry. Mrs Boyd-Porteous is keen on her early Mass. We might even have the holy visitors. We've had a monsignor before now, not to mention bishops.' She pronounced the first title with flagrant inaccuracy, and hissed mild loathing on the second.

'I'm sorry. I took it for granted that you'd be a Catholic,' the girl said, embarrassed by Mrs Naismith's religious aggression.

'It's no skin off my nose, because the man of the house isn't a Catholic, either. By your standards, he's even worse than I am. Mr Boyd-Porteous is a heathen.'

'I suppose you're Church of Scotland, then?'

'And so was Mrs Boyd-Porteous before she changed her mind.'

'I see,' Olive said.

'I wish *I* did,' Mrs Naismith said.

Olive made a favourable impression during her first days at Mickleyaird. Mr Boyd-Porteous was entertained by the interest she took in his garden.

'What are these?' Olive asked him.

'Buddleia,' he said.

'And this one?'

'Veronica.'

'Is it named after St Veronica?' the girl asked.

'I've no idea.'

'It was St Veronica who gave Christ her handkerchief to wipe his brow when he was carrying the cross to Calvary.'

'Now, I didn't know that. St Veronica and her handkerchief? Somehow I never thought of them blowing their noses in the first century AD, but I suppose they must have done.'

'So many bees and butterflies!' Olive said eagerly.

'Buddleia for butterflies, Veronica for bees,' Mr Boyd-Porteous said.

To the mistrustful Mrs Naismith, Olive O'Hagen was a wonder: a convent girl with table manners! An orphan who did not bolt her food, let alone ask for more! Mrs Naismith's mythology was stood on its head.

'She's not at all what you expected, is she?' Mrs Boyd-Porteous teased the housekeeper with a sly but detectable moral swank.

'Don't come it,' Mrs Naismith retorted, with her customary disregard for the conventions of talk between an employee and the lady of the house. 'She's nothing like what you expected, either. You went into a twist, like a cat caught in the rain, when you heard Mrs Buchanan's stories about the girls from St Justina's.'

'I am more interested in hearing what *you* expected,' Mrs Boyd-Porteous said.

'Thank God, but my experience of nunneries is nonexistent. So how would I know what to expect? I'll say this, though. She cleans the bath after she's used it, and she folds her towels as neat as you like and puts them back on the rail. Laundry in the laundry box, and no clothes folded over the backs of chairs. Not that I'm one hundred per cent convinced that our Miss O'Hagen isn't a little actress,' Mrs Naismith said.

'You do not frighten me in the slightest,' Mrs Boyd-Porteous said. 'I'm sure you overheard her at lunch yesterday when Father Struan was here. She never *tried* to sound particularly religious, and yet it was quite clear to anyone with eyes and ears that she is. What I hope you noticed, Gertrude, is that Olive was not in the least bit awkward or false.'

'I hope that place isn't training her for the nunhood, if that's the word,' Mrs Naismith said.

'Good gracious, no! Or – I don't think so,' Mrs Boyd-Porteous said, suddenly unsure.

'Well, there isn't a drop of makeup in her room,' Mrs Naismith said. 'Not so much as a wee bottle of cologne. The soap she brought with her isn't scented, and she still hasn't used that nice French soap you asked me to set out for her. And she's already in a convent, Mrs B.-P., even if it's an orphanage as well.'

'I hardly imagine that they'd *encourage* the use of cosmetics at

St Justina's,' Mrs Boyd-Porteous said. 'Apart from anything else, there is the expense to consider.'

'She's quite pale,' Mrs Naismith said.

'Not, I think, as pale as she was when she arrived.'

'Peely-wally,' the housekeeper said.

'Gertrude. Unless a girl's cheeks were positively crimson, you'd call her peely-wally, as you put it. Anyhow, if that's your worst complaint, I'm glad. I do wish you'd give Olive time to settle in and get used to us. All of us.'

Although she had settled into Mickleyaird more smoothly than either the Boyd-Porteouses or Mrs Naismith anticipated, Olive greeted each new experience with an eagerness of heart that her hostess found disquieting as well as satisfying. The girl's exhilaration over gathering flowers and helping arrange them in vases made clear how thoroughly she had been deprived of pleasures that Mrs Boyd-Porteous had always taken for granted. She was cheered by Olive's excited gratitude and tender curiosity, but it led her to worry whether she had done the right thing in introducing Olive to a style of life the girl had never known before and might never know again. Donating money to distant worthy causes was one thing, but Olive created a special predicament: the *object* of Mrs Boyd-Porteous's charity was in the house. It seemed cruel to offer Olive a taste of affluence and then withdraw it.

Several times as they drove one day to visit Mrs Buchanan at Forgallan House, Olive begged Mrs Boyd-Porteous to stop the car so that she could get out to look at a ruin, or a view, or lean over the parapet of a bridge and stare into the clear water.

Forgallan House was older and grander than Mickleyaird. Its intrinsic interest, together with the declining fortunes of its owner, determined that the house should be open to the public – admission £1.50 – throughout the summer months. Mrs Boyd-Porteous was apprehensive for Olive's comfort there.

'Forgallan House is somewhat *massive*,' she said. 'I've never been sure if it's Bunny Buchanan's fault or mine, or just the grandeur of the place, but I've never felt at home in Forgallan. It is not a welcoming sort of house, Olive. Please, be your usual delightful self, and we shall sail through this frightening experience. Bunny was terribly insistent that we should come, you know, and Forgallan *does* have the most intriguing little private chapel.'

They passed the notices that advertised the public visiting hours and the price of admission. 'Mrs Boyd-Porteous to visit Mrs Buchanan,' she told the caretaker, who manned a green shed where he took money, issued tickets, raised a barrier, and directed drivers to the car park. A gate marked 'PRIVATE' was opened to them. The attendant raised his cap.

'Don't feel privileged,' Mrs Boyd-Porteous told Olive. 'This is the former servants' entrance. The family have to use it when the house is open to the tourists.' As they left the car, she took a deep breath and said, 'Bunny Buchanan is such a bitter person that she brings out the good in one. Isn't that a terrible thing to say? Well, I've said it. I daresay we shall both leave feeling like saints.'

They were shown into a small, cramped sitting-room that Mrs Buchanan used when the rest of the house was being trodden through by the paying public, of whom the lady had a low opinion.

'I can't think why,' she said, 'but they revel in viewing the rooms in which they suppose one actually *lives*. I've heard comments on the state of the upholstery, or the curtains, or that such-and-such a painting is not by who it *is* by. Some people, too, seem to take an extraordinarily keen interest in what seems to be one's bedside reading. I say "seems", Esmée, because I take care to lay out rather serious historical or theological tomes, just to mislead them.' The mischievous humour of these remarks failed to force a way through Mrs Buchanan's lofty manner. 'Well, and how is this young lady's visit progressing, Esmée?'

'Oh, splendidly, quite splendidly!' Mrs Boyd-Porteous said.

'I'm having a marvellous time,' Olive said.

'Are you, indeed?' Mrs Buchanan said. She had not expected Olive to speak. 'And what do you think of Forgallan?'

'I think it's wonderful, Mrs Buchanan.'

'Most of the house was built a hundred and some years ago, as you may have observed.' Mrs Buchanan's voice implied that she placed little conviction in Olive's grasp of architectural history. 'But the bulk of the west side was formed out of the old Forgallan Castle, the ancient seat of the Wotherspoons.' She turned back to Mrs Boyd-Porteous. 'I see, Esmée, that the standard of dressmaking at St Justina's has not improved.' She nodded toward Olive and the dress she wore.

'Actually, Bunny, that's an old outfit of mine that my Mrs Naismith altered for Olive.'

'Oh? Really?'

'Would you think it too forward of me, Mrs Buchanan, if I asked to see the chapel?' Olive asked.

'It's on the tourist route,' Mrs Buchanan said curtly. 'My great-grandfather – This, you see, is *my* house; it was not my late husband's. I am a Wotherspoon –'

'Do you use it?' Olive broke in, as if unaware.

'Use what?'

'The chapel.'

'Well, yes. My youngest daughter was married in it a few years ago. Do you remember, Esmée?'

'Oh, Olive, it was the most beautiful wedding!'

'Does Father Struan say Mass in your chapel?' Olive asked. 'Oh, Mrs Buchanan, a chapel of your own!'

'Olive is a very religious young lady,' Mrs Boyd-Porteous said with considerable satisfaction.

'And from St Justina's? I am amazed, Esmée. Next I shall expect you to tell me that Miss O'Hagen is preparing to take the veil. Are you, Miss O'Hagen?'

'No, I'm not,' Olive said. Mrs Boyd-Porteous detected a note of annoyance.

'What, if I may ask, do you intend to do? Do you have a career in mind?' Mrs Buchanan arched her brows in exaggerated interest.

'I didn't get a place this year. They said it was because I'm too young – my birthday was only a few weeks ago,' Olive said.

'A summer baby!' Mrs Boyd-Porteous cried. 'Olive, I didn't know!'

'But it's as good as guaranteed for next year. I've a place to study English at the University of Edinburgh.'

'University?' Mrs Buchanan said, in a tone of spontaneous

disbelief. Good manners should have kept that under control, thought Mrs Boyd-Porteous, who was herself surprised by Olive's announcement.

'Olive is *extremely* clever,' Mrs Boyd-Porteous said.

'Obviously,' Mrs Buchanan said. 'The girls *I* took from St Justina's certainly didn't go to university. Oh, no! Wherever else they went, it certainly wasn't the University of Edinburgh. I could tell you a thing or two about the girls from St Justina's.'

'Bunny!' Mrs Boyd-Porteous said disapprovingly.

'Well, why not, Esmée? They gave me a great deal of trouble.'

Olive seemed to be included in Mrs Buchanan's dismissal of St Justina's. The girl rose and said stiffly, 'I would like to see the chapel, Mrs Buchanan. I'm sure I could find it if you were to tell me where it is.'

'It's not a particularly attractive chapel,' Mrs Buchanan said, resisting Olive's request. 'It's rather poky, to tell you the truth.'

'Oh, Bunny, no! It's perfectly delightful!' Mrs Boyd-Porteous interjected with gentle indignation.

'Actually, "hideous" is the word that comes most readily to *my* mind,' Mrs Buchanan said. 'Of course, I have never claimed to be a particularly devotional sort of Catholic. Oh, very well. I suppose you must, if you must.' Mrs Buchanan told Olive how to find the chapel. 'You'd better be quick about it,' she shouted after the girl, 'or Esmée and I shall eat all the cakes!'

When Olive was out of earshot, Mrs Buchanan said, 'I suppose she's eating you out of house and home. All of mine did. Eat, eat, eat ... Did I tell you? There was one girl, the same who rather fancied herself as a burglar, and she raided the kitchen, Esmée, in the middle of the night! Cook swore that the detestable glutton had grilled herself fifteen sausages! Fifteen!'

'Olive is very obviously *different*,' Mrs Boyd-Porteous said forcefully. 'And I think you were rude to her.'

'Me? Rude?'

'Yes, Bunny, *rude*. You showed her no consideration whatsoever.'

'And do you *believe* what she said about university?' Mrs Buchanan said with broad scepticism.

*

The chapel was small and cool. A religious tranquillity glowed in the varnish of its wooden panels and carved seating. Pools of red-and-blue light spilled from stained-glass windows and twitched on the stone floor near the altar. In the pews lay cushions and kneelers stitched over the years by women of the Wotherspoon family. A needlework Annunciation hung in a Gothic-arched frame; it was light and delicate, composed with obvious artistry. Other works by the same hand hung elsewhere on the chapel's walls among memorial plaques and devotional inscriptions.

Olive regained her equanimity in the chapel's calm, and walked about inspecting these fine embroideries and appliqués for some time. She thought them about the most interesting things she had ever seen. After a while, considering that she had been away for too long, especially after her risky display of temper, she started to make her way back to the sitting-room. Distant voices and the threatening resonance of hard heels on the stone floors added to her sensation that she was a trespasser or an unwanted guest. It was a feeling that she decided she was under no obligation to endure. Her face hardened, and she walked quickly away, not quite knowing where the corridor would lead. She came across a sign that said 'EXIT', and then, a little later, one that said 'TEAROOM'.

The café occupied what had once been a large storeroom on the ground floor. It was almost empty. Olive bought a cup of tea and sat down at a table. She felt exhausted with the effort of being good, well-mannered, and full of delight. She was torn between feeling comfort in Mrs Boyd-Porteous's jolly innocence and contempt for it. Well, if she'd gone too far with Mrs Buchanan she'd have to find a way to put it right with the Boyd-Porteouses.

In a few moments she found herself the last remaining customer. 'We'll be closing soon, dear,' said the waitress behind the tea counter. Olive was rising to leave, and calculating her next move, when the two women appeared in the doorway. The mistress of Forgallan House set her hands on her hips in the pose of one displeased but unsurprised.

'Olive!' cried Mrs Boyd-Porteous. 'Where've you been? Did

you get lost? We've looked everywhere for you!' Her tone was urgent, but she seemed neither unhappy nor angry.

'I must see to the guides,' said Mrs Buchanan. 'I'm sorry, Esmée, but I'll say goodbye. I have so much to attend to.'

'I'm sorry,' Olive said to Mrs Boyd-Porteous in the car. 'I'm sorry if I embarrassed you.'

'My dear, how could I blame you? No doubt Bunny Buchanan will tell everyone she knows about your "bad manners", but in my opinion you were magnificent.' She giggled as she craned over the steering wheel before turning on to the main road. 'I rather love you for it. Buying your own tea in the café! Rather than talk to that haughty crone! My dear, I shall cherish it until the day I die. By the way, she doesn't believe that you're going to university. She thought you said so as a lie, merely to impress her. Did you go round the entire house?'

'No, I didn't have time.'

'How can Bunny *bear* to run down that chapel?'

'I thought the chapel was lovely. And the needlework,' Olive said, pleased to move on.

'Oh, that needlework!' Mrs Boyd-Porteous enthused. 'By generations of Wotherspoon women, and Bunny Buchanan can't so much as sew on a button. Families! Oh, no, that sort of wonder does not run in families. How like you to have noticed it, Olive! It's so precious to me.'

'It was very beautiful,' Olive said.

'I do a little myself, you know,' Mrs Boyd-Porteous said. 'Embroidery mainly. I confess my deficiencies as a needle-woman, but if I may be so vain, I have mastered Florentine stitch.'

'Those cushions in your sitting-room?'

'Oh, yes, they're mine!'

'Would you teach me?' Olive asked. Her tone was hesitant.

In the days that followed, Mrs Boyd-Porteous applied herself to teaching Olive her repertoire of stitches. They sat together on the sitting-room sofa, or in an arbour outdoors. They visited a friend of Mrs Boyd-Porteous's whose skills in all forms of needle-work were a byword in excellence. They made sketches from plates in books, and started work on an Annunciation of their own.

'She should be showing Olive more of the countryside,' Ronald Boyd-Porteous complained to Mrs Naismith. 'The girl didn't come here to learn how to sew.'

'Well, she's a good girl, and she's a sight handier with a needle than I am,' the housekeeper said. She smiled, a little sheepish at acknowledging her change of heart.

'Still, it's nice to see,' he conceded. 'They really get on with it.'

'Olive likes it here,' Mrs Naismith said. 'Maybe too much. She'll miss Mickleyaird something terrible.'

'Has she said anything to you?' he asked.

'She hasn't, but I'd say it was a fair guess.'

'That's charity for you. One lot gives, the other receives, and those who receive can be forgiven for feeling a bit jealous of what the givers have got.' He looked questioningly at Mrs Naismith, whose downturned mouth and raised eyebrows registered disapproval. 'I didn't mean it like that, Gertrude. Anyway, how can envy be avoided? It's perfectly natural. All she has to do is compare St Justina's with here. It's inevitable. She's too intelligent not to have felt it already. Surely?' he said.

'For a start, I don't think she *is* jealous,' the housekeeper said. 'I just work here, and I'm not jealous. She likes Mickleyaird. She loves the place. Of course she'll miss it. You can make that easier for the girl,' Mrs Naismith said. 'Make sure you ask her back for next summer.'

Ronald Boyd-Porteous was moved by the sight of his wife and Olive together in the garden or sitting-room. At the same time, it made him uneasy over the decisions and indecisions of the past. For all his conscientious hard work, his chairmanship of committees, his international prestige in an important field, there had been an indolence in his life.

'You've become extremely fond of Olive,' he said to his wife during the dressing-gowned fifteen minutes before they went to bed. Outside, a warm August night had been cooled by the briefest of showers.

She turned to him from her dressing table, hairbrush in hand.

'I should think that you are, too, by the looks of things. I can't imagine anyone not being fond of Olive. I always knew that St Justina's was well run, but I had no idea how splendidly they could respond to a girl of her sensitivity. And perhaps we could help.'

'Yes, well, I imagine that she's their pride and joy. She'll have the resources of the Vatican backing her up, I should think.' Mrs Boyd-Porteous frowned with good-humoured impatience at her husband's flippancy. 'All the same, there's nothing to stop us from giving her a hand ourselves. Taking an interest,' he explained. 'Shall we ask her back next summer?'

'I've already taken care of that.' She resumed brushing her hair. 'The art shall not die,' she said, with a wave of her brush. 'We're planning some really quite *ambitious* tapestries.'

'It's very appealing,' he said with difficulty. 'Watching the two of you working away with your needles. Master and pupil. Or mother and daughter.' He felt the phrase linger on the air, the subject never broached. Even as he went on, the words 'mother and daughter' were what he heard. 'It's crossed my mind, over the past couple of weeks. I can't say I've been looking forward to it, Esmée, but I've been expecting you to ask –'

She put her hairbrush down and looked at him in the mirror.

Abruptly, he said, 'I'm going out for a smoke!'

Mr Boyd-Porteous did not stop until he reached the garden. He lit his cigarette. As he stood holding his lighter, he felt how moist and hot his palms were. He looked at the few stars in the cleared sky and groaned at the thought of his emergency. Rushing downstairs in his dressing gown and through the house to the garden was the most dramatic incident in his marriage. It was preposterous – he was an undemonstrative man! – that he should find himself standing on the damp lawn in his dressing gown. The scent of night-aromatic stocks went unnoticed. He could have avoided the truth by keeping to the discreet routines of his marriage; still, he was glad to have come so close to puncturing his restraint. He stamped on the half-smoked cigarette and climbed back upstairs, weary with his own weight.

He paused inside the bedroom door in a state of embarrassed sorrow. 'I know this is as likely to sound as selfish as everything else I seem to say, but I can't bear the thought of making fools of ourselves. Not after all this time. It would look like desperation on our part.'

'What are you talking about?'

'I know what you've been thinking. I can feel it. You want Olive to live here, with us – legally. You've been thinking about how to make official moves in that direction. Haven't you?'

His wife turned to him. 'You must think me extremely vulnerable, and very stupid,' she said, her words measuring sad surprise. 'To imagine that Olive could be my daughter? Olive is seventeen! She's ready to begin a life of her own!' He had trespassed too clumsily for it to be dismissed or forgiven as a simple misunderstanding. 'Is that your idea of starting a family – to adopt an adult?' She spoke with uncharacteristic bitterness. 'Did you honestly believe that's what I had in mind?'

'Yes,' he said firmly. He was sure his deductions were reasonable. 'The way you two sit together, laughing, sewing, talking . . . The way I've seen you *look*.'

She gazed at him with a kind of wistful horror. 'And you think I could be so pathetic as to want to adopt a seventeen-year-old girl . . . I wish you'd said nothing. After all, you say so little. I wish you'd left that subject dead. Unborn.'

'It was bound to come out sometime,' he said.

After a pause, she went on. 'I *did* think of it, but only for a second. Just like that – for one single moment. We have our own regrets, but we must leave Olive out of it!' Ronald Boyd-Porteous kept silent; he could see his wife's self-control slip from her grasp, and he was unsure of his own. 'It has nothing to do with Olive. She knows that she is welcome here at any time.' She switched off the lamp on her dressing table. 'And there shall be *other* girls from St Justina's.'

Primavera

MARIAN ELDRIDGE

AUNT CHRISSIE JENNAWAY invites Alvie Skerritt down to Melbourne for the August school holidays. She's Alvie's aunt, Joan Skerritt's sister, the one who swopped country for city, and married money.

Alvie can't wait. She's fed up with this hoon town, fed up with her cranky, jangling family. What is there here that she wants to do? She knows every shop window by heart. She would like someone to talk to, maybe, but what is it she wants to say? *What?* she demands.

Her father, Ray Skerritt – he's the shop steward out at the paper mill, and he's always on about something, job-sharing, industrial safety, Alvie's last maths test – he says, You're off to a silly life, just don't get ideas Alvie.

Why are men always so bossy, why can't they just leave you alone?

Alvie shrugs: I can take care of myself. Joan Skerritt, her mouth full of pins because she is hemming Alvie's new skirt for Melbourne, jabs Ray Skerritt with a look: Chrissie is my sister, Ray, do you *mind*?

Scenting battle, the little kids sparkle.

Alvie looks at her family and sighs.

. . . In what way silly, she wants to know. It's no big deal is it to want a bit of fun instead of the ever-present boiled cabbage stink of the paper mill, and a houseful of kids and trampled toys and homework and washing all over the place which as far as Alvie can see is about all that her mother has got from her father. A female's life is shithouse. So Cass Jawkins reckons. She's only in Alvie's year but she's got it sussed out: look after number one! Yeah right, says Alvie, in that sing-song surprised tone that everyone's using just now.

'Do stand still, Alv!' complains Joan Skerritt through the pins. 'Do you want me to get this hem straight or don't you?'

Alvie can't wait to get on that train.

But if the mill town's a bore, it turns out life in Melbourne is no great riot either. Dragging after Aunt Chrissie first thing to admire a floppy new pansy or a bulb poking through a mush of leaf litter. Watching Aunt Chrissie bid for an old chair that Alvie thinks should go straight to the tip. Having cakes and coffee together in posh little shops where Alvie's appetite shrivels just thinking what her father would say about the prices. Then home to Uncle Rupert who's a prune, and that enormous squeaky-clean house where from the fancy three-piece mirror in her bed-room Alvie catches her triple image looking sideways at her homemade skirt.

What's more, because it's school holidays, any day now that wimpy kid Philip Jennaway will turn up. Philip Jennaway is Uncle Rupert's son by his first marriage. Alvie remembers Philip as one of those top-of-the-class kids too dumb not to show it. He is not due at the Jennaways' until two or three days after Alvie arrives because, Aunt Chrissie explains, his mother always makes some difficulty about his spending the entire vacation with his father. Aunt Chrissie grows quite fierce about this. 'You'd think just this once – particularly when he hasn't any brothers or sisters of his own – but she always was a selfish woman.' Suddenly she lowers her voice. 'She refused him his conjugals, Alvie.'

Alvie takes a moment to realize it's not Philip she means but Uncle Rupert, that stooped grey man who during dinner will clear his throat and hawk, 'And what did you do today, young woman?'

What did you do, young woman? ... Alvie's thoughts go

skittering off to all the outings lately in the Gilberts' old panel van. Would Uncle Rupert swallow the story that the mattress Butch Gilbert has in the back is just a bit of showing-off to impress his mates? Despair like dirty bath-water washes over Alvie. She's fed up with flogging the same old line, 'Yes of course he behaves himself' to her parents, and to Butch Gilbert 'No you can't – next time maybe – right now I've got you-know-what, it's just started, I've got you know, *Charlie*.' That's what girls have to say. He falls for it every time.

Changing out of her jeans into her skirt for dinner because that's the custom at Jennaways', Alvie tiptoes across to the three-piece mirror. Well, Alvie? The whole room is holding its breath. Alvie holds her breath too, squeezes up her eyes, tries hard for the sting of tears in her nose – a gaggle of girls crying together, but no tears come. So she studies her reflection, trying to make sense of it, trying to put together what she sees: three skinny girls with small, tense breasts, flat stomachs, hip-bones sticking out like the wings on Uncle Rupert's leather chair. And inside, under the clothes, under the skin, the secret bones and veins and pulses, pumping blood, getting ready for Charlie, holding her together but all for what? She turns slowly, raising her arms, and thinks about a picture she has seen in some art book at school: three girls, arms lifted, absorbed in movement, oblivious of gawkers as wearing nothing but see-through nighties they dance bare-foot in a garden. *Asking for it, got up like that* snicker the gawkers as one of the girls gets jumped by some yobbo . . . She thinks about her mother, kitchen images mostly, and that time she was pregnant with Lurlene, tight as a watermelon, you could see her navel when the wind blew her smock. In Grade Five Cass Jawkins wouldn't believe that babies didn't come out through your navel. You could laugh at Cass Jawkins then. But not now, Cass Jawkins makes out she knows everything now. And what after all is there to get so excited about, says Cass Jawkins. Just a guy slobbering on you and a bit of discomfort, a bit of blood.

Yeah, just a bit of blood, echoes Alvie Skerritt. A female's life is ruled by blood.

*

But what does Alvie Skerritt know about anything? She knows enough to scrape through most exams. She knows that the first Mrs Jennaway wouldn't give Uncle Rupert his conjugals and that this is a terrible thing, not natural Aunt Chrissie declares. She knows from mooching around in the garden where Philip Jennaway once built a treehouse, now abandoned like elastics or marbles. And where will any of *that* get Alvie?

Your age Alvie is the springtime of your life, her father tells her. Alvie reckons it's more like going into a maths test with only bits of the formula inked on to her palm. They will all wake up to her one of these days – her parents, Butch Gilbert, knowing Cass Jawkins – and then what will she do?

Going downstairs for their pre-dinner sherry that makes Alvie secretly giddy, she finds that Philip has arrived. One glance at him and she ducks back upstairs to put on her special black lipstick. Oh golly, that Philip! My cousin in Melbourne's *gorgeous*, my cousin's a real hunk o' spunk, she practises telling Cass Jawkins. 'Hel*lo* nice to see you again Alvie,' he intones, and gives her a peck on the cheek. He has a faint moustache now and he wears his hair longer, spunky, she tells Cass Jawkins. 'White thanks Dad,' he says in that supercool voice. Uncle Rupert pours him a glass of wine instead of sherry and he stands swirling his glass and perving over it. This so intrigues Alvie that she practises with her sherry, moving her glass under her nose as she drinks in Philip. He'd be as tall now as Butch Gilbert, not as lunky though. His wrists escape from his coat sleeves like flyaway insects; Aunt Chrissie says straight after dinner she will get to those sleeves and lengthen them. At this Philip smiles, the old smile that Alvie can handle. Draining her glass, she catches his eye and tosses him a black, giddy simper. A tic jumps at the corner of his mouth.

'Chrissie,' he says – he directs all his comments at Aunt Chrissie but keeps glancing at Alvie. 'Chrissie, this is a survival thing, did you know that given a choice, in a maze say, slaters will turn right then left then right then left?' Well gee whizz, Phil.

It is arranged that Philip will take Alvie sight-seeing. Alvie sees Aunt Chrissie give Uncle Rupert a pleased little nod. Philip takes her first to the Museum, a sombre great building with a tarted-up cable tram at the entrance. Alvie's brain grows muzzy as Philip yacks on happily about the model steamships and the cutaway trains. They look at Phar Lap in a glass case. Phar Lap's coat gleams and muscles ripple as though he wants nothing better than to burst through the glass and gallop out of that winter-still room. Philip explains that his heart which was more than twice the weight of that of a normal horse is displayed miles away in the National Capital. Alvie looks from the dead gleaming horse to Philip and sees that little tic jump again when he catches her watching him. She wonders if he has ever kissed a girl. When they come out at last into the spring sun-shine which has cast a sherry-coloured glaze over everything, she takes hold of his hand, and keeps hold of it all the way home in the train.

Back in the Jennaways' garden, she tells him she has some-thing to show *him* – and she takes him through the tangled prunus and flowering currants to the platform constructed in the big leaning wattle. 'My old treehouse!' he says wonderingly. 'I made it years ago out of some bits of timber left over from something but I can't recall playing in it much.' Climbing up, he leans down to give her a hand but she laughs and pulls herself up. Twigs catch at their hair. They sit down. She puts her arm around him and leaning her head against his jumper, listens to his heart busy in its own secret world. 'I don't like cold dead places with old dead horses without hearts,' she mutters.

'What did you say? I can't hear you.'

For reply she raises her face and runs her tongue over his ear. He shudders, his lips touch hers. He tastes nice, she decides, better than Butch Gilbert or Herbie Mason who mash your face with their demanding smoky tongues. After a while she sits away. 'Let's leave some for tomorrow,' she says faintly.

The next day, and the next, and the next, they hurry home from the Art Gallery, Myer's Bargain Basement, a second trip to the Museum. When his tentative hands have gone far enough for that day according to the code of the girls back home, she draws back and asks him things about himself. Get them talking, says Cass Jawkins, it gives you a breather. But Alvie surprises herself by actually listening. Back home she never listens to Herbie or Butch. Philip says he doesn't know much about girls. He envies her, going to a mixed school. There's a girl on his tram but he doesn't know how to start off and anyway it doesn't matter now, does it? He envies people like Chrissie and his father, and now the Skerritts, some people are just lucky, able to love, he was coming to believe he was one of those people destined to miss out on all that.

What a screwed-up life! Alvie feels a pang of affection for that boring, bossy, jostling family back home.

'Does your mother have a boyfriend?' she asks one afternoon.

Philip shrugs. 'She's always going to the theatre and things with people – men – but she says they're all pigs. I guess that means me, too. She's joking of course but you know what? – she used to complain if Dad so much as came into the bathroom when she was having a shower.'

'What was he trying to do? Pinch her bottom?'

'Maybe.'

At this incongruous view of Uncle Rupert, Alvie laughs. She has a quick picture of herself: soap up to the chin in the old crazed bathtub at home, and in bursts Gorgeous to pinch her bottom – Who? David Bowie? Prince Andrew?

'Aren't you glad I'm not one of your museum pieces, Phil?' she asks, nudging him.

She is not prepared for what happens next. It's as though some crazy kid has thrown himself into Uncle Rupert's leather armchair and flung it over backwards. 'I could rape you, you know!' he blurts. As she twists her head angrily, thinking What a dumb thing to say, he throws himself off her, crying, 'Help me, Alvie! I don't know what I'm doing, I'm so crazy for you – I feel ashamed but why *should* I feel ashamed, you don't, do you? But then you're not a rapist, are you? My mother reckons a fellow that does that to a girl against her will deserves the knife.' She would, thinks Alvie. 'Maybe we'd better stop coming here – yes, that's the only thing, Alvie, stop coming here, stop kissing, stop going around together to museums and things.'

Alvie sits up and brushes twigs and wattle-bloom off her coat. 'Aunt Chrissie will think we've had a fight,' she says slowly. It's as though someone has copied out the right formula and passed it to her under the desk. She says, bending down to him, 'Do you really want to? Stop coming here, I mean? They haven't planned anything for us for tomorrow, Phil.' And watches her hand run over those forlorn shoulders until he turns to her, saying, 'You know I don't!'

'So . . . no more attempted assault, huh?' she jokes, but her voice sounds strange, dazed. Tomorrow she will know as much as anyone – her mother, Cass Jawkins. 'Only you'd better get something,' she continues. 'You know – get something? Glad-Wrap, that'll do.' So Cass Jawkins reckons.

But next morning she wakes with a familiar drag in the pit of her stomach, a heavy, fat cramping, and hurrying to the bathroom to make sure, she flies into a rage against all those forces – Butch Gilbert, Cass Jawkins, her own body – that are pushing her into this thing with Philip and then at the last moment like a stupid joke shoving Charlie in the way.

Perhaps Philip won't want to today, she thinks – perhaps he's forgotten – but no, when they set out at Aunt Chrissie's suggestion for a picnic in the Botanic Gardens, he turns aside at the Jennaways' front gate and pushes through the shrubbery to the treehouse. Savagely she thrusts aside his hand and climbs up by herself. 'Philip,' she says, and now she is nearly crying, Alvie Skerritt caught cheating at last. 'Listen, about us – there's *Charlie*.'

'Charlie?' Philip frowns, drawing away. 'Charlie?' At this reaction Alvie is offended. Because it's something that happens to half the world, isn't it? Just because *he* doesn't, he needn't back off as though she's diseased. She is so angry that she fails at first to take in Philip's hurt protest: 'You didn't tell me – only of course there would be, wouldn't there, lots, I suppose, queues – droves – I guess I was just an amusement.'

She is too busy saying caustically, 'Charlie's not my favourite friend, actually. Nor anyone's.' At this point she realizes Philip's mistake, and laughs. Philip says, 'Actually I don't much like two-timing myself' and tries to shake off her hand when she takes hold of his arm.

'Relax, relax,' she soothes, much as her mother soothes her

father when he's tensing everyone up about bombs or green belts or something. 'I can't help it, truly I can't.' She takes a deep breath. (A female has to make the most of these things, Alv.) 'That Charlie gets around – more than you ever will, Phil. He's what you might call unavoidable amongst the girls I hang around with.'

'All of them?'

'All of them. Sooner or later.'

Without another word Philip jumps down from the treehouse. Then, because he is a courteous boy brought up to help women, he turns back to assist Alvie. But refuses to look at her. So this time she takes his outstretched hand, and when she is standing on the ground again, sways against him. Puts her arms around him. Observes the familiar tic begin to twitch at the corner of his mouth. As soon as he kisses me, she tells herself, slipping her hands under his jumper, Just as soon as he kisses me I'll tell him what Charlie really is. Her hands move up and down that resisting back. But he has to kiss me first.

Away in a Niche

ALICE THOMAS ELLIS

THERE HAS BEEN a lot of talk recently about statues moving.
Well, they *do*. I know because I once spent Christmas in a
niche.

I had been shopping yet again on the endless Christmas round
and I stopped at our local church, for a sit down more than
anything else, because I was in no mood for praying. I sat there
going over my purchases in my mind and realizing I would have
to go out yet again since I had forgotten many things – wrapping
paper, and cloves for the bread sauce, and red apples for the
centre of the table, and more mundane things like cat's meat and
toothpaste. As I collected my carrier bags and genuflected pre-
paratory to leaving, I glanced to my left and caught the gaze of
our local saint: her mellifluous, impartial and, as I now thought,
annoyingly smug gaze.

'It's all right for you,' I told her. 'Stuck up there out of the
way in your plastered peace with your self-satisfied smirk.'

I would never have spoken like that normally but my feet
were hurting and my arms were nearly dragged out of their
sockets with the weight of the shopping. It was freezing outside
too. Still, that was no excuse for being rude to a saint, so I
apologized in an undertone, and then, just as I turned to go I
saw her eyes look swiftly to left and right, and she put her

painted plaster finger to her painted plaster mouth and leaned forward towards me.

Naturally I was astounded. I dropped one of my bags and heard something break and I gripped the back of a pew for support. Luckily there were only very few other people in the church, only one or two old women rapt in comtemplation of Our Lady and a comatose wino laid out on the floor. All the same, at my reaction she straightened up and resumed her stance in her niche, gazing into the distance with her small smile. After a moment I addressed her again.

'Did you just move,' I demanded, in a whisper, 'or am I going mad on top of everything else?'

Her eyes flickered down at me and her smile widened. I sat on the pew and looked sideways and up at her, and then I heard her speak. The gist of what she said was this: that she would carry my shopping home and take my place over Christmas if I would agree to take her place in the niche.

Well, it wasn't exactly up to my dream of spending Christmas alone in a small snowbound hotel at the end of the world, but it would certainly mean a rest, so I hardly hesitated at all before agreeing; and the next thing I knew I was looking across the church from the saint's erstwhile vantage point with my eyes on a level with the seventh Station of the Cross, and a weary-looking woman was gathering up a lot of carrier bags and genuflecting below my feet.

As she left she smiled up at me reassuringly and told me not to worry, she would take very good care of everyone and everything of mine.

I had a moment's misgiving because my motives in agreeing to this imposture had been completely selfish, arising from my great tiredness, from the prospect of for once being spared Uncle Fred's Christmas jokes, Cousin Amy's dissatisfaction with the arrangements no matter what they might be, and the early morning riot as the children tore the wrappings from their presents and discovered that I had forgotten to buy batteries to motivate their robots, toy cars, radios, etc. But then I reflected that my family could hardly be in better hands than those of a canonized saint, and that if I had any sense I would stop worrying and make the most of my rest. It would be ungrateful to spend Christmas fretting about those things I had left undone. I hoped the saint would be inspired to check the store cupboards and discover the lack of cloves; bread sauce without cloves is insipid.

Then I began to relax. The cat would point out unhesitatingly the lack of cat's meat; if anyone could not get by without toothpaste then they could hasten out and buy some. I felt the saint could be trusted to choose some decorative motif for the table centre, and as for the wrapping-paper – well, I found I really didn't care about that any more. I was perfectly comfortable standing in the niche because, after all, I had no bone or muscle to strain or stretch, being composed of plaster and paint on a wire armature, and I felt warm and secure in the silence which was stirred only by an occasional shuffle of ancient feet, a cough, a murmured incantation: I clutched my handful of plaster hyacinths (the saint's most potent emblem) and gazed with her own tranquillity across the aisles, my foot resting gently on a plaster boar's head.

Suddenly I became aware that someone was addressing me. I cautiously lowered my gaze and saw the top of a woman's head, nodding slowly up and down. '. . . I wouldn't want him to suffer,' she was saying; 'not too much anyway, for when he hasn't the drink he's been good enough to me.'

At this she looked up, her eyes met mine and I recognized her as my next door neighbour's cleaning lady. Simultaneously I realized that she was invoking the help of the statue, whom she believed to be the saint, to procure the death of her husband; had probably been doing a novena to this end, and I felt very much taken aback although not entirely surprised. The saint, you see, had gained her eminence in the community of saints not merely by the exemplary virtue of her ways but because she had been married by force to a perfect brute who used to beat her and tie her to trees and fling her down dungeons because she utterly refused to fulfil her conjugal obligations. One day, while he was chasing her round the woods, she ran into a wild boar who gored her to death; only just before she expired in a handy bed of hyacinths she forgave her husband his importunities, cruelties and misdemeanours and he repented and mended his ways amazingly, becoming a highly respected member of society and exceedingly devout. I was aware that some uneducated women, misunderstanding this tale and forgetting the saint's magnanimity and remembering only the horrible ways of her husband, were in the habit of asking her for assistance in marital matters, but I had not realized that anyone could be so misguided as to seek her intercession to the extent of asking for the death of a spouse.

My shock must have shown on my face for I felt my jaw drop and at that moment the woman looked imploringly up at me. My fingers momentarily relaxed and I felt a hyacinth slip from between them. Of course, the woman shrieked. I knew just how she felt. If I hadn't been so tired I might have shrieked myself when the saint spoke to me. The woman fled up the side aisle to the door and a moment later she was back dragging the curate with her. He had clearly been interrupted in the course of his tea, for he was eating bread and jam and had the reluctant air of a curate who knows that the cake will have been eaten by the time he returns.

'Look,' said the woman dramatically, pointing at the wretched hyacinth.

'It's only a hyacinth,' said the curate. The clergy are notoriously sceptical about miraculous happenings. They have to be.

'*She* dropped it on me,' insisted the woman, pointing up at me while I strove very hard to keep in countenance, much regretting my lapse although I felt I could not be held wholly to blame since she had greatly startled me. One does not expect one's neighbour's char to nurture murderous inclinations towards her husband, or at least not to be so open and frank about them. I had to remind myself that she supposed me to be the saint and not her employer's neighbour but I still considered her behaviour indiscreet.

She and the curate argued this way and that, and the tone of their discussion became quite heated. I stood in some embarrassment, vowing to be more careful until Christmas had passed. When I was alone again, reflecting on the nature of marriage, I had another worrying thought. My husband was an uxorious man and in view of the saint's attitude to conjugality I could see the possibility of serious misunderstanding. I hoped she would have the foresight to develop a heavy cold and insist on sleeping in the spare room.

The next morning as the congregation arrived for Mass I kept a wary eye on the door to see the saint enter in the guise of myself. She had brought the two older children, and I was relieved to see that her – my – nose was scarlet and our eyes were streaming. After Mass she came over to speak to me. In between a muttered *ave* and a paternoster and over the clicking of beads she whispered reassurances to me about the state of the house and the children's appetites and my husband's health. Even the cat, it seemed, had accepted her without question. I longed to ask her if she had remembered to buy the cloves, but after the events of the afternoon I dared not and stood smiling vacantly as she spoke to me in my own voice.

'Come *on*, Mummy,' said my children pulling at my skirt which the saint wore, and I felt a tremor in my plaster toes until I reminded myself that Mummy was, for the moment, not I but the tired-looking woman below with the dreadful cold.

'Goodbye, hyacinth lady,' said the younger of the two older children and I was glad to see that I – she – punished this affection with a little shake.

Relieved of anxiety about my family, I reverted to worrying about my neighbour's char. She was a nice, hard-working woman with many children, and as had now become evident, a husband so unbearable that she wished him dead. I would not have been so concerned had she not confided in me, for although she did not know that I had her secret I felt strangely responsible for her.

She came to look at me again on her way home from work, standing at my feet and gazing up at me with an expression of half-fearful expectancy. I was dreadfully tempted to speak, to offer her – not comfort, for I could think of none – but advice. I wanted to tell her to go to a marriage guidance counsellor, although I knew that the fact that she had come to me – or rather to the saint – meant that if this idea had occurred to her she had rejected it. She looked at me imploringly for a little longer and then left, her poor shoulders bowed with worry and disappointment and the prospect of a beating from her drunken husband, and I seethed in my niche with indignation and pity.

The next day was Christmas Eve and the saint called to see me in the afternoon with two of the younger children. She sat in the pew below me while the children went to look at the crib – at the lambs and the donkey and the star and the baby. She whispered that everything was ready for tomorrow, the capon stuffed, the potatoes peeled, the oyster soup ready to be reheated. Yes, she said kindly, she knew she must be sure and let it boil, she promised she wouldn't let my family suffer from food poisoning – not even Uncle Fred or Cousin Amy.

I was glad to see she had a sense of humour and relieved that she seemed to have a good grasp of the basic rules of cookery. This worry had not occurred to me before, but as she had flourished some centuries ago I would not have been surprised had she confessed an inability to master the intricacies of the gas stove, the food processor, the washing machine, etc. I wondered if she'd been driving the car.

The evening passed peacefully and I stood, half dreaming, content in my niche while one or two people asked my intercession in more reasonable matters – a girl wished to visit the Costa Brava and an old man wanted to win some money on a horse. I made a note to pass these requests on to the saint when we resumed our normal roles and personae.

As the time for Midnight Mass approached I watched the saint come in with all my family, even Uncle Fred and Cousin Amy, right down to the baby who peered at me over his father's shoulder with every sign of approval. Taking a chance, I blew him a swift kiss and he remarked 'Poggelich bah,' and laughed.

'Ssh,' said my husband.

'Pooh,' said my child, beaming at me.

I pulled myself together and stood quite still, gazing over their heads at the far wall.

Halfway through Mass there was a slight disturbance at the back of the church as some latecomers arrived. From the stumbling and slurred mutterings I gathered that they were drunk. This happened every year. Certain men who never attended Mass at any other time, not even to make their Easter Duties, would invariably, inevitably, roll up, paralytic, for Midnight Mass. Nobody minded as long as they weren't sick and didn't swear too loudly as they fell over attempting to kneel unsupported on the floor.

One of them reeled unsteadily down the aisle and came to a halt below my niche. He clutched at the end of the pew and knelt down. As he did so I caught sight of his face and recognized him despite the crossed eyes and hectically flushed nose as the husband of my neighbour's char. I glared down at him before recalling myself to the Mass. When it was over and the sleepy congregation made its slow way to the doors I saw that he had fallen fast asleep leaning against the pew's end. No one made any move to disturb him, but all left unanimously by way of the centre aisle as he slumped there, snoring gently, and suddenly I was seized by an irresistible compulsion.

Cautiously I loosened yet another hyacinth and dropped it on his head. He woke disoriented, half-blind with beer and sleep, and looked round pugnaciously. Whereupon I leaned swiftly forward, seized him by the collar so that he was forced to look into my face, and remarked in a low but positive tone, 'If you don't stop drinking and beating your wife, you bastard, you will be very, very sorry.' Then I dropped him and stood back in the niche, stone-still and silent.

I heard later that he had left the church, gone home and kissed his wife and all his children, thrown away the cans of beer he was keeping in the sideboard, helped wash up after Christmas dinner and taken his whole family for an outing on Boxing Day. His wife never knew exactly what had happened but she was delighted. When he stopped drinking he was able to go back to being a builder's labourer and he made so much money that she was able to give up her job cleaning for my neighbour and stay at home washing his labouring clothes. My neighbour was very put out but I felt that that really couldn't be helped.

The saint came back the day after Boxing Day. I thought that she – I – looked very tired, but she seemed content and said that she had left everything as she imagined I would wish to find it and Cousin Amy had not been too obnoxious. There were quite a few left-overs still, but she was sure I would be able to sort everything out when I got home. She apologized that the bread sauce had been a bit tasteless because she hadn't been able to find any cloves but everything else had been very good. When she was back in her niche and I in my self I thought that she looked rather relieved, and I was a bit annoyed to find that she had left me with the remains of her cold, although she had got over the initial worst stages of sore throat, raw chest and itching nose.

When I got home I went round the house on a tour of inspection. The spare room, chill and exquisitely clean, smelt strongly of hyacinths; while the bed in my own room was unmade and the curtains undrawn. Whilst I was remedying these deficiencies, pondering the exclusive ways of sanctity and wondering whether the slight ache in my limbs was due to the saint's cold, the position I had been obliged to maintain or possibly to some subconscious memory of the agressive attentions of thc wild boar, my husband peered round the door. 'You're better,' he said in a tone of relieved surprise. Remembering the Saint's magnanimity towards her own husband who had been much, much worse than mine, I forebore to ask what had prevented him from making the bed himself. For the rest I found the house remarkably tidy with an unusual air of order and propriety; the children cheerful and amiable. Only the baby was sitting in his pram, thumb in mouth, looking puzzled and faintly forlorn. When I picked him up he looked at me for a long moment, then took his thumb out of his mouth, put his arms around my neck and would not be parted from me until he fell asleep long past his bedtime when the moon was high.

Martyrs

DESMOND HOGAN

ELLA WAS AN Italian woman whose one son had been maimed in a fight and was now permanently in a wheel-chair, still sporting the char-black leather jacket he'd had on the night he'd been set upon. Ella's cream waitress outfit seemed to tremble with vindication when she spoke of her son's assailants. 'I'll get them. I'll get them. I'll shoot them through the brains.' The chrome white walls listened. Chris's thoughts were set back that summer to Sister Honor.

The lake threw up an enduring desultory cloud that summer – it was particularly unbudging on Indiana Avenue – and Chris sidled quickly by the high-rise buildings which had attacked Mrs Pajalich's son. Sister Honor would have reproached Ella with admonitions of forgiveness but Chris saw – all too clearly – as she had in Sister Honor's lucid Kerry coast blue eyes the afternoon she informed her she was reneging on convent school for State high school that Sister Honor would never forgive her, the fêted pupil, for reneging on a Catholic education for the streams of State apostacy and capitalistic indifference. Chris had had to leave a Catholic environment before it plunged her into a lifetime of introspection. She who was already in her strawberry black check shirt, orientated to a delicate and literary kind of introspection.

Sister Honor's last words to her, from behind that familiar desk, had been 'Your vocation in life is to be a martyr.'

The summer before university Chris worked hard – as a waitress – in a cream coat alongside Mrs Pajalich. Beyond the grey grave-stone citadels of the city were the gold and ochre cornfields. At the end of summer Chris would head through them – in a Grey-hound bus – for the university city. But first she had to affirm to herself. 'I have escaped Sister Honor and her many mandates'.

Ella Pajalich would sometimes nudge her, requesting a bit of Christian theology, but inevitably reject it. Ella had learnt that Chris could come out with lines of Christian assuagement. How-ever the catastrophe had been too great. But that did not stop Ella, over a jam pie, red slithering along the meringue edges, from pressing Chris for an eloquent line of Heaven-respecting philosophy.

Rubbing a dun plate that was supposed to be white, Chris wondered if Heaven or any kind of Elysium could ever touch Ella's life; sure there were the cherry blossoms by the lake in spring under which she pushed her son. But the idea of a miracle, of a renaissance, no. Mrs Pajalich was determined to stick the café bread knife through someone. If only the police officer who allowed his poodle to excrete outside her street-level apartment. Ella had picked up the sense of a father of stature from Chris and that arranged her attitude towards Chris; Chris had a bit of the Catholic aristocrat about her, her father an Irish-American building contractor who held his ground in windy weather outside St Grellan's on Sunday mornings, his granite suit flap-ping, a scarlet breast-pocket handkerchief leaping up like a fish, his black shoes scintillating with his youngest son's efforts on them and his boulder-like fingers going for another voluminous cigar. 'Chris you have the face of fortune. You'll meet a nice man. You'll be another Grace Kelly. End up in a palace.' Chris saw Grace Kelly's face, the tight bun over it, the lipstick like an even scimitar. She saw the casinos. Yes she would end up living beside casinos in some mad, decadent country, but not Monaco, more likely some vestige of Central or South America.

'Chris, will you come and visit me at Hallow'een?' The dreaming Chris's face was disturbed. 'Yes, yes, I will.'

Summer was over without any great reckoning with Sister Honor and Chris slid south, through the corn, to a city which rose over the corn, its small roofs, its terracotta museums by the clouded river, its white capitol building, a centre-piece, like a Renaissance city.

Sister Honor had imbibed Chris from the beginning as she would have a piece of revealing literature; Chris had been established in class as a reference point for questions about literary complexities. Sister Honor would raise her hand and usher Chris's attention as if she was a traffic warden stopping the traffic. 'Chris, what did Spenser mean by this?' Honor should have known. She'd done much work in a university in Virginia on the poet Edmund Spenser; her passion for Spenser had brought her to Co. Cork. She'd done a course in Anglo-Irish literature for a term in Cork University. Red Irish buses had brought her into a countryside, rich and thick now, rich and thick in the Middle Ages, but one incandesced by the British around Spenser's time. The British had come to wonder and then destroy. Honor had come here as a child of five with her father, had nearly forgotten, but could not forget the moment when her father, holding her hand, cigar smoke blowing into a jackdaw's mouth, had wondered aloud how they had survived, how his ancestry had been chosen to escape, to take flight, to settle in town in the Mid-West and go on to creating dove-coloured twentieth-century skyscrapers.

Perhaps it had been the closeness of their backgrounds which had brought Chris and Honor together – their fathers had straddled on the same pavement outside St Gellen's Catholic Church, they'd blasted the aged and lingering Father Dunne with smoke from the same brand of cigars. But it had been their over-probing interest in literature which had bound them more strongly than the aesthetic of their backgrounds – though it might have been the aesthetic of their backgrounds which drove them to words. 'Vocabularies were rich and flowing in our backgrounds,' Sister Honor had said. 'Rich and flowing.' And what did not flow in Sister Honor she made up for in words.

Many-shaped bottoms followed one another in shorts over the

verdure around the white Capitol building. The atmosphere was one of heightened relaxation; smiles were fifties-type smiles on girls in shorts. Chris found a place for herself in George's bar. She counted the lights in the constellation of lights in the jukebox and put on a song for Sister Honor. Buddy Holly. 'You Go Your Way and I'll Go Mine'. A long-distance truck driver touched her from behind and she realized it was two in the morning.

She had imagined Sister Honor's childhood so closely that sometimes it seemed that Sister Honor's childhood had been her childhood and in the first few weeks at the University – the verdure, the sunlight on white shorts and white Capitol building, the Fall, many-coloured evening rays of sun evoking a primal gust in her – it was of Sister Honor's childhood she thought and not her own. The suburban house, hoary in colour like rotten bark, the Maryland farm she visited in summer – the swing, the Stars and Stripes on the verdant slope, the first or second edition Nathaniel Hawthorne books open and revealing mustard, fluttering pages – like an evangelical announcement. In the suburbs of this small city Chris saw a little girl in a blue crinoline frock, mushrooming outwards, running towards the expectant arms of a father. Red apples bounced on this image.

Why had she been thinking of Sister Honor so much in the last few months? Why had Sister Honor been entering her mind with such ease and with such unquestioning familiarity? What was the sudden cause of this tide in favour of the psyche of a person you had tried to dispose of two years beforehand? One afternoon on Larissa Street Chris decided it was time to put up barriers against Sister Honor. But a woman, no longer in a nun's veil, blonde-haired, half the colour of dried honey, still tried to get in.

Chris was studying English literature in the university – in a purple-red, many-corridored building – and the inspection of works of eighteenth- and nineteenth-century literature again leisurely evoked the emotion of the roots of her interest in literature, her inclination to literature, and the way Sister Honor had seized on that interest, and so thoughts of Sister Honor – in the context of her study of literature – began circulating again. Sister Honor, in her mind, had one of the acerbic faces of the

Celtic saints on the front of St Grellan's, a question beginning
on her lips, and her face lean, like a greyhound's stopped in the
act of barking.

'Hi, I'm Nick.'

'I'm Chris.'

A former chaperone of nuclear missiles on a naval ship, now
studying Pascal, his broad shoulders cowering into a black
leather jacket, accompanied Chris to George's bar one Saturday
night. They collected others on the way, a girl just back from an
all-Buddhist city in California, a young visiting homosexual
lecturer from Cambridge, England, a girl from the People's
Republic of China who said she'd been the first person from her
country to do a thesis at Harvard – hers was on nineteenth-
century feminist writers. George's bar enveloped the small
group, its low red, funeral parlour light – the lights in the
window illuminating the bar name were both blue and red.

Autumn was optimistic and continuous, lots of sunshine; girls
basked in shorts as though for summer; the physique of certain
girls became sturdier and more ruddy and brown and sleek with
sun. Chris found a tree to sit under and meditate on her background, Irish Catholic, its sins against her – big black aggressive
limousines outside St Grellan's on Sunday mornings unsteadying
her childhood devotions, the time they dressed her in emerald
velvet, cut in triangles, and made her play a leprechaun, the time
an Irish priest showed her his penis under his black soutane and
she'd wondered if this was an initiation into a part of Catholicism
– and her deliverance from it now. The autumn sun cupped the
Victorian villas in this town in its hand, the wine red, the blue,
the dun villas, their gold coins of autumn petals.

Chris was reminded sometimes by baseball boys of her acne –
boys eddying along the street on Saturday afternoons, in from
the country for a baseball match – college boys generally gave
her only one or two glances, the second glance always a curious
one as she had her head down and did not seem interested in
them. But here she was walking away from her family and sometimes even, on special occasions, she looked straight into
someone's eyes.

What would Sister Honor have thought of her now? O God, what on earth was she thinking of Sister Honor for? That woman haunts me. Chris walked on, across the verdure, under the Capitol building beside which cowboys once tied their horses.

The Saturday night George's bar group was deserted – Nick stood on Desmoines Street and cowered further into his black leather jacket, muttering in his incomprehensible Marlon Brando fashion of the duplicity of the American Government and armed forces – Chris had fallen for a dance student who raised his right leg in leotards like a self-admiring pony in the dance studio. The plan to seduce him failed. The attempted seduction took place on a mattress on the floor of his room in an elephantine apartment block which housed a line of washing machines on the ground floor which insisted on shaking in unison in a lighted area late into the night, stopping sometimes as if to gauge the progress of Chris's and her friend's love-making. In the early stages of these efforts the boy remembered he was a homosexual and Chris remembered she was a virgin. They both turned from one another's bodies and looked at the ceiling. The boy said the roaches on the ceiling were cute.

Chris made off about three in the morning in a drab anorak blaming Catholicism and Sister Honor, the autumn river with its mild, offshooting breeze leading her home. Yes, she was a sexual failure. Years at convent school had ensured a barrier between flowing sensuality and herself. Always the hesitation. The mortification. Dialogue. 'Do you believe we qualify, in Martin Buber's terms, for an I–thou relationship, our bodies I mean.' 'For fuck's sake, my prick has gone jellified.' Chris knew there was a hunch on her shoulders as she hurried home. At one stage, on a bend of the river near the road, late, home-going baseball fans pulled down the window of a car to holler lewdnessess at her.

She'd never been able to make love – 'our bodies have destinies in love,' Sister Honor rhetorically informed the class one day – and Chris had been saving her pennies for this destiny. But tonight she cursed Sister Honor, cursed her Catholicism, her Catholic-coated sense of literature and most of anything Sister

Honor's virginity which seemed to have given rise to her cruelty. 'Chris, the acne on your face has intensified over Easter. It is like an ancient map of Ireland after a smattering of napalm.' 'Chris, your legs seem to dangle, not hold you.' 'Chris, walk straight, carry yourself straight. Bear in mind your great talent and your great intelligence. Be proud of it. Know yourself, Chris Gormley.' Chris knew herself tonight as a bombed, withered, defeated thing. But these Catholic-withered limbs still held out hope for sweetening by another person.

Yes, that was why she'd left convent school – because she perceived the sham in Sister Honor, that Sister Honor had really been fighting her own virginity and in a losing battle galled other people and clawed at other people's emotions. Chris had left to keep her much-attacked identity intact. But on leaving she'd abandoned Sister Honor to a class where she could not talk literature to another pupil.

Should I go back there sometime? Maybe? Find out what Honor is teaching. Who she is directing her emotions to. If anybody. See if she had a new love. Jealousy told Chris she had not. There could never have been a pair in that class to examine the Ecclesiastes like Honor and herself – 'A time of war, and a time of peace'. Chris had a dream one night in which she saw Honor in a valley of vines, a Biblical valley, and another night a dream in which they were both walking through Spenser's Cork, before destruction, by birches and alders, hand in hand, at home and at peace with Gaelic identity and Gaelic innocence or maybe, in another interpretation of the dream, with childhood bliss. Then Sister Honor faded – the nightmare and the mellifluous dream of her – the argument was over. Chris settled back, drank, had fun, prepared for autumn parties.

The Saturday night George's bar group was resurrected – they dithered behind one another at the entrance to parties – one less sure than the other. Chablis was handed to them, poured out of cardboard boxes with taps. A woman in black, a shoal of black balloons over her head, their leash of twine in her hand, sat under a tree in the garden at a party one night. She was talking loudly about an Egyptian professor who had deserted her. A girl approached Chris and said she'd been to the same convent as Chris had been. Before the conversation could be pursued the room erupted into dancing – the girl was lost to the growing harvest moon. Chris walked into the garden and comforted the lady in black.

'Dear Sister Honor.' The encounter prompted Chris to begin a letter to Honor one evening. Outside the San Francisco bus made its way up North Dubuque Street, San Francisco illuminated on front, just about passing out a fat negro lady shuffling by Victorian villas with their promise of flowers in avenues that dived off North Dubuque Street, bearing her unwieldy laundry. But the image of Sister Honor had faded too far and the letter was crumpled. But for some reason Chris saw Honor that night, a ghost in a veil behind a desk, telling a class of girls that Edmund Spenser would be important to their lives.

Juanito was a Venezuelan boy in a plum red tee-shirt, charcoal hair falling over an almost Indian face which was possessed of lustrous eyes and lips that seemed about to moult. He shared his secret with her at a party. He was possessed by demons. They emerged from him at night and fluttered about the white ceiling of Potomac apartments. At one party a young man, Jose from Puerto Rico, came naked, crossed his hairy legs in a debonair fashion and sipped vodka. So demented was he in the United States without a girlfriend that he forgot to put on clothes. Juanito from Venezuela recurred again and again. The demons were getting worse. They seemed to thrive on the season of Hallow'een. There was a volcanic rush of them out of him now at night against the ceiling.

But he still managed to play an Ella Fitzgerald number, 'Let's Fall in Love', on a piano at a party. Jose from Puerto Rico found an American girlfriend for one night but she would not allow him to come inside her because she was afraid of disease, she told him, from his part of the world.

Chris held a party at her apartment just before the mid-term break. Juanito came and Jose. She'd been busy preparing for days. In a supermarket two days previously she'd noticed as she'd carried a paper sack of groceries at the bottom left-hand corner of her college newspaper, a report about the killing of some American nuns in a Central American country. The overwhelming feature on the page however had been a blown-up photograph of a bird who'd just arrived in town to nest for the winter. Anyway the sack of groceries had kept Chris from viewing the newspaper properly. The day had been very fine and Chris, crossing the green of the campus, had encountered the bird who'd come to town to nest for the winter or a similar bird. There was goulash for forty people at Chris's party – more soup than stew – and lots of pumpkin pie, apple pie and special little coffee buns, specked by chocolate, which Chris had learned to make from her grandmother. The party was just underway when five blond college boys in white tee-shirts entered bearing candles in carved pumpkin shells, flame coming through eyes and fierce little teeth. There were Japanese girls at Chris's party and a middle-aged man frequently tortured in Uruguay but who planned to return to that country after this term at the college. He was small, in a white tee-shirt, and he smiled a lot. He could not speak English too well but he kept pointing at the college boys and saying 'nice'. At the end of the party Chris made love in the bath not to one of those boys who'd made their entrance bearing candles in pumpkin shells but to a friend of theirs who'd arrived later.

In the morning she was faced by many bottles and later, a few hours later, a ribboning journey through flat, often unpeopled land. The Greyhound bus was like her home. She sat back, chewed gum, and watched the array of worn humanity on the bus. One of the last highlights of the party had been Jose emptying a bottle of red wine down the mouth of the little man from Uruguay.

When she arrived at the Greyhound bus station in her city she understood that there was something different about the bus station. Fewer drunks around. No one was playing the jukebox in the cafe. Chris wandered into the street. Crowds had gathered on the pavement. The dusk was issuing a brittle blue spray of rain. Chris recognized a negro lady who usually frequented the bus station. The woman looked at Chris. People were waiting for a funeral. Lights from high-rise blocks blossomed. The negro woman was about to say something to Chris but refrained. Chris strolled down the street, wanting to ignore this anticipated funeral. But a little boy in a football tee-shirt told her 'The nuns are dead.' On the front page of a local newspaper, the newspaper vendor forgetting to take the money from her, holding the newspaper from her Chris saw the news. Five nuns from this city had been killed in a Central American country. Four were being buried today. One was Honor.

When Chris Gormley had left the school Sister Honor suddenly realised now that her favourite and most emotionally involving pupil – with what Sister Honor had taken to be her relaxed and high sense of destiny – had gone, that all her life she had not been confronting something in herself and that she often put something on front of her prize pupils, to hide the essential fact of self-evasion. She knew as a child she'd had a destiny and so some months after Chris had gone Honor flew – literally in one sense but Honor saw herself as a white migrating bird – to Central America with some nuns from her convent.

The position of a teaching nun in a Central American convent belonging to their order had become vacant suddenly when a nun began having catatonic nightmares before going, heaving in her frail bed. With other sisters she changed from black to white and was seen off with red carnations. The local newspaper had photographed them. But the photograph appeared in a newspaper in Detroit. A plane landed in an airport by the ocean, miles from a city which was known to be at war but revealed itself to them in champagne and palm trees. A priest at the American Embassy gave them champagne and they were photographed again. There was a rainbow over the city that night. Already in that photograph when it was developed Honor looked younger. Blonde hair reached down from under her white veil, those Shirley Temple curls her father had been proud of and sometimes pruned to send snippets to relatives.

In a convent twenty miles from the city Honor found a TV and a gigantic fridge. The reverend mother looked often into the fridge. She was fond of cold squid. A nearby town was not a ramshackle place but an American suburb. Palm trees, banks, benevolent-faced American men in panama hats. An American zinc company nearby. The girls who came to be taught were chocolate-faced but still the children of the rich – the occasional chocolate-faced girl among them a young American with a tan. Honor that autumn found herself teaching Spenser to girls who watched the same TV programmes as the girls in the city she left. An American flag fluttered nearby and assured everyone – even the patrolling monkey-bodied teenage soldiers – that everything was all right. Such a dramatic geographical change, such a physical leap brought Honor in mind of Chris Gormley.

Chris Gormley had captivated her from the beginning, her long, layered blonde hair, her studious but easy manner. Honor was not in a position to publicly admire so she sometimes found herself insulting Chris. Only because she herself was bound and she was baulking at her own shackles. She cherished Chris though – Chris evoked the stolidity and generosity of her own background; she succeeded in suggesting an aesthetic from it and for this Honor was grateful – and when Chris went Honor knew she'd failed here, that she'd no longer have someone to banter with, to play word games with, and so left, hoping Chris one day would make a genius or a lover – for her sake – or both. Honor had been more than grateful to her though for participating in a debate with her and making one thing lucid to her – that occasionally you have to move on. So moving on for Honor meant travel, upheaval, and finding herself now beside a big reverend mother who as autumn progressed kept peering into a refrigerator bigger than herself.

A few months after she arrived in the convent however things had shifted emphasis; Honor was a regular sight in the afternoons after school throwing a final piece of cargo into a jeep and shooting – exploding off in a cantankerous and erratic jeep – with other nuns to a village thirty miles away. She'd become part of a catechetics corps. Beyond the American suburb was an American slum. Skeletal women with ink hair and big ink eyes with skeletal children lined the way. Honor understood why she'd always been drawn to Elizabethan Irish history. Because history recurs. For a moment in her mind these people were the victims of a British invasion. At first she was shy with the children. Unused to children. More used to teenage girls. But little boys graciously reached their hands to her and she relaxed, feeling better able to cope.

The war was mainly in the mountains; sometimes it came near. But the children did not seem to mind. There was one child she became particularly fond of – Harry after Harry Belafonte – and he of her and one person she became drawn to. Brother Mark, a monk from Montana. He had blond hair, the colour of honey, balding in furrows. She wanted to put her fingers through it. Together they'd sit on a bench – the village was on an incline – on later afternoons that still looked like autumn, vineyards around, facing the Pacific which they could not see but knew was there from the Pacific sun hitting the clay of the vineyards, talking retrospectively of America. Did she miss America? No. She felt an abyss of contentment here among the little boys in white vests, with little brown arms already bulging with muscles. Brother Mark dressed in a white gown and one evening, intuiting her feelings for him – the fingers that wanted to touch the scorched, blue and red parts of his head – his hand reached from it to hers. To refrain from a relationship she volunteered for the mountains.

What she saw there would always be in her face, in her eyes. Hornet-like helicopters swooped on dark rivers of people in mountain-side forests and an American from San Francisco – Joseph Dinani – his long white hair like Moses's scrolls, hunched on the ground in an Indian poncho, reading the palms of refugees for money and food. He'd found his way through the forests of Central America in the early 1970s.

There were bodies in a valley, many bodies, pregnant women, their stomachs coming over water like rhinoceroses bathing. Even after that there'd be an alarm in her eye and her right eyebrow was permanently estranged from her eye. She had to leave to tell someone but no one in authority for the moment wanted to know. The Americans were in charge and nothing too drastic could happen with the Americans around.

She threw herself into her work with the children. For some hours during the day she taught girls. The later hours, evening

111

closing in in the hills, the mountains, she spent with the children.

They became like her family. Little boys recognized the potential for comedy in her face and made her into a comedienne. In jeans and a blouse she jived with a boy as a fighter bomber went over. But the memory of what she'd seen in the mountains drove her on and made her every movement swifter. With this memory was the realization, consolidating all she felt about herself before leaving the school in the Mid-West, that all her life she'd been running from something – boys clanking chains in a suburb of a night-time Mid-West city, hosts of destroyers speeding through the beech shade of a fragment of Elizabethan Irish history – and now they were catching up on her. They had recognized her challenger. They had singled her out. Her crime? To treat the poor like princes. She was just an ordinary person now with blonde curly hair, a pale pretty face, who happened to be American.

The reverend mother, a woman partly Venezuelan, partly Brazilian, partly American, took at last to the doctrine of liberation and a convent, always anarchistic, some nuns in white, some in black, some in jeans and blouses, became more anarchistic. She herself changed from black to white. She had the television removed and replaced by a rare plant from Peru. An American man in a white suit came to call on her and she asked him loudly what had made him join the CIA and offered him cooked octopus. Honor was producing a concert for harvest festivites in her village that autumn.

There was a deluge of rats or mice – no one seemed sure which – in the tobacco-coloured fields that autumn and an influx of soldiers, young, rat-faced soldiers borne along, standing, on front of jeeps. Rat-eyes imperceptibly took in Honor. They had caught up with her, a little girl in a white dress crossed the fields, tejacote apples upheld in the bottom of her dress. A little boy ran to Honor. They were close at hand. At night when her fears were most intense, sweat amassing on her face, she thought of Chris Gormley, a girl at school in the Mid-West with whom she'd shared a respite in her life, and if she said unkindnesses to her she could say sorry now but that out of frustration comes the tree of one's life. Honor's tree blossomed that autumn.

Sometimes rain poured. Sometimes the sky cheerily bright-
ened. Pieces moved on a chess table in a bar, almost of their
own accord. In her mind Honor heard a young soldier sing a
song from an American musical, 'Out of My Dreams and Into
Your Heart'.

The night of the concert squashes gleamed like moons in the
fields around the hall. In tight jeans, red check shirt, her curls
almost peroxide, Honor tightly sang a song into the microphone.
Buddy Holly. 'You go your way and I'll go mine, now and
forever till the end of time'. A soldier at the back shouted an
obscenity at her. A little boy on front, in a grey tee-shirt from
Chicago, smiled his pleasure. In her mind was her father, his
grey suit, the peace promised once when they were photographed
together on a broad pavement of a city in the Mid-West, that
peace overturned now because it inevitably referred back to the
turbulence which gave it, Irish-America, birth. And she saw the
girl who in a way had brought her here.

There was no panic in her, just a memory of an Elysium of
broad, grey pavements and a liner trekking to Cobh, in Co. Cork.
'Yea, though I walk through the valley of the shadow of death,
I will fear no evil: for thou art with me; thy rod and thy staff
they comfort me.' In the morning they found her body with that
of other nuns among ribbons of blood in a rubbish dump by a
meeting of four roads. No one knew why they killed her because
after the concert a young, almost-Chinese skinned soldier had
danced with her under a yellow lantern that threw out scarlet
patterns.

Afterwards Chris would wonder why her parents had not
contacted her; perhaps the party with its barrage of phone calls
had put up a barrier. But here now, on the pavement, as the
hearses passed, loaded with chrysanthemums and dahlias and
carnations, she, this blonde, long-haired protegée of Sister
Honor, could only be engulfed by the light of pumpkins which
lit like candles in suburban gardens with dusk, by the lights of
windows in high-rise blocks, apertures in catacombs in ancient
Rome, by the flames which were emitted from factory chimneys
and by the knowledge that a woman, once often harsh and for-
bidding, had been raised to the status of martyr and saint by a

113

church which had continued since ancient Rome. An elderly lady in a blue macintosh knelt on the pavement and pawed at a rosary. A negro lady beside Chris wept. But generally the crowd was silent, knowing that it had been their empire which had put these women to death and that now this city was receiving the bodies back among the flame of pumpkins, of windows, of rhythmically issuing factory fires, which scorched at the heart, turning it into a wilderness in horror and in awe.

Carnation Butterfly

CHRISTOPHER HOPE

EILEEN MAUNDY PUSHED aside her typewriter one bright morning and decided to walk in her garden. It was an admission of defeat. The sticking point was the central character of her new novel, *The Settler's Niece*. The girl in question was Linda who had come to Africa from the Cotswolds to visit her aged, ferocious uncle and who discovered by inexorable, painful illuminations (brilliant and intimate observation of the hairline cracks in the female psyche under pressure being a feature of Maundy's work), that nothing in her foreign English upbringing had prepared her for the racial hatreds which obsessed her old uncle and his country. Her treatment of the initial stages of the girl's painful education was satisfactory. Cool innocence met scalding reality and the resultant burns were revealed with delicate precision. The groundwork was there. But the slow dawning of knowledge was not enough. In this unique land suffering was daily bread, and evil as ordinary as sunshine. That much was clear to Linda. But how to make the fatal knowledge burst in the girl? It needed some perverse act, a violent moment of vision, some brutal, unanswerable revelation.

To look at Eileen Maundy was to disbelieve her depth of feeling about such matters. With her fair hair drawn firmly back behind her head, her features neatly angular without being pinched, her small expressive hands and her preference for fine yet unassuming clothes, she looked like a little dressmaker, or as a seamstress might have looked, or a governess. She saw herself, first of all, with just this clarity and she was quite charmingly rueful about the ironies which abounded in the life of herself and her husband, Travers. Their agreeable life, their garden, their double garage and their swimming pool; his work in the personnel department of a big gold mining company; her sense of imminent disaster which suffused all her writing. She had come to terms with the revolution, which, she said in her quiet matter-of-fact voice, would one day put paid to all this, and the neat little hand swept away the garden, the double garage, the swimming pool, and ended in a forefinger on her breast.

All her work explored what someone called 'the bitter fruits of racialism'. Ironic retribution in *Before The Deluge*; the corruptions of power in *Under The Stone*; the virulent gene handed down by the fathers of imperialism and colonialism which inflamed and infected the lives of their heirs, minutely explored in the famous trilogy: *The Hun At The Gate*, *The Prime Minister's Cousin*, and *Children Of Drought*. 'Invalids of history or muscular hostages?' ran the concluding question in *Under The Stone*. All her work was darkened by this sense of foreboding, of the cataclysm to come, of blood and darkness. '. . . do you dream of the future?' the mysterious dwarf Loco is asked in *The Hun At The Gate*. 'I have no future, but still I have dreams . . .' Loco replies. It was quite simply, as Eileen herself explained it, a wish to make amends. Though others said it should more properly be called a compulsion. The compulsion was given notable expression in the striking short story, *A Spinster's Prayer*, in which a young secretary who has been brutally attacked and stabbed by a blind beggar is shown at the last to have anticipated the attack and even forgiven it:

> *She opened her mouth to tell him she understood but no sound came, only a bubble of blood forced up from her punctured lungs gathered at her lips and broke, like a prayer.*

Keeping his head down Solomon the gardener saw her come out of the house. She was coming to enjoy the garden, the purposeful stride told him that and the towelling robe and the dark glasses. She was coming to the pool, to stretch out for a few hours in the sunshine. Doubtless she would be full of advice. He dug his knees more deeply into the soft turf with a grunt of annoyance and went on cutting the tails of the dahlia tubers which he was planning to plant.

Her garden was stamped with the glistening blue of the pool, its surface flickering back the sunshine as the breeze shifted direction, bouncing the light like a playful child with a mirror making her blink. The wagtails made careful rocking little runs across the lawns. A hedge of roses fenced the garden from the street, the heavy silent suburban street now in mid-morning empty but for the occasional delivery man on his bicycle, pedalling from the pharmacy, grocer, butcher, heavy black bicycles loaded with drugs, meat, flowers. The roses in the hedge were tall, pink mixed with red and flaming orange. As she watched, Solomon let himself out of the gate and busied himself on the pavement.

Solomon obdurate, incorrigible, resisted all suggestions she made with genuine civility and tact. He would not discuss politics with her; declined her invitation to throw off the heavy, sweaty blue overalls and dress in the crisp whites she bought him; preferred not to take his meals with them and even flatly refused her offer to teach him to write. Yet he continued to expect her to bail him out of the police station when he got blind drunk, or was picked up for being without his pass, though she tried often to explain to him that his behaviour played right into the hands of those who exploited him by selling him the drink as well as those who arrested him for suffering from its effects.

From the hedge drifted the plush meaty petals of the blown roses, lying at her feet in fragrant drifts. She touched a large plump yellow rose with an orange tinge, its petals fallen open in the sunshine and in its abandonment to the heat reminding her of the sort of open-mouthed lazy pleasure a dog shows when he lies on his back and spreads his paws and has his belly scratched. The hedge was a good symbol. Perhaps she would have Linda, the old man's niece, facing the hedge just as she did now, thinking it beautiful. It would measure the depth of her deception. For Linda of course couldn't see the thorns for the petals. She couldn't see that it was there not to be admired but to be gone through. Couldn't see that she was no longer in a country of soft, domestic gardens but in the heart of Africa. Yes, Linda would have to go through that hedge. She would have to bleed.

Solomon wished she would come away from his hedge. He had planted a nicely balanced mixture of Hybrid Polyanthus, blending Floribundas, Paulson's Pink, Red Ripples, Floradora and Orange Triumph to make an effective mixture, strong without being garish. It was a good hedge and he was pleased with it, though mildew was something of a problem and he had been careful to dust regularly with powdered sulphur. He caught a glimpse of her legs through the hedge. Soon she would go over to the poolside. She would want her heavy iron chair with the faded cushions; a brute of a thing, difficult to carry. Only that morning he had locked it in the shed.

Eileen Maundy knew Solomon was on the other side of the hedge but she preferred not to speak to him. She couldn't imagine what he was doing outside on the pavement. Stepping even closer to the hedge she peered through its tangle of stem and thorn and saw with a shock that her gardener was down on his knees staring up at her and it was with a stabbing sense of shock and dismay that it occurred to her that he was looking at her legs. She moved away hurriedly, her shock and anger made all the worse by the cool observer within her which both saw and mocked her reaction, the very reaction she herself had deftly pinpointed in various books as the despicable, women's magazines' mish-mash of fears and phobias about the supposed lecherous proclivities of black men. So it was that when she flushed it was with anger and embarrassment.

On his knees behind the hedge Solomon reflected on the clear signs of mildew he had detected. Regular sulphur dusting should have been enough to control it but then he remembered that rose trees grown in a corridor of the garden where they are exposed to draughts developed mildew rather easily and it occurred to him that the cold east wind that sometimes blew between the high walls and fences of the big houses on their street might well be providing the draught. Perhaps he would try an experiment, perhaps he would burn some paper and gauge the strength of the wind as it passed the hedge.

A column of smoke climbed above the hedge. He was sitting on the ground watching it when she came out of the garden gate.

'Why are you burning paper on the pavement?'

Briefly Solomon contemplated telling her about his theory of the draught but decided against it. He lifted his round, bearded face. He rubbed his jaw. He shrugged. 'I don't know, Madam.'

She ignored the 'Madam', though she had begged him not to use it. 'I don't mind, Solomon, but what do you think the neighbours feel? They see you out here setting fire to pieces of paper and the next thing you know one of them will have called the police. You can't light fires on the pavement.'

Solomon nodded sheepishly.

'Then why do it?'

Again Solomon contemplated telling her of his theory. Instead with his bare feet he stamped out the flames. She had to look away. When the fire was out he followed her into the garden. He chose a corner as far away as possible and began examining a bed of lilies, *lilium regale*; little white trumpets opened their mouths showing their pale yellow throats. On the outside as the flower narrowed to the stem it became suffused with pink. He was pleased with them but when he looked at the next bed containing his snapdragons his heart sank. Several of the flowers evidenced a listless drooping spirit. Here were the unmistakable signs of wilt.

Eileen Maundy noticed his stricken look as he hunched over the flower-bed and she felt slightly mollified. Perhaps after all he did understand her concern. Solomon, she decided, was all very well at his job. He was devoted to his flowers and kept everything in the garden quite beautifully, but when he got outside that front gate he was absolutely hopeless, he simply didn't understand that out in the world he was a natural victim, prey to the monsters who cruised this vicious society. On reflection she decided that in Solomon's lack of understanding of his position there was a resemblance to the incomprehension of her character, Linda.

Half-hidden in the banks of stocks and sweet peas Solomon watched her making her way to the pool. He felt his mood, already depressed by the discovery of an unmistakable darkening of the lower stems among these flowers which pointed to a bad case of 'black leg', now sinking still further.

Eileen Maundy stepped out of her robe and flung it on the grass. She'd forgotten to wear a hat which was foolish in that heat but she was not going back for it. Beneath her robe she wore a brief, dark blue bikini on which little yellow yachts and seagulls disported themselves. She noticed with some disappointment that the big white iron chair with faded cushions on which she enjoyed lounging by the pool had not been put out but she told herself, half-amused at her own petulance, that she was certainly not going to ask 'Mr Solomon' to fetch it for her. She spread her robe and sat crossed-legged and rubbed suntan oil on to her back and shoulders. Then she stretched herself out in the robe, her cheek on the soft towelling and reaching behind her she undid the straps of her bikini top with a quick deft movement. Out of the corner of her eye she noticed how the grass yellowed at the roots and in the heat heard it ticking faintly like a clock. She smelt the earth, its sweetness strangely interlaced with fumes of chlorine from the pool behind slapping and licking its tiled edges. The sun lay on her back and shoulders.

The breathing woke her, laboured, very close, a shuffling on the grass, then a grunt. Wide-eyed suddenly in the brilliant sunshine she saw before her eyes little hairy cells shimmer and dance. The surface of her skin was hot from the sun but just beneath it the flesh itself was icy and she could feel the oil sliding down her back and sides. Small beads of perspiration crawled in her hair and eyebrows. She could not or perhaps, she told herself with the last vestiges of rationality, she would not move. She would not look. It was closer now, and the breathing louder. A shadow fell across her legs. This was her nightmare, the bloody future. The breathing behind her was loud and quick, she felt his almost unbearable strain. Her mind refused to believe what was happening and yet with her body she knew. With her body she saw him rearing directly above her and she tensed, digging her toes into the turf, waiting for the fall. He reared, high and terrible, and then something heavy hit the grass behind her.

In that moment she made the passage from the clarity of darkest imagination into the brief, banal light of truth, as she was later to describe it to sympathetic friends adding that, paradoxically, her undoing had proved to be the making of her. She had lifted herself literally by the toes and was on her feet running for the house. Later she refused to admit that she had misunderstood or even misapprehended what was happening to her. In a way she insisted she knew, it was not a question of whether the knowledge was right or wrong, it was the knowledge itself that she wanted. It had given her the key to the door that blocked her way to the illumination she had desperately searched for. She had it, as half-naked, fumbling and blinded with tears, she ran into the house and locked the doors and sat down at her desk and without bothering to wipe away the tears that splashed on to the page, she began to write:

The girl at first failed to notice anything but the beauty of the country. Her large bedroom with its high ceilings and the cobwebs in the corner, with the green slatted blinds on the windows which she enjoyed leaving open wide at night. In the morning the sun streamed through. There was so much sun. The great garden beyond, its bougainvillaea and its magnolias richly foaming. She barely noticed the gardener whom she regarded as some sort of employee and perhaps imagined he went home at night to his own house with rooms, curtains and carpets on the floor. She looked at Africa but she didn't watch it. She didn't learn to watch others just as they were watching her. So it was that she never watched the gardener in his scratching, delving, harmless trade. She left the windows open behind the closed green curtains as she undressed one evening, let her dress slip to the floor, hooked it on one foot and flicked it across the room in a whirling arc to land on the chair, tongue caught between her teeth in a characteristic grimace of concentration. So it was that hitting her from behind his rush carried her across the room and down on her bed, face pressed into the pillow, unable to scream, to breathe, to think — knowing only the weight and strength of him, feeling him tear at the last of her clothes, forcing her to bear his weight, to feel fright, pain, then nothing but the crushing, tearing knowledge of Africa around, upon, within her . . .

Solomon stared after the running woman, her breasts bouncing furiously. He watched her disappear into the house and slam the door. He felt a touch of annoyance. The heavy iron chair with which he had staggered across the garden stood uselessly by the poolside. Well, at least now he could get back to work. He'd noticed several of the carnation buds were not opening, their insides burnt out. This was a real blow coming as it did after the other diseases he had detected. The wilt was worst of all. That was incurable. He bent close to the carnations. Some of the plants had spotted leaves and were turning black at the base and dying. Well, he knew he could do something about that. The symptoms were clear, a case of carnation butterfly. He would need a fungicide spray.

Credit

FRANCIS KING

THAT WAS THE day when the cable, four days old, caught up with them in the hotel in which, as though in some long since abandoned palace, they had the freedom to wander from dusty, cavernous bedroom to dusty, cavernous sitting-room, to a bathroom always susurrant with the lisping of a cistern hung askew on the peeling wall, to a terrace on which some ferocious emerald green vine had all but suffocated the rose trained along its trellis. 'We'll have to return as soon as we can,' Bill told Alice, holding out the cable to her, although he had already read out its contents. 'Is that necessary?', she asked perversely, even though she herself had for days now been wishing to put an end to what had become for her a secret martyrdom of greasy, unclean food, rickety and lumpy beds, maimed and suppurating beggars, and children as exasperatingly persistent as the omnipresent flies. 'Yes, it is necessary,' Bill answered. 'The funeral is on Monday.' 'Won't that be a little premature to try on Mac's shoes for size?' Bill did not answer that. Instead, he said: 'It's probably just as well that our tour has been curtailed like this. We've been spending an absolute fortune. Far more than I'd expected.'

That was also the day when Bill discovered that their driver, an Indian Christian called Joseph, could only, for all his interest

123

in the museums, temples and ruins that they visited, be illiterate. Joseph was a daily, living contradiction of all that they had been told, even by the Indians themselves, about Indians being inefficient, unpunctual and dishonest. 'Oh, if only we could take him back to England,' Bill exclaimed more than once, looking out of the grimy window of some hotel to see the ramshackle car, newly washed yet again, waiting for them, half an hour before they required it, in the drive, with Joseph bending over it solicitously, a shammy-leather cloth in his hand, to add a final polish. Joseph would jump out with alacrity to open the car doors for them, would haggle for them whenever they made a purchase, and would insist each day that they should check the mileage, so that there was no possibility of his tampering with the clock.

Bill made his discovery of the illiteracy when – Alice having taken to her bed on the pretext of a migraine – Joseph was driving him out, on the last of their days in India, to some Jain temples perched on an island in the middle of a turbulent river. Joseph, hundreds of miles from his northern home, had never been there before. As they lurched and bumped over a road that was often little more than a dusty track, he kept shaking his head to himself and frowning at his reflection in the driving-mirror. 'What's the matter?', Bill eventually asked. Joseph shrugged his bony shoulders. 'Do you think we've lost the way?' It seemed kinder to Bill to say 'we' than 'you'. Joseph shrugged again. Then, at a crossroads, he stopped the car. 'Maybe we have taken the wrong direction, sir,' he said. 'Oh, no – look!', Bill exclaimed, leaning forward from the sagging back seat and pointing ahead of them. Joseph squinted through the windshield at the signpost, its English and Hindi emerging uncertainly through a film of ochre dust. He looked profoundly unhappy. 'Yes, sir,' he said, his voice rising in what was a half interrogation. 'To the left,' Bill said. 'It says to the left, doesn't it?' 'Ah, yes, sir, to the left!'

That was also the day when Bill saw his first white hitchhiker. In a village, strung out along the road, he stood, blond, close-cropped head bare, outside a shack that seemed to be a petrol station, vegetable and fruit store and café all in one. A rucksack on his back, he wore what had clearly once been an elegant blue-and-white seersucker suit and had a no less clearly once elegant attaché case beside him. On his feet he had the kind of wooden clogs usually worn on beaches. He smiled ruefully as he raised his thumb, as though to tell them, 'Yes, I know you won't stop.'

Joseph, who had already shown that he had no use for Indian hitchhikers, now made it plain that he had no use for white ones either, as he accelerated. 'Stop, Joseph, stop!' Bill cried out, leaning forward and putting a hand on the driver's shoulder. 'Stop! We might as well give the poor beggar a lift. Plenty of room – and it can be no fun standing around in this heat.'

'That's very kind of you, sir,' the hitchhiker said, as he clambered into the front seat beside Joseph. Frowning and pursing his lips, Joseph had already disposed of the rucksack and attaché case in the boot. The youth's accent was American.

'It's lucky we're bound for the same destination.'

'On this road there's probably no other. A truck took me as far as that village. The driver said I'd catch a bus. That was at least six hours ago.'

Bill leaned forward to see the newcomer better. Big-boned but pitifully emaciated – the knuckles looked huge in the sun-burned hands, the nails far from clean, that he had placed behind his scraggy neck as though to ease away some ache – he would have been handsome if the sun had not stripped the skin from his forehead and nose, as though some searing flame had passed across them. An acrid odour emanated either from his body or his clothes.

Bill fumbled in the breast-pocket of his safari suit and took out a packet of the lemon glucose sweets that he and Alice had been advised to carry around with them to combat thirst. He held the packet out: 'How about one of these?' The boy took three, digging into the packet with a forefinger. 'Thanks. I've had no breakfast, except some tea. No supper either, for the matter of that.' He put all three sweets into his mouth simul-taneously and began to suck voraciously.

'Have you been in India long?', Bill asked. He did not really wish to know or even to talk at all, so intense had become the midday heat, but he felt obliged to make an effort.

The youth swivelled round in his seat. 'Well, I suppose the price of a ride like this is always to tell one's lifestory.' He smiled. He was not being offensive.

'No need for that.'

But the youth went on. 'I came here for a vacation – my godfather, he's English, is with the United Nations in Delhi. Then, instead of going back to the job that's awaiting me as an accountant in a bank in Philadelphia, I decided to bum my way around for a while.' He paused. 'Now I don't think I'll ever go back home.'

'Never?' Bill had begun to think, as the boy spoke, of his own imminent return: the funeral, the protestations about the 'tragedy' of Mac's early death, even though few people in the office had liked the sour bastard, the subsequent jostlings for his job.

'Never . . . probably,' the boy added in sudden qualification, as though he had now for the first time realized the full implications of that 'never'.

'Then what will you do?' Bill wanted to add: 'You can't bum around forever.'

'I hope my visit to the temples will decide for me.' The youth fell silent for a moment, chin on chest, his eyes fixed on the grey road ahead of them. Then he swivelled around again in his seat. 'There's an ashram there,' he said. 'I'll stay there awhile. Maybe I'll stay there for the rest of my life.' He gave a little, choking laugh. 'Who knows?'

'Who knows?', Bill echoed. Secretly he was thinking: 'What an idiot!'

'They have something,' the boy said meditatively. He did not specify who 'they' or what the 'something' were. 'Yep, they have something.'

'Haven't you got a family – a girlfriend – back in America?'

'Had.' To Bill the monosyllable was chilling.

After that Bill made no further effort to prolong the conversation, until, after a series of precipitous hairpin bends, negotiated by Joseph with a blithe insouciance, they arrived at the village caught, like a random scurf of rocks, wood, corrugated iron and thatch, in an elbow of the wide, turbid river. As, his body aching and stiff as though from a fall, Bill clambered out of the car, a number of men in nothing but loin-cloths, some of them daubed with ash, clustered around with begging-bowls outstretched in claw-like hands. The boy laughed: 'I'll probably soon be holding out a bowl myself.' Bill had taken out some loose change from his trouser pocket, with Joseph looking on benignly, as he always did when Bill or Alice gave anything to a beggar.

'Do you want me to hire a boat for you, sir?' Joseph asked, when the coins had been distributed.

'Is that how one gets across?' It was a stupid question, Bill realized as soon as he had asked it. How else would one get across to the island, since there was clearly no bridge?

'There is also a public boat,' Joseph said meaningfully, looking at the American. He clearly thought that the youth should travel on it, instead of with his master.

'Get us a boat,' Bill said, with unwonted sharpness. Then he turned to the American, who had taken off his seersucker jacket and was now carefully folding it up, as though it had just been washed and ironed, instead of being creased and saturated with dust. 'I take it you want to cross over at once?'

'Fine. Thanks.'

Joseph found a boatman, a white-haired man, with a lean muscular body, naked, like the beggars, but for a loin-cloth. He and Joseph both extended hands to help, as Bill and the American clambered aboard. Bill placed himself gingerly on one of the two narrow, horizontal slats that served as seats, put up a hand to shade his eyes and looked across the river to where the temples rose up, shimmering like a mirage in the afternoon glare. The American made his way, the boat tipping perilously to now one side and now the other, up to the prow. Joseph hesitated and then walked over to join him. From the stern the boatman propelled them with a single oar that looked like a vast wooden shovel.

'Beautiful,' the boy said, smiling out towards the temples, his eyes half closed against the slanting sunlight.

'Beautiful,' Bill agreed. 'But you should get yourself some sunglasses,' he added irrelevantly. 'This light is dangerous.'

The boy laughed. 'Too late now.'

'I have a spare pair in the car. I could have let you have those.'

'Too late now,' the boy repeated with a kind of suppressed joy.

Its opaque, brown waves edged with a yellow froth, the water swirled around them. At one point, as Bill peered down at it, he was digusted to see the swollen carcass of a dog, one side showing a purple gash. Momentarily it surged into sight and then was plucked away by one of the criss-cross currents. On the far shore, three thin, tall men were bathing. Some white lengths of cloth – Bill assumed them to be loin-cloths – flapped out like sails from the rocks to which they had somehow been fastened.

The American, standing motionless at the prow, once again smiled into the dry, hot wind. Then he shifted his stance, swinging his seersucker jacket, which had previously been dangling from a forefinger, up on to his shoulder. Something glittered momentarily in the sunlight, as Bill glanced over. The youth let out what was more a scream than a shout. 'My credit cards! My credit cards!' he pointed downwards into the swirling water. 'My credit cards have fallen in!'

With extraordinary speed Joseph tore off his clothes, revealing, to Bill's amazement, long cotton drawers reaching to his bony knees and a long cotton vest. Shouting something to the boatman he jumped over the side of the boat. After a momentary hesitation, the boatman jumped in after him, but prudently held on to the side of the boat with one hand, so that it should not be swept away on the flood. The river at that point was sufficiently shallow for both of them to stand. Joseph disappeared under the murky waters again and yet again. The American, kneeling in the boat, leant over and peered down. From time to time he shouted: 'There! *There*! No, not there! I think that I can see it.'

'See what?' Bill asked. Receiving no answer, he repeated, 'See what?'

'The wallet. The crocodile-skin wallet. My godfather gave it to me. For my birthday. Oh Christ! Christ! All my credit cards! All of them!'

The two Indians eventually clambered back dripping, into the boat. Joseph picked up his shirt and began to dry himself on it. The boatman threw back his head and unaccountably laughed, showing a few teeth stained with betel-nut. 'Gone,' Joseph said. 'Impossible to find.' He sounded breathless after all his diving. 'A lot of money?', he asked.

'Not money. My credit cards. All my credit cards. Fortunately any money I have – and there's not much of that – is in another pocket.'

'You can always get the credit cards replaced,' Bill said, as the boatman once again took up the shovel-like oar.

But stricken, his bony hands clasped around his knees as he huddled in the bottom of the boat, oblivious to the bilge that was staining his clothes yet further – he might be some sack thrown down there carelessly, Bill thought – the American made no answer.

When they had reached the further bank with a scrape and a jolt, Joseph elbowed aside the boatman to help Bill ashore. He made no attempt to help the boy, who jumped free clumsily, all but falling over on the mudflat. 'I will tell the boatman to wait for us, sir. He says that it will take about an hour and a half to see the temples.'

'Which way is the ashram?' the American asked, struggling back into his jacket despite the heat.

Joseph turned to ask the boatman. Then simultaneously the two of them pointed. 'That way, sir,' Joseph said. 'You walk straight ahead. Not far.'

'That way?' the boy asked dubiously. It was as though he imagined that they might be misdirecting him.

Joseph nodded. Then he said to Bill: 'We go this way, sir.'

Suddenly Bill felt an unreasoning sadness at saying goodbye to the boy. 'Are you sure you don't want to change your mind and come back with us?'

'Quite sure.' It sounded ungracious, even angry.

'I'm sorry about those credit cards.'

The boy shrugged and began to walk away with long, effortful strides, mumbling, 'Well, maybe . . .' He reached some steps, halted, turned half round. What he said next Bill could barely catch, but in retrospect he decided that it was 'Maybe it was a sign.'

The boy hastened up four or five of the steps. Then again he turned, raising a hand in a final salutation as he called out: 'Thanks! Thanks a lot!'

At the hotel desk when they were paying their bill, in the car as they drove out to the airport, at the airport itself – Joseph saw to all the interminable formalities for them, queuing patiently and persistently, while they sat silent and motionless under a slowly churning fan – Bill's hand would keep straying in near-panic to the breast-pocket of his jacket. Eventually, as they shuffled on to the tarmac, Alice noticed the repeated gesture. 'Why do you keep touching that pocket?' she asked sharply. 'Have you lost something? Are you frightened of losing something?'

'Of course not! What *are* you talking about?'

He only stopped touching the pocket when they were safely aboard the aeroplane.

Smile

DEBORAH MOGGACH

WE HAD TO wear these SMILE badges. It was one of the rules. And they'd nailed up a sign saying SMILE, just above the kitchen door, so we wouldn't forget. It's American, the hotel. Dennis, the chief receptionist, even says to the customers, 'Have a nice day,' but then he's paid more than I am, so I suppose he's willing.

I was on breakfasts when I was expecting. Through a fog of early-morning sickness I'd carry out the plates of scrambled eggs. The first time I noticed the man he pointed to the SMILE badge, pinned to my chest, then he pulled a face.

'Cheer up,' he said. 'It might never happen.'

I thought, *it has*.

Looking back, I suppose he appeared every six weeks or so, and stayed a couple of nights. I wasn't counting, then, because I didn't know who he was. Besides, I was on the alert for somebody else, who never turned up and still hasn't, being married, and based in Huddersfield, and having forgotten about that night when he ordered a bottle of Southern Comfort with room service. At least I'm nearly sure it was him.

I was still on breakfasts when I saw the man again, and my

apron was getting tight. Soon I'd be bursting out of the uniform.

He said, 'You're looking bonny.'

I held out the toast basket, and he took four. Munching, he nodded at my badge. 'Or are you just obedient?'

It took me a moment to realize what he meant, I was so used to wearing it.

'Oh yes, I always do what I'm told.'

He winked. 'Sounds promising.'

I gave him a pert look and flounced off. I was happy that day. The sickness had worn off; I was keeping the baby, I'd never let anybody take it away from me. I'd have someone to love, who would be mine.

'You've put on weight,' he said, six weeks later. 'It suits you.'

'Thanks,' I said, smiling with my secret. 'More coffee?'

He held out his cup. 'And what do you call yourself?'

'Sandy.'

I looked at him. He was a handsome bloke; broad and fleshy, with a fine head of hair. He had a tie printed with exclamation marks.

I've always gone for older men. They're bound to be married of course. Not that it makes much difference while they're here.

When he finished his breakfast I saw him pocketing a couple of marmalade sachets. You can tell the married ones; they're nicking them for the kids.

When I got too fat they put me in the kitchens. You didn't have to wear your SMILE badge there. I was on salads. Arranging the radish roses, I day-dreamed about my baby.

I never knew it would feel like this. I felt heavy and warm and whole. The new chef kept pestering me, but he seemed like a midge – irksome but always out of sight. Nobody mattered. I walked through the steam, talking silently to my bulge. This baby meant the world to me. I suppose it came from not having much of a home myself, what with my Dad leaving, and Mum moving in and out of lodgings, and me being in and out of Care. Not that I blame her. Or him, not really.

I'd stand in the cooking smells, look at my tummy and think, *You're all mine, I'll never leave you.*

When she was born I called her Donna. I'd sit for hours, just breathing in her scent. I was always bathing her. It was a basement flat we had then, Mum and me and Mum's current love-of-her-life Eddie, and I'd put the pram in the area way so Donna could imbibe the sea breezes. Even in our part of Brighton, I told myself you could smell the sea.

I'd lean over to check she was still breathing. I longed for her to smile – properly, at me. In the next room Mum and Eddie would be giggling in an infantile way, they seemed the childish ones. Or else throwing things. It was always like this with Mum's blokes.

I'd gaze at my baby and tell her, *You won't miss out. You'll have me; I'll always be here.*

Behind me the window pane rattled as Mum flounced out, slamming the door behind her.

I went back to work, but in the evenings, so I could look after Donna during the day and leave her with Mum when she was sleeping. They put me in the Late Night Coffee Shop. It had been refurbished in Wild West style, like a saloon, with bullet holes printed on the wallpaper and fancy names for the burgers. The wood veneer was already peeling off the counter. Donna had changed my world; nothing seemed real any more, only her.

I had a new gingham uniform, with a flounced apron and my SMILE badge. I moved around in a dream.

One night somebody said, 'Howdee, stranger.'

It was the man I used to meet at breakfast.

He put on an American accent. 'Just rolled into town, honey. Been missing you. You went away or something?'

I didn't say I'd had a baby; I liked to keep Donna separate.

He inspected the menu. 'Can you fix me a Charcoal-Broiled Rangeburger?'

It was a quiet evening so we hadn't lit the charcoal. Back in the kitchen I popped the meat into the microwave and thought how once I would have fancied him, like I fancied the bloke from Huddersfield, like I almost fancied Dennis in Reception. But I felt this new responsibility now. Why hadn't my parents felt it when I was born? Or perhaps they had, but it had worn off early.

When I brought him his meal he pointed to my badge. 'With you it comes naturally.' He shook salt over his chips. 'Honest, I'm not just saying it. You've got a beautiful smile.'

'It's added on the bill.'

He laughed. 'She's witty too.' He speared a gherkin. 'Somebody's a lucky bloke.'

'Somebody?'

'Go on, what's his name?'

I thought, *Donna.*

'There's nobody special,' I said.

'Don't believe it, lovely girl like you.'

I gave him my enigmatic look – practice makes perfect – and started wiping down the next table.

He said. 'You mean I'm in with a chance?'

'You're too old.'

'Ah,' he grinned. 'The cruel insolence of youth.' He munched his chips. 'You ought to try me. I'm matured in the cask.'

Later, when he finished his meal, he came up to pay. He put his hand to his heart. 'Tell me you'll be here tomorrow night. Give me something to live for.'

I took his Access card. 'I'll be here tomorrow night.'

During breakfasts he'd paid the cashier; that's why I'd never seen his name.

I did now. I read once, on the Access card.

Finally, I got my hands to work. I pulled the paper through the machine, fumbling it once. I did it again, then I passed it to him.

'What's up?' he said. 'Seen a ghost?'

That night Donna woke twice. For the first time since she was born I shouted at her.

'Shut up!' I shook her. 'You stupid little baby!'

Then I started to cry. I squeezed her against my nightie. She squirmed and I squeezed her harder, till her head was damp with my tears.

*

Even my Mum noticed. Next day at breakfast she said, 'You didn't half make a racket.' She stubbed her cigarette into her saucer. 'Got a splitting headache.'

I didn't answer. I wasn't telling that last night I'd met my father. I couldn't tell her yet. She'd probably come storming along to the hotel and lay in wait in his room.

Or maybe she'd be indifferent. She'd just light another fag and say, *Oh him. That bastard.*

I couldn't bear that.

The day seemed to drag on for ever. Overnight, Brighton had shrunk. It seemed a small town, with my father coming round each corner, so I stayed indoors.

On the other hand Eddie had grown larger. He loafed around the flat, getting in the way. I needed to talk, but nobody was the right person. Just once I said to him, raising my voice over the afternoon racing,

'Did you know I was called Alexandra?'

'What?'

'My Mum and Dad called me that, but when I was twelve I changed it to Sandy.'

'Did you then?' He hadn't turned the volume down. Then he added vaguely, 'Bully for you.'

I didn't know how to face him. On the other hand, I would have died if he didn't turn up. I waited and waited. I nearly gave up hope. I had to wait until 10.30. I felt hot in my cowgirl frills.

He came in and sat down at the table nearest my counter. I walked over with the menu, calm as calm. I didn't think I could do it.

'I thought you weren't turning up,' I said.

'Me?' His eyes twinkled. 'You didn't trust me?' He took the menu. 'Oh no, Sandy, you give me a chance and you'll find out.'

'Find out what?'

'That I'm a man of my word.'

I couldn't answer that. Finally I said, 'Oh yeah?' with a drawling voice. 'Tell us another.'

'Honest to God, cross my heart.'

I looked at him, directly. His eyes were blue, like mine. And his nose was small and blunt, a familiar little nose in his large, flushed face. I wanted to hide my face because it suddenly seemed so bare. He must be blind, not to recognize me. I was perspiring.

Then I thought: why should he recognize me? He last saw me when I was four. Has he ever thought of me, all these years?

Taking his order into the kitchen, my mind was busy. I stood in front of the dead charcoal range, working out all the places I'd lived since I was four . . . Shepperton, Isleworth, Crawley . . . There was nothing to connect me to Brighton.

SMILE, said the sign as I walked out.

'You travel a lot?' I said, putting his plate in front of him.

'A conversation at last!' He split the ketchup sachet and slopped it over his chips, like blood. He nodded. 'For my sins. So what's my line of business, Sandy?'

'You're a rep.'

'How did you guess?'

'Your hands.'

He looked down with surprise, and opened out his palms. There were yellowed calluses across his fingers.

'You're an observant lass. Do I dare to be flattered?' He put out his hand. 'Here. Feel them.'

I hesitated, and then I touched his fingers. The skin was hard and dry. I took away my hand.

'You've always been a salesman?' I asked.

'Well . . .' He winked. 'Bit of this, bit of that.'

'Bit of what?' I wanted to know.

'Now that would be telling.'

'You've been all over the place?'

'It's the gypsy in my soul,' he said. 'Can't tie me down.'

There was a pause. Then I said, 'Eat up your dinner.'

He stared at me. 'What's got into you?'

'Nothing.'

There was a silence. I fiddled with my frills. Then I went back to the counter.

*

When he paid he said, 'I know you don't like old men but it's Help The Aged Week.'

'So?' I put on my pert face.

'You're off at half eleven?'

I nodded.

'Let me buy you a drink.' He paused. 'Go on. Say yes.'

The bar had closed. Besides, it was against the rules for me to go there. You're only allowed to smile at the customers.

But who knows where a smile might lead? It had led me here.

He had a bottle of Scotch in his room, and he ordered me a fresh orange juice from Room Service. When it arrived I hid in the bathroom.

His things were laid out above the basin. I inspected them all: his toothbrush (red, splayed), his toothpaste (Colgate); electric shaver; aftershave (Brut, nearly finished). I wanted to take something home but that was all there was. The towels belonged to the hotel so there was no point. I wondered where he kept the marmalade sachets. But they weren't for me.

'Welcome to my abode,' he said, pulling out a chair.

I sat down. 'Where is your abode?'

'Pardon?'

'Where do you live?'

He paused. 'You don't want to hear about my boring little life.'

'Go on,' I said, giving him a flirtatious smile. 'Tell me.'

He hesitated, then he said shortly, 'Know Peterborough?'

'No.'

'Well, there.' His tone grew jaunty. Eyes twinkling, he passed me my glass. 'A fresh drink for a fresh young face. How old are you, Sandy?'

'Nineteen.'

'Nineteen.' He sighed. 'Sweet nineteen. Where have you been all my life?'

I tried to drink the orange juice; it was thick with bits. There was a silence. I couldn't think what to say.

He was sitting on the bed; the room was warm and he'd taken off his jacket. The hair was an illusion; he was thinning on top but he'd brushed his hair over the bald patch. Far away I heard a clock chiming.

I wasn't thirsty. I put down the glass and said, 'What do you sell?'

He climbed to his feet and went over to his suitcase, which had a Merriworld sticker on it. He snapped it open.

'Let me introduce Loopy.'

He passed me a rubbery creature dressed in a polka-dot frock. She had long, bendy arms and legs and a silly face. He fetched a pad of paper, knelt down on the floor and took her from me. Her arms ended in pencil points. Holding her, he wrote with her arms: TO SANDY WITH THE SMILE. Then he turned her upside down and said, 'Hey presto.' He started rubbing out the words with her head.

'Don't.' I pulled his hand back. I took the paper, which still had TO SANDY WITH, and put it in my apron pocket.

He said, 'Rubber and pencils all in one. Wonder where the sharpener ought to be . . .'

'What?'

'Just my vulgar mind.'

'Where do you take these things?'

'Ramsdens. Smiths. That big shopping centre.'

I knew all the places; I connected him with them. I'd bought Donna's layette at Ramsdens.

He took out a clockwork Fozzy Bear, a Snoopy purse and a magnetic colouring book.

'So you sell toys,' I said.

'It's the child in me,' he said. 'I'm just a little boy at heart.'

'Are you?'

'Happy-go-lucky, that's me.'

'Anything for a laugh?'

'No use sitting and moaning.' He took another drink. 'Got to enjoy yourself.'

I gazed at the scattered toys. 'Just a game, is it?'

'Sandy, you've only got one life. You'll learn that, take it from me.' He shifted closer to my legs.

'Anything else in there?' I pointed to the suitcase.

He leaned back and took out a box. 'Recognise it?'

I shook my head.

'Ker-Plunk.'

'What?'

'You were probably still in nappies. It's a sixties line, but we're giving it this big re-launch.' He patted the floor. 'Come on and I'll give you a game.'

He took out a plastic tube, a box of marbles and some coloured sticks. 'Come on.' He patted the floor again.

I lowered myself down on the carpet, tucking my skirt in. This damn uniform was so short.

'Look – you slot these sticks in, like this.' He pushed them into perforations in the tube, so they made a platform; then with a rattle he poured the marbles on top, so they rested on the sticks.

'Then we take it in turns to pull out a stick *without*,' he wagged his finger at me, 'without letting a marble drop through.' We sat there, crouched on the floor. 'If it does, you're a naughty girl.'

I pulled out a stick. He pulled out one. I pulled out another.

'Whoops!' he said, as a marble clattered through the sticks.

'Bad luck!' he cried. 'I'm winning!'

Sometimes his marbles fell through, sometimes mine. I won.

'Can't have this,' he said. 'Got to have another game.'

He poured himself some more Scotch, and settled down on the floor again, with a grunt. We collected the sticks and pushed them into the holes, then poured the marbles on top.

I didn't want to play, but then I didn't want to leave, either. We pulled out the sticks; the marbles clattered down the tube.

He slapped his thigh. 'Got you!'

Outside the window, the clock chimed again. Sitting there amongst the toys I thought, *Why did you never do this with me before? At the proper time?*

'Your turn,' he said. 'Stop day-dreaming.'

I pulled out a stick. My throat felt tight and there was an ache in my chest.

'Whoops!' he cried. 'Bad luck!'

I felt a hand slide around my waist. The fingers squeezed me. He shifted himself nearer me, so our sides were touching.

'Silly game, isn't it,' he said.

I moved back, disentangling myself. 'I must go.'

'But we haven't finished!' He looked at me, his face pink from bending over the game.

I climbed to my feet. 'Mum'll be worried.'

'Come on, you're a big girl now.' He held up his hand. 'Come and sit down.'

'No.'

He winked. 'Strict, is she?'

I shrugged. He climbed to his feet and stood beside me. We were the same height.

'What about a kiss then?'

I looked into his eyes. Then his face loomed closer. I moved my head; his lips brushed my cheek. I felt them, warm and wet. I bent down and picked up my handbag. My hands were shaking.

'Must go,' I said, my voice light.

He saw me to the door, his hand resting on my hip. 'Can I see you home?'

'No!' I paused. 'I mean, no thanks.'

He opened the door. 'I'm leaving tomorrow, but I'll be back next month. Know what I'd love to do?'

'What?'

'Take you down to the pier. Never been to the pier. Eat ice-creams.' He squeezed my waist, and kissed my cheek. 'Know something?'

I whispered, 'What?'

'You make me feel years younger.' He paused. 'Will you come?'

I nodded. 'OK,' I said.

He buttoned me into my coat, and smoothed down the collar. He stroked my hair.

'You're a lovely girl,' he murmured. 'Tell your Mum to keep you locked up. Say I said so.'

I couldn't bear to wait at the lift, so I made for the stairs. As I went he called, 'Tell her it's my fault you're late.' His voice grew fainter. 'Tell her I'm the one to blame.'

*

Six weeks took an age to pass. I'd looked at the ledger in Reception; he was booked for 15 April.

Donna was sleeping better, but for the first time in my life I slept badly. I had such strong dreams, they woke me up. I'd lie there, next to her calm face, and gaze at the orange light that filtered in from the street. I'd put his piece of paper under my pile of sweaters. That was all of him I had, so far. I said nothing to my Mum.

On 15 April Eddie knocked on the bathroom door.

'You're planning to stay there all day?'

I was washing my hair. 'Go away!' I shouted.

At seven o'clock prompt I was on station in the Coffee Shop. Time dragged. 8.00 . . . 8.13 . . . Each time I looked at my watch, only a minute had passed.

9.30. The doors swung open. It wasn't him. Business was slow that night; the place was nearly empty.

10.30 . . . 11.00 . . .

At 11.30 I closed up and took the cash to Dennis, in Reception.

'Not got a smile for me?'

I ignored him and went home.

When I got back, Mum was watching the midnight movie. I was going to my room but she called, 'Had a flutter today.'

I nodded, but she turned.

'Don't you want to see what I've bought?' She reached down and passed me a carrier bag. 'Put it on Lucky Boy and he won, so I splashed out at Ramsdens.'

I stared at her. 'Ramsdens?'

'Go on. Look. It's for little Donna.'

I went over, opened the carrier bag and drew out a huge blue teddy bear. 'Cost a bomb,' she said. 'But what the hell.'

Next day I made enquiries at Reception. He'd checked in, they said, during the afternoon as usual. But then he'd come back at six and checked out again.

Later I went to Ramsdens and asked if the Merriworld representative had visited the day before.

The girl thought for a moment, then nodded. 'That's right. Jack.' She paused to scratch her ear-lobe. 'Jack-the-lad.'

'So he came?'

She pursed her lips. 'Came and went.'

'What do you mean?'

She looked at me. 'What's it to you?'

'Nothing.'

She shrugged. 'Dunno what got into him. Left in a hurry.'

He'd seen Mum. He'd seen her buying the bloody teddy bear.

He didn't come back. Not once he knew she was in Brighton. At Ramsdens, six weeks later, there was a new rep called Terry. I checked up. Not that I had much hope. After all, he'd scarpered once before.

But Donna smiled. It wasn't because of the teddy, she was too young to appreciate that, though Mum would like to believe it.

And it wasn't wind, I could tell. It was me. She smiled at me.

Master of Ceremonies

JOHN MURRAY

MY GRANDFATHER ENJOYED putting enormous fear into women . . .

Thus as early as I can remember my gentle old grandmother shook with nerves, like some wired electrical contraption. And her daughter, my mother, normally the one so fearless, one might say the bold fighter outside of her father's house, was also harshly cut to size by this irascible old man.

Even so it was untrue to say that he was cruel to all women and gentle with all men. Rather, any man whom he considered womanish – that is, in his terms talkative, gossipy, nervous, without any centre of gravity – he also endeavoured to bully and mock. His nephew Sid being a good example, one of the men whose conversation my grandfather would punctuate with noisy spittings into the fire, whose opinions he would openly scoff at, whose exaggerations which nervous old Sid used to manufacture to impress us all, he would greet with a leer of fine contempt. Perhaps others felt the same way as my grandfather with regard to the jabberings of Sid. Certainly many of them, including nervous women, would treat him rather brusquely.

The old man never bullied me, nor attacked my own father. We were both very quiet, very shy and it was obvious he respected us for that. Confident women too, ones so self-contained they made even him uneasy, he would leave well alone with his tongue. He was kind to small children, respectful to quiet men, hardworking, vain, Labour to the bone, compendiously bitter, prodigious of memory and story. He lived in the changeless past as others live in a vacuum of motion or talk. At home he liked to sit pensive and rock himself in the armchair, his personal armchair, planted there for at least one or two millennia so it seemed. From time to time his voice would rise up for a story and the household would turn its ears to the unchallenged master of ceremonies.

My grandmother and mother would listen because they were afraid to do anything else. I listened because I was a child and I was gripped by his brilliant tales. My father either attended or read away quietly in a corner. Most often I was the only really attentive audience, for who can be attentive when she or he is panicking? Thus he would turn to me, the nine-year-old, and focus his art upon me. One good listener being worth a thousand compliant faces of course. We became that age-old partnership, the story-teller and his single-minded solitary listener.

My grandparents' house was a small, sad terraced two-up, two-down, with no bathroom and no inside toilet. At the fronts it faced a parallel row of terraces and along the backs it had shabby allotments and the enormous aged gasworks. The smell of that gas I loved, it salted my nose, it salted the whole town and particularly its poorest end which was congregated there, in rows and rows of terraces identical to this one. From their back window you beheld the yard, roughly cobbled and walled in high on either side, blocked in at the front where the tall, painted gate was the towering means of exit. Out into the yard I would go if I needed fresh air or to urinate. I would enter the outside toilet, a small, narrow affair with the usual wind, stone and faecal smell, and leaving the door on the latch, would proceed to pee across the lettering that said *Shanks Twyford*, trying each time to follow the sequence of the letters and then starting again if I erred in my urinary progress. I never sat and squatted in that lavatory as I had a fear of being somehow locked inside in that eerie darkness. Besides, sometimes when I was in there, the neighbours would start their terrible show and that would be enough to get me skedaddling back into the house again and safety.

'There it goes again,' grumbled my grandfather stonily as I returned. 'That crazy idiot upsetting that laal lass. And this goes on from morning till night every single day . . .'

My mother looked deeply pitying. I felt much afraid. My father went on reading. My grandmother went on shaking. The bitch dog Lassie continued quaking in skinny sympathy. She was a little Lakeland terrier, already in her teens, safe with my grandmother and aware of the two faces of her master. He predictably would love her and terrorize her by turn.

'Will you hark at that racket?' he asked my mother with a poisoned face. 'If I was that bairn I'm bloody sure I'd blare twice as hard if I had to endure that damn soft bawlin.'

Through the walls and also from the outside, over the wall of the yard, we could hear the neighbour playing his piano to accompany what sounded like opera or something as remarkable issuing from his lips. He was not playing and singing for his own entertainment but because his teenage daughter was weeping. His daughter was fifteen years old but was unable to sit upright or do anything but lie and most times cry. After the age of twelve months her body had ceased to grow and all the growth had continued in her head. Thus she had an enormous head and a tiny little body, hydrocephalic or macrocephalic, I believe, being the medical diagnosis.

'He says that it sometimes cheers her up,' remarked my grandmother pacifically. 'He says sometimes the singing stops the kiddie crying.'

'Pah,' snorted her husband quickly. 'There's many a time that laal lass is quiet, asleep or day-dreamin mebbe. And then that clown starts his mad caterwaulin and the poor little beggar sets off yawling and bawlin . . .'

My mother remarked with that melting, tender voice, 'It's such a shame. It's such a cross for that poor little girl.'

My grandmother nodded, shook and agreed. She was shaking in the armchair that was placed against the window facing the yard. Her husband in his rocker was seated stiffly opposite, adjacent to the roaring coal fire. To his right was the table and round that were my parents and myself. I always sat the very nearest to my grandfather, like some shield, and my father always sat most remote as he went on with his quiet reading. The little bitch Lassie meanwhile was propped on my grandmother's pinny, as bright as a little sparrow and with that toothy grin little terriers often have in their senility.

'And she has such a pretty face,' said grandmother gently. 'It's an enormous one and yet it's such a bonny face that little creature has . . .' 'The poor little beggar,' repeated my mother, her eyes glistening with strong compassion.

There were a few seconds respite. Grandfather's railway clock ticked away with its steady, sombre sound. The fire hissed and laughed in the old, black-painted grate. The aria singing bellowed on like pure insanity. Was the father weeping too as he sang for his miserable daughter? She never seemed to gain any relief at all from her keening and crying, sobbing and moaning that wafted through the thin, old walls.

'I think,' said my grandfather with provocation, 'that that bairn should never have been allowed to live.'

There was the slightest, tensest pause. My mother kept quiet but my grandmother who was indeed capable of rebellion and even quaking annoyance from time to time, muttered with impatience.

'*You* can't say that. Don't be wicked! Wisht with you, man!'

Everything in the room, even the wall-clock tautened. For we had been through this sequence many times. Grandfather was quite unmoved by the righteousness of my grandmother's tone. She had had religion and a lay-preacher father. He had always taken as much of that business, of religion, as he wanted. No more than a sneering trifle.

'It's plain fact,' he persisted, at first only loudly self-defensive. 'What joy does that poor laal bugger have, lyin on her back all her damn days? What sort of a dog's life is yon, woman?'

'*You* cannot say,' my grandmother retorted, her shakes suddenly changing into the simple flush and movement of human emotion. Just then it was plain that her shakes were only her bottled-up heart, nothing more. Even I, a child, could see as much as that.

'What the deuce,' she went on, 'you can't be lettin babies die, just because they're not a hundred per cent. There's no sense in that, that's wicked, foolish talk is that . . .'

'Oh?' he scoffed violently. 'You know where wickedness is, my lass? Wickedness is in lettin that kid lie there year after year with a halfwit like that driving it crackers. That's what I call cruelty. And I'll say it again, they should just have let the poor thing die when they saw it was going to be like the monster it is. The doctors should just have let that bloody kiddie die!'

'But,' my grandmother protested with a red and passionate face, her shakes again suddenly transformed into the vibrations of her temper and her faith, 'the baby didn't start to go queer until it was twelve months. You can't go and kill a twelve-month-old baby even if you're ready to kill one that's just been born. Don't talk so damn wicked, man!'

She was sat upright, her neck muscles were juddering, her head and trunk vibrant with the taste of her convictions. I admired her for once instead of feeling only pity for her. All the same there was something faintly comic in the set of her jaw and it was this which her husband proceeded at once to seize on.

'Look there!' he addressed us all sneeringly. 'The missus gettin in a lather and bawlin at the rest of us!'

'No,' my grandmother yelped sharply and shamefacedly. 'No I am not!'

'Oh but you are my lass,' he taunted heartlessly. 'Great red face, neck shaking, hands going all over the shop. Look there, son, at your grandmother!' he added, as he looked to me for supportive mockery.

My grandmother hid her head. My mother attempted to change the subject and remarked in a rush on the volume of people up in the town centre. My father had hastily resumed his book. I was simply watching it all, helpless and riveted.

'And now she's datherin,' the old man went on victoriously. 'Just look at her shakin away! Shakin and shakin like a bumble bee or a bit of grass! What is it then? Is it your *nerves*? Is it your nerves, makin you shake, my lass? I tell you, I wouldn't let *myself* shake like that! Would I hell! I'd pull myself together and stop myself. What – you're a nervous wreck you are, missus.

You and the dog together, both shaking like a pair of bloody tambourines . . .'

He went on as cruelly as this for some time. At last my grandmother started to weep, and then attempted to hold and retract her tears. Finally she darted into the back kitchen and called from there with a shaky, anxious voice, to ask us if we'd all like a cup of tea and a bite to eat. My mother dashed through supposedly to give her a hand, but I could hear her whispering in a thick and supportive voice, to ignore what her father had said. Just ignore him was her solemn advice.

But already the tormentor had resumed another tale and with me his listener he went on to exploit his gift of perfect recall.

Tea had commenced. Darkness was falling already, on a warmish evening at the tail end of April. My grandfather rose midway through the tea and switched on his massive old valve radio. Laboriously he fiddled through wavebands and volume controls until he had us all listening to *The Archers*. The radio as ever took a minute or so to warm up. It was like an animal, as big as a little old goat perhaps, and the many knobs on the front gave it a face and a personality of its own. Valve radios, surely they have a power and a magic second to none. That boom, crackle, inner world of the sound, that cave and echo wonder of it all. *The Archers* actually bored me to tears but just the resonant, foggy roar of the machine itself was enough to make my guts as warm and secure as an infant's.

Walter Gabriel made entrance and my grandfather laughed and chuckled away. He and my grandmother listened to the programme every evening and as my mother wistfully remarked were half-convinced that the Archers were real people living in a real village and having their dramas at a regular time of the day, just as we chose to eavesdrop on them.

Immediately it finished the old man went and firmly switched it off. Then he returned to the rocker while my mother and grandmother saw to the pots. My father rose and offered his help but was returned to the sitting room to keep the old man company. It was dark outside but naturally no electric light went on until grandfather decreed it. Instead we sat in the gloaming with that roaring fire from the grate, and he and my father lit up their evening pipes. If my father happened to be near enough the fire then he was able to keep on his reading; if not he was forced to be a listener too. But eventually grandfather would realize the strain on my father's eyes and gently rise to switch the light on for him. Left to themselves, he and his wife often sat in the firelit darkness until they wended their way to bed at nine or ten.

In the gloaming the stories were even better. Grandfather punctuated them with prods at the fire and with the slow mechanics of his pipe. He would lean down from his rocker and poke with the bright new alloy poker Sid had fetched him. Impurities in the coal might spark up and glow out green, blue, yellow and black. I gazed into the grate and saw the perfection of embers, incandescence. I listened to all that sissing and singing from the flames. My father would gaze like myself in a reverie at the fire. Much later I was to learn that certain primitive people made a god or a totem out of fire and it wasn't at all possible to forecast as much just then.

And from time to time the old man's pipe would empty so that he would take out his tobacco tin, a shiny, polished, circular bewitching tin more like an empty watchcase than a tobacco pouch. He would snap it open and pull out his twist tobacco, a material which looks like nothing so much as dried dog shit. Or like a dark brown rope which needs to be cut and rubbed before it can be pressed into the pipe. Then the old man had to light it. He had no taste for matches, particularly in the sacred time of evening gloaming. If the light was on I could see the colours of the spills which he poked down into the blasting fire. He had a box at his feet which contained spills of all colours: blue, green, red and yellow. He would pull out a spill and light it slowly in the flames. Bent down to the grate for this, this leisurely lighting would be done in a meditative way. Then he might cast the remnant into the fire, return to his private chair, then most likely his latest, strangest recollection.

My grandfather had no time for matches though to be sure he needed at least one to light the fire in the morning, just as my grandmother needed some in her shaky hands for the gas cooker in the tiny, primitive kitchen she kept. Separate, greatly elevated from these were my grandfather's *special* matches, and these were something to which one might devote a whole treatise, had one the time and the skill to tease out their mysterious significance as kernel memories.

Those special matches were a souvenir someone had fetched him from a Morecambe tobacconist's about a decade earlier. They were in effect like match versions of his spills, for they were all the colours of the rainbow too, those match-heads where the phosphorus was dyed red, yellow, blue, green and even some chalk-coloured whites were to be found. All the colours were jammed together in what was a cylinder-shaped box with a plastic, transparent top. The reds were together, the blues together, the yellows together, and they were all framed within an oval top which made them appear like a set of lustrous, beautifully-coloured families. Of course, the box was never opened. The matches were never used. They stayed pristine, unstruck, perfect and blindingly coloured.

I have never ever seen colours like the colours of those matches. They shone like stars or like angels. They were so beautiful they could hypnotize me for minutes at a time. I wanted to eat them, swallow them, inhale them, partake of them, enjoy and imbibe and impress on myself their lustre and other-wordly radiance . . .

My grandmother saw me looking at those matches and commented tenderly on how rapt I seemed. My grandfather looked at them and then me proudly and unselfishly. My grandmother asked me if I wasn't going to put the calendar right for her today, as I did every other time I came visiting. I rose shyly and stepped self-consciously as I made over to the sideboard to do the job that was mine.

It was a little brass holder with a moulded horse emblem on the top. Inside the holder went three different sizes of card. At the front of the holder went the smallest proclaiming the weekday Tuesday. Behind it the lesser giving the number of the month, the twenty-seventh. After that, the particular month, which was April. It was a laborious, endless business getting it all to rights, particularly when as now the calendar hadn't been put right for a month or so. That cheap little ornament-calendar had the innocent grace of all familiar, simple things. Its smallness, its friendly brass mimicry of a horse. I felt my grandparents' eyes trained upon me as I did my job and I performed it with a sense of duty and a sense of untold, unexplainable necessity. As if I was marking time for them always.

The old man had been retired for over a dozen years, but he maintained a part-time job. He was out working in some shopkeeper's greenhouses for thirty or more hours a week and in 1961 was being paid two pounds ten and sixpence for this. His relatives talked of the exploitation involved but my grand-father was coolly indifferent to anything but the work itself. He liked to be busy and would have been even harsher if left to his memories and nothing besides. In any case, what point was an abundance of money to such as *him*?

Those hours he was working were the ones where my grand-mother was left to bathe her broken nerves. She went out and shopped, took Lassie out down by the back of the gasworks, sat on her own in the house and shook and cooked and waited. She lived in a permanent melancholy apprehension that was excited and maintained by her husband, Jackie Spade. Her pleasures were her relatives, her packets of sweets, her daily listen to *The Archers* and presumably her sleep. The doctor gave her tablets but they made no real difference to her terrors. If the doctor had had any sense of metaphor he might have given the pills to my grandfather instead. As it was, my grandfather would have as soon approached a doctor as approach a clergyman. He thought of medicine and the ill as feeble and despicable. My grandmother, left to her own devices, used to perform a soothing nervous tic with her hands. She would cause them to revolve round and round each other just as if carding some imaginary wool. There remained nonetheless the problem of her neck; nothing that she knew of could stop the bouncings and twitchings of that agile limb.

Except for one remarkable thing. A friend of a friend of the man for whom my grandfather did his part-time job, one day gave my grandfather a television. We couldn't think why the old man should have accepted such a gift seeing that he had long made plain his hatred for that invention and seeing that he was as resistant to charity as he was to the pills of doctors. Later we learnt that he had perhaps parted with some cash, or it might have been so many weeks' wages given in part-payment via his employer. However, economics aside, his authority had to find some way of addressing itself to the invasion of this impudent-faced intruder.

His relationship with the television was from the start a dubious one. His wife naturally fell in love with it from the very first half hour. She also soon found the televisual equivalent of *The Archers* in terms of that novel, realistic series called *Coronation Street*, and another less demanding show called *Yorkie*, starring Wilfred Pickles, was soon to draw her to the screen like a love-starved addict.

My grandfather noticed this particular fascination. He noticed several things as he observed his wife now so fascinated with something new that effectively he, Jack Spade, had taken a rear seat in the audience. This new machine had much more power to it than the ageing, weary old radio. The only radio programme his wife showed any passion for was *The Archers* but with the television it seemed she would have gawped at anything, given the chance. Jack Spade commented on that with some sarcasm and some disdain. He used the word 'brainwashed' and watched with pleasure as she started and flushed. She strove to deny the addiction but in his own cruel way he was right. She knew he was right and the tears welled up in her cornflower-blue, meek eyes. Thus she always watched in panicking doubt her *Coronation Street* and said little prayers all the time that she watched it. Impermanence, anxious impermanence, was always a part of her despicable addiction.

To start with, my grandfather kept the television down below the wireless and covered with a cloth, just as if it was a budgerigar taking a permanent night's rest. The radio sat on top of the table and in order for the TV to be switched on, the two must change places and thereby the radio be humiliated and demoted. Was it that the old man was just sentimental and wished not to see the old replaced by the new? After all, he could not exactly help himself from being just as glued to *Coronation Street*, especially if he thought that no one was looking at his line of gaze . . .

If his wife wished to watch any other programme she had to ask him to put the TV up there for her. She would no more have switched it on herself than have stolen his personal rocking chair. And for those first five weeks it suited him to make much heavy weather of it all and to do the replacement and the switching on with something of an effort and a show of generosity. He carried it out with painstaking resistance. He lingered long over the performance in order to enjoy her lasting apprehension.

Weeks passed and my grandfather became most unnerved. His wife's enjoyment of *Coronation Street* was so profound that when it was on it left him feeling old and helpless and almost like an accessory to the room. To his room! All else aside it was impossible for him just to ruminate and daydream with that infernal blaring. It dominated the room, overwhelmed the atmosphere in a way that the radio could never hope to do. It dominated his wife, where formerly he had dominated his wife. There was an irritating competition there. There had to be a stop put somewhere.

One night my grandmother made her very last request for him to put on his television. It was seven twenty-five and it was a Monday. Last Wednesday had been a real cliffhanger where Ena Sharples had been left for dead. 'Jack,' she mumbled to the old man very frightenedly. Her hands dathered as usual, her neck twitched and begged for some kind of attention and tenderness, even if it only be in other folks' lives on that magical ridiculous seventeen inch screen.

'No,' he refused expressionlessly, rocking in his rocker, fingering his dark brown twist tobacco.

'Please!' she begged, not knowing whether to be relieved or to weep now that the blow had fallen.

'No,' he repeated calmly, and then added for good measure. 'You're getting brainwashed by that thing, my lass! It's taking you over. It's making you soft! You're sat there like a cow with your nose an inch from that screen and it's the only thing that gives you any interest in life. You should give yourself a shake!

You should be ashamed of yourself! Isn't it a fact that it's brainwashing you that blasted telly?'

'No,' she wept, just as Lassie squatted on her haunches and begged for a look from her double.

'I think so,' he said, almost conversationally.

'Please,' she implored, her shakes letting loose like ten cannons.

'No,' he said, suddenly happily, 'and that's final. I said no and I meant it, lass! And tomorrow I'm giving it back to that feller, that television. I hate it! It rules everything. What, all our folks, all our relatives and their bairns do nowt but watch that bloody thing. All day, all night, like machines. They're mad! They want their heads looked! I'm damned if I'm gonna be ruled by a thing like yon from mornin till night . . .'

Until, two years later, he was seventy-eight. In my mother's opinion her parents were getting far too old to fend for themselves so she scoured about for a house close to ours, so that she could minister as a daughter should. Soon she had acquired a tiny cottage that was hardly ten yards from our own. The old man made enough protests but eventually agreed to the move. His wife was delighted of course, for not only would she have an escape from her husband, she would also have access to a nineteen-inch television.

I was growing up just as they were growing very old. My secondary schooling corresponded to those last six years of my grandfather's life. My father had got him an allotment in the village and every day – rain, shine, wind, drought – the old, determined, stern and wrinkled man peddled his two miles there and back. My grandmother sat with my mother through much of the day and twice a week for all those years she would come across to watch her *Coronation Street*. She must have watched at least six hundred episodes before she died. She had gained that much freedom, that three hundred hours, for not even Jack Spade would have presumed to bar the door against her evening exits.

In 1968, at just turned eighteen, I won myself a place at one of our ancient universities. The results came on a day when my parents were out shopping and there was no one with whom I might share my ecstatic news. I, who hardly went near my grandparents from one year to the next, I suddenly remembered two people to whom I could relate my present glories. I scuttered off those ten yards to inform them of the prowess of their magical grandson. I was elated with pride and vanity and pleasure. I had worked like a single-minded maniac to get my prize and now I was basking like a pampered lapdog.

My grandmother was tickled to the skies. She took out a dusty bottle of sherry, her hands quaking as she poured, and drank to my success. My grandfather sat in his rocker, nodding himself backwards and forwards and digesting the news with curiosity. He shook his head up and down with that emphasis of old and repeated the syllables of that famous university town. 'Very good,' he said with solemn scrutiny. 'Well, well. That's done it an make no mistake.'

My grandmother echoed the magical syllables too. That city to her, to him, to me also in my provincial fantasies, was halfway between Eldorado and Olympus. Getting into *that* university was tantamount to having won through the labours of an epic hero. I saw the pride on their faces and knew now why it meant so very much to me, that victory. One's own pride was only one's pride for others, a means of glowing before others who could perhaps not really see what was there at one's roots.

'Here's to you,' said my quaking grandmother, her neck going to left and right as she spoke, adding as she toasted how proud and pleased my two parents would be.

'Oh aye,' said my grandfather with proprietorial wisdom, as if it was only he had ever really understood me and my ways. '*I* knew how brainy this feller was. I knew all along about this feller. What, I can mind how sharp he was as a bairn. I could have telled you all how well this lad would do in time . . .'

He nodded backward and forward in his chair and sucked away wisely at his pipe.

'But you know,' he said obscurely, 'you should rest your brains, lad, sometimes. Too much bookwork can be a bad thing for you. You should relax your brains now and again.'

My heart stabbed painfully. *What* was it he saw? Anything,

155

nothing, the roots of my ambition? And where would the memory of such as Jackie Spade fit within the portals of that church university, that town for the elect, the chosen, the blessed ones?

'This lad'll end up one of the gentry,' concluded my grandfather. 'This lad'll end up among the toffs. And good for him! You go out there son and beat the bloody lot of them, toffs and all!'

He was dead about six months later. In the early winter of 1969 he found himself too weak to cycle down to the allotments. For two, perhaps three months he was there struggling with the final blows, upstairs in his bed, tossing and turning and forgiving no one in his steady way. He begged for no contrition, no unction, no attentions. He wanted no nursing. He told the nurses to let him die, without self-pity or dramatizing, and he meant it. Because in the last few weeks it was bed-washing, rubber rings and all that monstrous palaver. And along with that his mind would take him for walks all over the past. He who had lived in the past in word now lived in the past in thought and substance. He believed himself to be back down the pits (where he had worked before the railways) and he cursed the unyielding nature of the coal and the earth and I was told he swore obscenely as he did so.

They told me to go and see him and I would not. My grandmother asked, my mother asked, my father suggested it but I would not go and see him. Besides, as my grandfather had shrewdly seen, I just hadn't the time to bless myself these days. I still had A levels to sit and as everyone knows those things are closer to God than are grandfathers. Like a well-oiled machine I studied, fretted, keened and quietly suffered. Those who can guess what I am talking about will know what I am talking about. I never paid him his last respects. I refused to go and see him on his death bed. I stayed where I was and I studied.

When he died it turned out that he had left me, me uniquely of his many grandchildren, one of his special Victorian sovereigns. My grandmother handed me that along with the little horse emblem calendar, the unstruck perfect matches, the look of a far-away widow.

She wept long after the death of her tormentor. She lived another nine months was all. We could judge how affected she was by his absence inasmuch as she used to fall asleep watching her *Coronation Street* where before she was as alert as her little bitch Lassie had long ago been.

She spent all her time sleeping, falling asleep, thinking about doing so . . . and thinking perhaps of all the years she had endured under Jackie – the emphatic – Spade. People said it was his nagging must have kept her alive. Others that it was that that had left her so exhausted when she was only seventy-five. By early 1970 she was in bed and breathless and in three weeks she was dead.

I had felt nothing when he died and I felt nothing again when his wife went. By then I was in the ancient city which left me for some reason no time to feel sorrow nor loss nor anything whatever. I remember trying to cry over the death of my gentle, long-haired grandmother, she who would have been as near to blamelessness of character as anyone. Nothing would come. Not even a single drop could be squeezed.

Until all of ten years after. I was lying awake in a distant Midlands township, in a town that my grandfather would have hated. It was a town that had no taste, smell, vigour, past, future. It had two dozen supermarkets, DIY shops, traffic islands, multi-storey car parks, hypermarkets, new estates, prosperity – in a word fuckall. My wife and I were living on an estate of semis where the neighbours were to say the least far less vigorous than the cadavers who dwelt in the adjacent cemetery. In fact the cemetery was the only beautiful thing in that Midlands town. It had a few weeds, a look of age, an air of being lived in as it were.

I saw his matches in the gloaming, as I lay awake, thinking just as he always did of the past. I saw the colours of his *special* matches in their brightness, their beauty, their glory. The memory had come because of first simply thinking of Cumberland. Rootless at home, rootless in exile, it was all one and the same was it not? Little terriers, little bitch terriers cracking stones between their teeth in grey and smoky backyards. Old men bullying old women. Ambitious children trying to win their way

157

from the backyards of the future. All those handsome, televisual dreams of Getting On and Doing Very Well At All Costs.

And then the floodgates opened up. All at once the colours of the matches turned into smell and turned into grief. I could smell them, him, her, Lassie and her small tin box, that house, that fire, the gas works, the cream cakes bought by my mother. I could see it all like gold and would have sold my body and soul just to have smelt it all for good.

Cruising at Fifty

PHILIP OAKES

THEY DELIVERED THE car on the last day of shooting, parking it beside Rex Merritt's trailer so that it was the first thing he saw when he returned from the set. His pleasure was just as intense as he had expected. He stroked the sleek green bonnet and eased himself behind the wheel to inhale the scent of the upholstery. Leather smelled like money, he thought; but so did the best tweed and the best cologne. Perhaps it was all in the mind, but not all minds were experienced enough to make the comparisons.

Tough on them, he decided. After thirty years of acting in films he was entitled to some of the fringe benefits, especially at the end of six weeks' location in Yorkshire where it had rained two days out of three and his co-star had been a prize bitch from Tulsa whose career was being groomed by a one-time hairdresser from Beverly Hills. He and Merritt had not got on. At their first meeting Merritt had called him Goldilocks and the relationship had not improved.

'It just slipped out,' Merritt told the director, Norman Peel. 'I didn't mean to hurt his feelings.'

Peel took off his glasses and massaged the dents they had made on either side of his nose. 'We need his co-operation,' he said patiently. 'She does what he tells her to do. She's where the money is. Don't make life difficult.'

'I'll try,' said Merritt. And he had done his best to keep his word. He had slipped up the day he told an interviewer in tones of the purest admiration that his co-star's talents were all before her. The quip had been widely quoted and the film had nearly foundered as a result. But now it was over and he was on his way home.

The car was his fiftieth birthday present to himself. No one, thought Merritt, deserved it more. It was his reward for out-lasting producers, agents, fellow-actors, the whole appalling industry. At mid-century he was a survivor. He had served his time in repertory, achieved star billing before he was twenty-five, gone to Hollywood at twenty-seven and returned tactfully to England ten years later. His timing had been perfect. The great names had faded. TV had devoured the studios. But he was still in demand. And the new car was his prize for succeeding against the odds.

By the time he reached the motorway it was raining again. Cars and lorries ahead of him were each contained in a nimbus of spray. He switched on a symphony concert to take his mind off the weather. The road was the colour of old putty, scored by skid marks and blotted by oil. After an hour's driving his head ached and he pulled into a service station.

'Nice little wagon,' said the attendant at the pump.

'Not bad.'

'New, is it?'

'New today,' he admitted. 'I'm just running it in.'

The attendant scraped the windscreen with a rubber flange then polished it with a cloth. 'No burn-ups then. You can't go putting the old foot down yet awhile.'

'I don't need to,' said Merritt. 'She cruises at fifty.'

He was heading for the exit when the girl stopped him, stepping in front of the car as though she had not seen him. She wore jeans and a denim jacket and her short streaked hair was plastered to her head. 'Going to London?' she asked.

'Near enough.'

'Give us a lift then.'

Her accent was sub-Cockney, but curiously classless. She did not stoop to speak through his window but remained upright with one thumb hooked through her tote bag, so that he found himself bending forward to catch what she said. 'Where do you want to get to?'

'Away from here.' She shifted the weight of the tote bag and rested the other hand on her hip. 'Fulham would be nice.'

'I'm not going that far.'

'It doesn't matter. Anywhere.'

He opened the door and she slid in beside him, stowing the bag between her feet.

'You're wet through,' said Merritt. 'Take your jacket off.'

'It doesn't matter,' she repeated.

'The seat matters. Please take it off.'

She shrugged her shoulders and obeyed. Beneath the tee-shirt he saw the ripple of her rib-cage and the sharp points of her breasts. No brassière, he thought, and instinctively looked straight ahead. It meant nothing, he told himself. No one even bothered to burn bras any more. They had lost their magic. But out of the corner of his eye he looked again and as he did so he saw her smile.

'You can look if you want to,' she said. 'I don't mind.'

'Look at what?'

'If you don't know then I can't tell you.' She rummaged in the dashboard. 'Got any ciggies?'

'Sorry, I don't smoke.'

'Can I roll my own?'

'If you must.'

'It doesn't matter.' She slumped down in her seat and he drove on in silence. After a while he heard her humming quietly in time to the wipers.

'What's the tune?' he asked.

'I don't know. I've only just made it up.'

'Are you a musician?'

'Christ, no.' She flicked the hair from her forehead. 'I've known a few, mind.'

'What kind?'

'How many kinds are there?' She raised her right hand and extended the fingers, one by one. 'Heavy Metal. New Wave.

161

New Romantics. That's as far as I go. They're not so different. Just blokes.' She nodded towards the radio. 'Even them, the classical lot. I bet they're just the same.'

'Very likely,' said Merritt.

She studied him surreptitiously, glancing at his profile, then looking away as if matching it with a picture she had filed in her mind. 'Do I know you from somewhere?' she asked.

'It's possible.'

'What are you then? Someone on the telly?'

'Sometimes,' he said. 'Mostly I make films.

'What's your name?'

He told her and she wagged her head thoughtfully. 'My mum used to go really mad for you. That was when she was my age.'

'Thanks a lot. How old's that?'

'How old do you think?'

'Eighteen,' he suggested.

She hunched her bony shoulders. 'If you like. Not that it matters.'

'Of course it matters,' said Merritt. 'What's your name?'

She sighed and drew her initials on the windscreen with a grimy finger. The letters ran together and she wiped them out. 'Cissie Lynch,' she said.

Merritt patted the knee next to his. 'Now we've been introduced.'

He felt curiously relieved, as though he had brought a difficult negotiation to its close. As a young man he had been unable to remember names, a problem he had struggled to overcome when his first wife told him it meant he was uninterested in the person he was addressing. What she said was entirely true. But it was important, Merritt realized, that no one should detect his indifference.

So he made the effort and it had been worthwhile. On the set he had trained himself to remember the names of the entire unit, from the stars to the chippies. There was no side to Rex Merritt, they said. He was a prince.

Dusk deepened into night and his headlights, burning through the rain, seemed to carry the car on rods of neon. His headache

162

returned and Merritt wound down his window to let the wind flog his face.

'Are you okay?' asked the girl.

'I need to get off the road. Where are we?'

'Near Northampton. There's a sign.'

Merritt peered through a curtain of spray. 'It's not too far to London. Do you want to get out here and try for another lift?'

'What are you going to do?'

'Find somewhere to stay.'

'Me too,' she said. 'I'm with you.'

'You've not been invited.'

'Not yet.' She met his scrutiny without flinching and as he took the next turn-off he felt her hand climb his back and massage the muscles at the base of his neck.

'That feels good.'

'I can do better than that.'

'Not while I'm driving.'

She gave a sneaky laugh and his heart lurched in his chest. Women had always regarded him as sympathetic, including the two he had married and subsequently divorced. But the truth was that in the final analysis, sometimes in the first, he did not like them much. They could be convenient and companionable. Some had been therapeutic. But, by and large, he found them trivial, vindictive and, thank God, disposable. He lived alone, except for a manservant, in a mansion flat overlooking Hampstead Heath. Women came and went by invitation.

They were, mostly, attached to his own profession; actresses or publicists or make-up girls. 'I suppose you get us from the wardrobe,' one of them complained as he led her to the door. And he had smiled and promised to phone her and then crossed her name from his address book. He did not like to be reminded that he was making use of the facilities.

The girl in the car was different. She was not impressed by his name or reputation. She did not belong to the acting clan. He knew nothing of her background and he did not wish to know. They were passing strangers who would not meet again. Already he thought of their time together as a small and dirty secret which he need never reveal to another soul. He pressed

163

his head against her hand and sighed with pleasure and anticipation.

'Are you really eighteen?'

'More or less.'

'More? Or less?'

'Don't worry about it,' she said.

He did not care. He felt dizzy with lust. To the left he saw the
lights of a motel and he turned into the forecourt. He paid for a
cabin and drove on past parked cars and dividing trellises to the
end of the line. There was a double bed and in the bathroom
there were twin toothbrushes in matching mugs.

'Cosy,' she said.

Standing behind her, he reached beneath the tee-shirt and held
her breasts. She did not move away and he pressed harder. 'Can
we get something to eat?' she said.

'I expect so. What would you like?'

'I could manage a steak.'

'All right, then.'

'And a bottle of wine.'

He let her go and made the parody of a bow. 'Anything else,
madam?'

'I want a shower,' she said. 'And I want to watch telly. How
about you?'

'You know what I want.'

He ordered the meal on the house phone and watched her
closely as she undressed.

She had a lean, almost hairless body. On her lower belly there
was a scar the colour of rust. 'My appendix,' she said, 'gone but
not forgotten.' Without warning, he felt his eyes prick with tears.
She was so young, he thought; more vulnerable than she knew.

She closed the bathroom door behind her and he heard the
tattoo of water against porcelain. He picked her clothes up and
folded them over a chair. Her tote bag was surprisingly heavy
and, mildly curious, he loosened the cord and felt inside. There
was a wallet, a compact, a packet of tobacco, a blue plastic comb
and a pistol. A pistol, thought Merritt, hearing the words as if
he had spoken them aloud. What in Christ's name was she doing
with that in her bag?

He was not only shocked but frightened. Violence terrified him. He put the pistol on the bed and saw the duvet sink beneath its weight. When he ran a finger over the blue steel it came away with a faint slick of oil. He broke open the chamber and saw that it was fully loaded. He closed his mind to the possibilities of how it might be used. Or indeed, he thought in a flash of panic, how it had already been used.

Distantly he heard her humming an old Beatles tune and imagined her shrouded in steam, her face tilted upwards as if to receive a benediction. He had not been mistaken about her vulnerability. But it was not for him to exploit. She was unlike all the others he had used and discarded because she cared nothing for his name or reputation. Her indifference was absolute and he felt his security dissolve. They were not only a generation, but a race apart. He stared at the pistol dimpling the duvet and measured his fear.

She opened the bathroom door and saw the gun. 'Nosy,' she said.

Merritt spread his hands. 'Sorry.'

'Sorry for what?'

'Looking in your bag.'

'It doesn't matter.' She was wearing a towel pleated between her breasts and she loosened it to pat herself dry. Beads of water streaked her spine and she handed the towel to Merritt. 'Do my back.'

He did as he was told and she grinned at him over her shoulder. 'Nasty shock, was it?'

'Yes, it was.'

'At your time of life too.' She clicked her tongue. 'Bad for the system.'

'I'll survive.'

'That's what they all say. Don't you believe it.' Naked, she sat on the bed. 'All right, then. What do you want to know first?'

'Nothing,' said Merritt. 'Tell me nothing.' He felt himself under threat. The more he knew, the more he would be involved. 'Just be quiet,' he begged her.

'You wanted to know how old I am. Have another guess.'

'I don't want to hear.'

'Sixteen,' she said. 'How would that go down with the folks?'

'You lied to me,' said Merritt. 'I could explain.'

She picked up the gun and weighed it in her hand. 'As for this,' she said, 'you'll die laughing when you hear about this.'

Merritt shook his head desperately. 'No,' he said, 'keep it to yourself.' He edged away but she pursued him, the gun clasped between her breasts. Her mouth curved in a half smile and she licked her lips as though she was tasting blood, or the promise of it. 'Please,' he heard himself whisper, 'please stop this.'

'Stop what?'

'Leave me alone.'

'That's not what you wanted half an hour ago.'

'It's what I want now.'

'Oh yes.' She nodded wisely. 'And you always get what you want, don't you? No argument. No hassle. Lucky old you.'

'It's not like that.'

'Oh yes it is,' she said. 'That's exactly how it is. Don't tell me any different. The world's made for people like you. Nice job, nice car, nice bit on the side.' She shivered but made no attempt to cover herself with the towel and he realized she was shaking not from the cold but with rage. 'It shouldn't be so easy,' she said. 'You ought to know what it's like for other people. You ought to be told.'

She drew breath and he sensed revelation about to engulf him. He would be involved. He would be made responsible. Unless he escaped at that very moment, Merritt realized, he was lost. As she opened her pale mouth he ran from the room, his hands over his ears.

The rain had stopped but his car was pebbled all over as if it had been drenched with a hose. He wrenched open the door and breathed its essence.

It no longer smelled simply of money, but of sanctuary. For several seconds he sat with his hands on the wheel until his pulse slowed from a canter to a steady beat. The door of the cabin remained closed. No one called after him. He was safe, he told himself, as he started the engine. He was innocent of crimes committed and crimes still planned.

The memory of his desire returned briefly like an illness recalled over the years. But by the time he had reached the motorway it was gone, to be replaced by incredulity that he had been so stupid, so unwary.

He remembered the gun and the flare of naked flesh and for one fearful moment he allowed himself to speculate on what she had been about to tell him. He would never know and he powerfully desired not to know. But he would never cease to wonder. At mid-century he had been made a gift of disquiet. Instinctively he reduced speed and drove home, cruising at fifty.

Fen Hall

RUTH RENDELL

WHEN CHILDREN PAINT a picture of a tree they always do the trunk brown. But trees seldom have brown trunks. Birches are silver, beeches pewter colour, planes grey and yellow, walnuts black and the bark of oaks, chestnuts and sycamores green with lichen. Pringle had never noticed any of this until he came to Fen Hall. After that, once his eyes had been opened and he had seen what things were really like, he would have painted trees with bark in different colours but next term he stopped doing art. It was just as well, he had never been very good at it, and perhaps by then he wouldn't have felt like painting trees anyway. Or even looking at them much.

Mr Liddon met them at the station in an old Volvo estate car. They were loaded down with camping gear, the tent and sleeping bags and cooking pots and a Calor gas burner in case it was too windy to keep a fire going. It had been very windy lately, the summer cool and sunless. Mr Liddon was Pringle's father's friend and Pringle had met him once before, years ago when he was a little kid, but still it was up to him to introduce the others. He spoke with wary politeness.

'This is John and this is Roger. They're brothers.'

Pringle didn't say anything about Roger always being called Hodge. He sensed that Mr Liddon wouldn't call him Hodge any more than he would call *him* Pringle. He was right.

'Parents well, are they, Peregrine?'

Pringle said yes. He could see a gleam in John's eye that augured teasing to come.

Hodge, who was always thinking of his stomach, said: 'Could we stop on the way, Mr Liddon, and buy some food?'

Mr Liddon cast up his eyes. Pringle could tell he was going to be 'one of those' grown-ups. They all got into the car with their stuff and a mile or so out of town Mr Liddon stopped at a self-service shop. He didn't go inside with them which was just as well. He would only have called what they bought junk food.

Fen Hall turned out to be about seven miles away. They went through a village called Fedgford and a little way beyond it turned down a lane that passed through a wood.

'That's where you'll have your camp,' Mr Liddon said.

Of necessity, because the lane was no more than a rough track, he was driving slowly. He pointed in among the trees. The wood had a mysterious look as if full of secrets. In the aisles between the trees the light was greenish-gold and misty. There was a muted twittering of birds and a cooing of doves. Pringle began to feel excited. It was nicer than he had expected. A little further on the wood petered out into a plantation of tall straight trees with green trunks growing in rows, the ground between them all overgrown with a spiky plant that had a curious prehistoric look to it.

'Those trees are poplars,' Mr Liddon said. You could tell he was a schoolteacher. 'They're grown as a crop.'

This was a novel idea to Pringle. 'What sort of crop?'

'Twenty-five years after they're planted they're cut down and used for making matchsticks. If they don't fall down first. We had a couple go over in the gales last winter.'

Pringle wasn't listening. He had seen the house. It was like a house in a dream, he thought, though he didn't quite know what he meant by that. Houses he saw in actual dreams were much like his own or John and Hodge's. Suburban Surrey semi-detached. This house, when all the trees were left behind and no twig or leaf or festoon of wild clematis obscured it, stood basking in the sunshine with the confidence of something alive, as if secure in its own perfection. Dark mulberry colour, of small Tudor bricks, it had a roof of many irregular planes and gables and a cluster of chimneys like candles. The windows with the sun on them were plates of gold between the mullions. Under the eaves swallows had built their lumpy sagging nests.

'Leave your stuff in the car. I'll be taking you back up to the wood in ten minutes. Just thought you'd like to get your bearings, see where everything is first. There's the outside tap over there which you'll use of course. And you'll find a shovel and an axe in there which I rely on you to replace.'

It was going to be the biggest house Pringle had ever set foot in – not counting places like Hampton Court and Woburn. Fen Hall. It looked and the name sounded like a house in a book, not real at all. The front door was of oak, studded with iron and set back under a porch that was dark and carved with roses. Mr Liddon took them in the back way. He took them into a kitchen that was exactly Pringle's idea of the lowest sort of slum.

He was shocked. At first he couldn't see much because it had been bright outside but he could smell something dank and frowsty. When his vision adjusted he found they were in a huge room or cavern with two small windows and about 400 square feet of squalor between them. Islanded were a small white electric oven and a small white fridge. The floor was of brick, very uneven, the walls of irregular green-painted peeling plaster with a bubbly kind of growth coming through it. Stacks of dirty dishes filled a stone sink of the kind his mother had bought at a sale and made a cactus garden in. The whole place was grossly untidy with piles of washing lying about. John and Hodge, having taken it all in, were standing there with blank faces and shifting eyes.

Mr Liddon's manner had changed slightly. He no longer kept up the hectoring tone. While explaining to them that this was where they must come if they needed anything, to the back door, he began a kind of ineffectual tidying up, cramming things into the old wooden cupboards, sweeping crumbs off the table and dropping them into the sink.

John said: 'Is it all right for us to have a fire?'

'So long as you're careful. Not if the wind gets up again. I don't have to tell you where the wood is, you'll find it lying about.' Mr Liddon opened a door and called. 'Flora!'

A stone-flagged passage could be seen beyond. No one came. Pringle knew Mr Liddon had a wife, though no children. His parents had told him only that Mr and Mrs Liddon had bought a marvellous house in the country a year before and he and a couple of his friends could go and camp in the grounds if they wanted to. Further information he had picked up when they didn't know he was listening. Tony Liddon hadn't had two halfpennies to rub together until his aunt died and left him a bit of money. It couldn't have been much surely. Anyway he had spent it all on Fen Hall, he had always wanted an old place like that. The upkeep was going to be a drain on him and goodness knows how he would manage.

Pringle hadn't been much interested in all this. Now it came back to him. Mr Liddon and his father had been at university together but Mr Liddon hadn't had a wife then. Pringle had never met his wife and nor had his parents. Anyway it was clear they were not to wait for her. They got back into the car and went to find a suitable camping site.

It was a relief when Mr Liddon went away and left them to it. The obvious place to camp was on the high ground in a clearing and to make their fire in a hollow Mr Liddon said was probably a disused gravel pit. The sun was low, making long shafts of light that pierced the groves of birch and crabapple. Mistletoe hung in the oak trees like green birds' nests. It was warm and murmurous with flies. John was adept at putting up the tent and gave them orders.

'Peregrine,' he said. 'Like a sort of mad bird.'

Hodge capered about, his thumbs in his ears and his hands flapping. 'Tweet, tweet, mad bird. His master chains him up like a dog. Tweet, tweet, birdie!'

'I'd rather be hunting falcon than Roger the lodger the sod,' said Pringle and he shoved Hodge and they both fell over and rolled about grappling on the ground until John kicked them and told them to give him a hand, he couldn't do the lot on his own.

It was good in the camp that night, not windy but still and

171

mild after the bad summer they'd had. They made a fire and cooked tomato soup and fish fingers and ate a whole packet of the biscuits called iced bears. They were in their bags in the tent, John reading the *Observer's Book of Common Insects*, Pringle a thriller set in a Japanese prison camp his parents would have taken away if they'd known about it, and Hodge listening to his radio, when Mr Liddon came up with a torch to check on them.

'Just to see if you're OK. Everything shipshape and Bristol fashion?'

Pringle thought that an odd thing to say considering the mess in his own house. Mr Liddon made a fuss about the candles they had lit and they promised to put them out, though of course they didn't. It was very silent in the night up there in the wood, the deepest silence that Pringle had ever known, a quiet that was somehow heavy as if some great dark beast had lain down on the wood and quelled every sound beneath under its dense soft fur.

He didn't think of this for very long because he was asleep two minutes after they blew the candles out.

Next morning the weather wasn't so nice. It was dull and cool for August. John saw a brimstone butterfly which pleased him because the species was getting rarer. They all walked into Fedgford and bought sausages and then found they hadn't a frying pan. Pringle went down to the house on his own to see if he could borrow one.

Unlike most men Mr Liddon would be at home because of the school holidays. Pringle expected to see him working in the garden which even he could see was a mess. But he wasn't anywhere about. Pringle banged on the back door with his fist – there was neither bell nor knocker – but no one came. The door wasn't locked. He wondered if it would be all right to go in and then he went in.

The mess in the kitchen was rather worse. A large white and tabby cat was on the table eating something it probably shouldn't have been eating out of a paper bag. Pringle had a curious feeling that it would somehow be quite permissible for him to go on into the house. Something told him – though it was not a something based on observation or even guesswork – that Mr Liddon wasn't in. He went into the passage he had seen the day before through the open door. This led into a large stone-flagged hall. The place was dark with heavy dark beams going up the walls and across the ceilings and it was cold. It smelled of damp. The smell was like mushrooms that have been left in a paper bag at the back of the fridge and forgotten. Pringle pushed open a likely looking door, some instinct making him give a warning cough.

The room was enormous, its ceiling all carved beams and cobwebs. Even Pringle could see that the few small bits of furniture in it would have been more suitable for the living room of a bungalow. A woman was standing by the tall, diamond-paned, mullioned window, holding something blue and sparkling up to the light. She was strangely dressed in a long skirt, her hair falling loosely down her back, and she stood so still, gazing at the blue object with both arms raised, that for a moment Pringle had an uneasy feeling she wasn't a woman at all but the ghost of a woman. Then she turned round and smiled.

'Hallo,' she said. 'Are you one of our campers?'

She was at least as old as Mr Liddon but her hair hung down like one of the girls' at school. Her face was pale and not pretty yet when she smiled it was a wonderful face. Pringle registered that, staring at her. It was a face of radiant kind sensitivity, though it was to be some years before he could express what he had felt in those terms.

'I'm Pringle,' he said, and because he sensed that she would understand. 'I'm called Peregrine really but I get people to call me Pringle.'

'I don't blame you. I'd do the same in your place.' She had a quiet unaffected voice. 'I'm Flora Liddon. You can call me Flora.'

He didn't think he could do that and knew he would end up calling her nothing. 'I came to see if I could borrow a frying pan.'

'Of course you can.' She added, 'If I can find one.' She held the thing in her hand out to him and he saw it was a small glass bottle. 'Do you think it's pretty?'

He looked at it doubtfully. It was just a bottle. On the window

173

sill behind her were more bottles, mostly of clear colourless glass but among them dark green ones with fluted sides.

'There are wonderful things to be found here. You can dig and find rubbish heaps that go back to Elizabethan times. And there was a Roman settlement down by the river. Would you like to see a Roman coin?'

It was black, misshapen, lumpy, with an ugly man's head on it. She showed him a jar of thick bubbly green glass and said it was the best piece of glass she'd found to date. They went out to the kitchen. Finding a frying pan wasn't easy but talking to her was. By the time she had washed up a pan which she had found full of congealed fat he had told her all about the camp and their walk to Fedgford and what the butcher had said: 'I hope you're going to wash yourselves before you cook my nice clean sausages.'

And she told him what a lot needed doing to the house and grounds and how they'd have to do it all themselves because they hadn't much money. She wasn't any good at painting or sewing or gardening or even housework, come to that. Pottering about and looking at things was what she liked.

'"What is this life, if full of care, we have no time to stand and stare?"'

He knew where that came from. W. H. Davies, the Supertramp. They had done it at school.

'I'd have been a good tramp,' she said. 'It would have suited me.'

The smile radiated her plain face.

They cooked the sausages for lunch and went on an insect-hunting expedition with John. The dragonflies he had promised them down by the river were not to be seen but he found what he said was a caddis, though it looked like a bit of twig to Pringle. Hodge ate five Mars bars during the course of the afternoon. They came upon the white and tabby cat with a mouse in its jaws. Undeterred by an audience, it bit the mouse in two and the tiny heart rolled out. Hodge said faintly, 'I think I'm going to be sick,' and was. They still resolved to have a cat watch on the morrow and see how many mice it caught in a day.

By that time the weather was better. The sun didn't shine but it had got warmer again. They found the cat in the poplar plantation, stalking something among the prehistoric weeds John said were called horse-tails. The poplars had trunks almost as green as grass and their leafy tops, very high up there in the pale blue sky, made rustling whispering sounds in the breeze. That was when Pringle noticed about tree trunks not being brown. The trunks of the Scotch pines were clear pinkish-red, as bright as flowers when for a moment the sun shone. He pointed this out to the others but they didn't seem interested.

'You sound like our auntie,' said Hodge. 'She does flower arrangements for the church.'

'And throws up when she sees a bit of blood, I expect,' said Pringle. 'It runs in your family.'

Hodge lunged at him and he tripped Hodge up and they rolled about wrestling among the horse-tails. By four in the afternoon the cat had caught six mice. Flora came out and told them the cat's name was Tabby which obscurely pleased Pringle. If she had said Snowflake or Persephone or some other daft name people called animals he would have felt differently about her, though he couldn't possibly have said why. He wouldn't have liked her so much.

A man turned up in a Land Rover as they were making their way back to camp. He said he had been to the house and knocked but no one seemed to be at home. Would they give Mr or Mrs Liddon a message from him? His name was Porter, Michael Porter, and he was an archaeologist in an amateur sort of way. Mr Liddon knew all about it, and they were digging in the lower meadow and they'd come on a dump of nineteenth-century stuff. He was going to dig deeper, uncover the next layer, so if Mrs Liddon was interested in the top now was her chance to have a look.

'Can we as well?' said Pringle.

Porter said they were welcome. No one would be working there next day. He had just heard the weather forecast on his car radio and gale force winds were promised. Was that their camp up there? Make sure the tent was well anchored down, he said, and he drove off up the lane.

Pringle checked the tent. It seemed firm enough. They got into it and fastened the flap but they were afraid to light the candles and had John's storm lantern on instead. The wood was silent no longer. The wind made loud siren-like howls and a rushing rending sound like canvas being torn. When that happened the tent flapped and bellied like a sail on a ship at sea. Sometimes the wind stopped altogether and there were a few seconds of silence and calm. Then it came back with a rush and a roar. John was reading Frohawk's *Complete Book of British Butter-flies*, Pringle the Japanese prison camp thriller and Hodge was trying to listen to his radio. But it wasn't much use and after a while they put the lantern out and lay in the dark.

About five minutes afterwards there came the strongest gust of wind so far, one of the canvas-tearing gusts but ten times fiercer than the last: and then, from the south of them, down towards the house, a tremendous rending crash.

John said, 'I think we'll have to do something.' His voice was brisk but it wasn't quite steady and Pringle knew he was as scared as they were. 'We'll have to get out of here.'

Pringle put the lantern on again. It was just 10.

'The tent's going to lift off.' said Hodge.

Crawling out of his sleeping bag, Pringle was wondering what they ought to do, if it would be all right, or awful, to go down to the house, when the tent flap was pulled open and Mr Liddon put his head in. He looked cross.

'Come on, the lot of you. You can't stay here. Bring your sleeping bags and we'll find you somewhere in the house for the night.'

A note in his voice made it sound as if the storm were their fault. Pringle found his shoes, stuck his feet into them and rolled up his sleeping bag. John carried the lantern. Mr Liddon shone his own torch to light the way. In the wood there was shelter but none in the lane and the wind buffeted them as they walked. It was all noise, you couldn't see much, but as they passed the plantation, Mr Liddon swung the light up and Pringle saw what had made the crash. One of the poplars had gone over and was lying on its side with its roots in the air.

For some reason – perhaps because it was just about on this

spot that they had met Michael Porter – John remembered the message. Mr Liddon said OK and thanks. They went into the house through the back door. A tile blew off the roof and crashed on to the path just as the door closed behind them.

There were beds up in the bedrooms but without blankets or sheets on them and the mattresses were damp. Pringle thought them spooky bedrooms, dirty and draped with spiders' webs, and he wasn't sorry they weren't going to sleep there. There was the same smell of old mushrooms and a smell of paint as well where Mr Liddon had started work on a ceiling.

At the end of the passage, looking out of a window, Flora stood in a nightgown with a shawl over it. Pringle, who sometimes read ghost stories, saw her as the Grey Lady of Fen Hall. She was in the dark, the better to see the forked lightning that had begun to leap on the horizon beyond the river.

'I love to watch a storm,' she said, turning and smiling at them.

Mr Liddon had snapped a light on. 'Where are these boys to sleep?'

It was as if it didn't concern her. She wasn't unkind but she wasn't involved either. 'Oh, in the drawing room, I should think.'

'We have seven bedrooms.'

Flora said no more. A long roll of thunder shook the house. Mr Liddon took them downstairs and through the drawing room into a sort of study where they helped him make up beds of cushions on the floor. The wind howled round the house and Pringle heard another tile go. He lay in the dark, listening to the storm. The others were asleep, he could tell by their steady breathing. Inside the bags it was quite warm and he felt snug and safe. After a while he heard Mr Liddon and Flora quarrelling on the other side of the door.

Pringle's parents quarrelled a lot and he hated it, it was the worst thing in the world, though less bad now than when he was younger. He could only just hear Mr Liddon and Flora and only disjointed words, abusive and angry on the man's part, indifferent, amused on the woman's, until one sentence rang out clearly. Her voice was penetrating though it was so quiet.

'We want such different things!'

He wished they would stop. And suddenly they did, with the coming of the rain. The rain came, exploded rather, crashing at the windows and on the old sagging depleted roof. It was strange that a sound like that, a loud constant roar, could send you to sleep . . .

She was in the kitchen when he went out there in the morning. John and Hodge slept on, in spite of the bright watery sunshine that streamed through the dirty diamond window panes. A clean world outside, new-washed. Indoors the same chaos, the kitchen with the same smell of fungus and dirty dishcloths, though the windows were open. Flora sat at the table on which sprawled a welter of plates, indefinable garments, bits of bread and fruit rinds, an open can of cat food. She was drinking coffee and Tabby lay on her lap.

'There's plenty in the pot if you want some.'

She was the first grown up in whose house he had stayed who didn't ask him how he had slept. Nor was she going to cook breakfast for him. She told him where the eggs were and bread and butter. Pringle remembered he still hadn't returned her frying pan which might be the only one she had.

He made himself a pile of toast and found a jar of marmalade. The grass and the paths, he could see through an open window, were littered with broken bits of twig and leaf. A cock pheasant strutted across the shaggy lawn.

'Did the storm damage a lot of things?' he asked.

'I don't know. Tony got up early to look. There may be more poplars down.'

Pringle ate his toast. The cat had begun to purr in an irregular throbbing way. Her hand kneaded its ears and neck. She spoke, but not perhaps to Pringle or the cat, or for them if they cared to hear.

'So many people are like that. The whole of life is a preparation for life, not living.'

Pringle didn't know what to say. He said nothing. She got up and walked away, still carrying the cat, and then after a while he heard music coming faintly from a distant part of the house.

*

There were two poplars down in the plantation and each had left a crater four or five feet deep. As they went up the lane to check on their camp, Pringle and John and Hodge had a good look at them, their green trunks laid low, their tangled roots in the air. Apart from everything having got a bit blown about up at the camp and the stuff they had left out soaked through, there was no real damage done. The wood itself had afforded protection to their tent.

It seemed a good time to return the frying pan. After that they would have to walk to Fedgford for more food, unless one of the Liddons offered a lift. It was with an eye to this, Pringle had to admit, that he was taking the pan back.

But Mr Liddon, never one to waste time, was already at work in the plantation. He had lugged a chain saw up there and was preparing to cut up the poplars where they lay. When he saw them in the lane he came over.

'How did you sleep?'

Pringle said, 'OK, thanks,' but Hodge, who had been very resentful about not being given a hot drink or something to eat, muttered that he had been too hungry to sleep. Mr Liddon took no notice. He seemed jumpy and nervous. He said to Pringle that if they were going to the house would they tell Mrs Liddon – he never called her Flora to them – that there was what looked like a dump of Victorian glass in the crater where the bigger poplar had stood.

'They must have planted the trees over the top without knowing.'

Pringle looked into the crater and sure enough he could see bits of coloured glass and a bottleneck and a jug or tankard handle protruding from the tumbled soil. He left the others there, fascinated by the chain saw, and went to take the frying pan back. Flora was in the drawing room, playing records of tinkly piano music. She jumped up, quite excited, when he told her about the bottle dump.

They walked back to the plantation together, Tabby following, walking a little way behind them like a dog. Pringle knew he hadn't a hope of getting that lift now. Mr Liddon had already got the crown of the big poplar sawn off. In the short time since the storm its pale silvery green leaves had begun to wither. John asked if they could have a go with the chain saw but Mr Liddon said not so likely, did they think he was crazy? And if they wanted to get to the butcher before the shop closed for lunch they had better get going now.

Flora, her long skirt hitched up, had clambered down into the crater. If she had stood up in it her head and shoulders, perhaps all of her from the waist up, would have come above its rim, for poplars have shallow roots. But she didn't stand up. She squatted down, using her trowel, extracting small glass objects from the leafmould. The chain saw whined, slicing through the top of the poplar trunk. Pringle, watching with the others, had a feeling something was wrong about the way Mr Liddon was doing it. He didn't know what though. He could only think of a funny film he had once seen in which a man, sitting on a branch, sawed away at the bit between him and the tree trunk, necessarily falling off himself when the branch fell. But Mr Liddon wasn't sitting on anything. He was just sawing up a fallen tree from the crown to the bole. The saw sliced through again, making four short logs now as well as the bole.

'Cut along now, you boys,' he said. 'You don't want to waste the day mooning about here.'

Flora looked up and winked at Pringle. It wasn't unkind, just conspiratorial, and she smiled too, holding up a small glowing red glass bottle for him to see. He and John and Hodge moved slowly off, reluctantly, dawdling because the walk ahead would be boring and long. Through the horse-tails, up the bank, looking back when the saw whined again.

But Pringle wasn't actually looking when it happened. None of them was. They had had their final look and had begun to trudge up the lane. The sound made them turn, a kind of swishing lurch and then a heavy plopping, sickening, dull crash. They cried out, all three of them, but no one else did, not Flora or Mr Liddon. Neither of them made a sound.

Mr Liddon was standing with his arms held out, his mouth open and his eyes staring. The pile of logs lay beside him but the tree trunk was gone, sprung back roots and all when the last saw cut went through, tipped the balance and made its base heavier than its top. Pringle put his hand over his mouth and held it there. Hodge, who was nothing more than a fat baby really, had begun to cry. Fearfully, slowly, they converged, all four of them, on the now upright tree under whose roots she lay.

The police came and a farmer and his son and some men from round about. Between them they got the tree over on its side again but by then Flora was dead. Perhaps she died as soon as the bole and the mass of roots hit her. Pringle wasn't there to see. Mr Liddon had put the plantation out of bounds and said they were to stay in camp until someone came to drive them to the station. It was Michael Porter who turned up in the late afternoon and checked they'd got everything packed up and the camp site tidied. He told them Flora was dead. They got to the station in his Land Rover in time to catch the 5.15 for London.

On the way to the station he didn't mention the bottle dump he had told them about. Pringle wondered if Mr Liddon had ever said anything to Flora about it. All the way home in the train he kept thinking of something odd. The first time he went up the lane to the camp that morning he was sure there hadn't been any glass in the tree crater. He would have seen the gleam of it and he hadn't. He didn't say anything to John and Hodge, though. What would have been the point?

Three years afterwards Pringle's parents got an invitation to Mr Liddon's wedding. He was marrying the daughter of a wealthy local builder and the reception was to be at Fen Hall, the house in the wood. Pringle didn't go, being too old now to tag about after his parents. He had gone off trees anyway.

Cocktails at Doney's

WILLIAM TREVOR

'YOU'VE FORGOTTEN ME,' were the first words Mrs Faraday spoke
to him in the Albergo San Lorenzo. She was a tall, black-haired
woman, wearing a rust-red suede coat cut in an Italian style. She
smiled. She had white, even teeth, and the shade of her lipstick
appeared subtly to match the colour of her coat. Her accent was
American, her voice soft, with a trace of huskiness. She was
thirty-five, perhaps thirty-seven, certainly not older. 'We met a
long time ago,' she said, smiling a little more. 'I don't know
why I never forget a face.'

She was married to a man who owned a paper mill near some
town in America he'd never heard of. She was a beautiful woman,
but he could remember neither her nor her husband. Her name
meant nothing to him and when she prompted him with the
information about her husband's business he could not remember
any better. Her eyes were brown, dominating her classic features.

'Of course,' he lied politely.

She laughed, clearly guessing it was a lie. 'Well, anyway,' she
said, 'hullo to you.'

It was after dinner, almost ten o'clock. They had a drink in
the bar since it seemed the natural thing to do. She had to do
with fashion; she was in Florence for the Pitti Donna; she always
came in February.

'It's nice to see you again. The people at these trade shows can be tacky.'

'Don't you go to the museums as well? The churches?'

'Of course.'

When he asked if her husband accompanied her on her excursions to Florence she explained that the museums, the churches, and the Pitti Donna would tire her husband immensely. He was not a man for Europe, preferring local race-tracks.

'And your wife? Is she here with you?'

'I'm actually not married.'

He wished he had not met Mrs Faraday. He didn't care for being approached in this manner, and her condemnation of the people at the trade exhibitions she spoke of seemed out of place since they were, after all, the people of her business world. And that she was married to a man who preferred race-tracks to culture was hardly of interest to a stranger. Before their conversation ended he was certain they had not ever met before.

'I have to say good-night,' he said, rising when she finished her drink. 'I tend to get up early.'

'Why, so do I!'

'Good-night, Mrs Faraday.'

In his bedroom he sat on the edge of his bed, thinking about nothing in particular. Then he undressed and brushed his teeth. He examined his face in the slightly tarnished looking-glass above the wash-basin. He was fifty-seven, but according to this reflection older. His face would seem younger if he put on a bit of weight; chubbiness could be made to cover a multitude of sins. But he didn't want that; he liked being thought of as beyond things.

He turned the looking-glass light out and got into bed. He read *Our Mutual Friend* and then lay for a moment in the darkness. He thought of Daphne and of Lucy – dark-haired, tiny Lucy who had said at first it didn't matter, Daphne with her pale-blue, trusting eyes. He had blamed Daphne, not himself, and then had taken that back and asked to be forgiven; they were both of them to blame for the awful mistake of a marriage

183

that should never have taken place, although later he had said that neither of them was, for how could they have guessed they were not suited in that way? It was with Lucy he had begun to know the truth; poor Lucy had suffered more.

He slept, and dreamed he was in Padua with a friend of another time, walking in the Botanical Gardens and explaining to his friend that the tourist guides he composed were short-lived in their usefulness because each reflected a city ephemerally caught. 'You're ashamed of your tourist guides,' his friend of that time interrupted, Jeremy it was. 'Why *are* the impotent so full of shame, my dear? Why *is* it?' Then Rosie was in the dream and Jeremy was laughing, playfully, saying he'd been most amusingly led up the garden path. 'He led me up it too, my God,' Rosie cried out furiously. 'All he could do was weep.'

Linger over the Giambologna birds in the Bargello, and the marble reliefs of Mino da Fiesole. But that's enough for one day; you must return tomorrow.

He liked to lay down the law. He liked to take chances with the facts, and wait for letters of contradiction. *At the height of the season there are twelve times as many strangers as natives in this dusty, littered city. Cascades of graffiti welcome them – the male sexual organ stylized to a Florentine simplicity, belligerent swastikas, hammers and sickles in the streets of gentle Fra Angelico . . .*

At lunchtime on the day after he had met her Mrs Faraday was in Doney's with some other Americans. Seeing her in that smart setting, he was surprised that she stayed in the Albergo San Lorenzo rather than the Savoy or the Excelsior. The San Lorenzo's grandeur all belonged to the past: the old hotel was threadbare now, its curtains creased, its telephones unresponsive. Not many Americans liked it.

'Hi!' she called across the restaurant, and smiled and waved a menu.

He nodded at her, not wishing to seem stand-offish. The people she was with were talking about the merchandise they had been inspecting at the Pitti Donna. Wisps of their conversation drifted from their table, references to profit margins and catching the imagination.

He ordered tagliatelle and the chef's salad, and then looked through the *Nazione*. The body of the missing schoolgirl, Gabriella, had been found in a park in Florence. Youths who'd been terrorising the neighbourhood of Santa Croce had been identified and arrested. Two German girls, hitchhiking in the south, had been made drunk and raped in a village shed. The *Nazione* suggested that Gabriella – a quiet girl – had by chance been a witness to drug-trafficking in the park.

'I envy you your job,' Mrs Faraday said, pausing at his table as he was finishing his tagliatelle. Her companions had gone on ahead of her. She smiled, as at an old friend, and then sat down. 'I guess I want to lose those two.'

He offered her a glass of wine. She shook her head. 'I'd love another cappucino.'

The coffee was ordered. He folded the newspaper and placed it on the empty chair beside him. Mrs Faraday, as though she intended to stay a while, had hung her red suede coat over the back of the chair.

'I envy you your job,' she said again. 'I'd love to travel all over.'

She was wearing pearls at her throat, above a black dress. Rings clustered her fingers, earrings made a jangling sound. Her nails were shaped and painted, her face as meticulously made up as it had been the night before.

'Did you mind,' she asked when the waiter had brought their coffee, 'my wondering if you were married?'

He said he hadn't minded.

'Marriage is no great shakes.'

She lit a cigarette. She had only ever been married to the man who owned the paper mill. She had had one child, a daughter who had died after a week. She had not been able to have other children.

'I'm sorry,' he said.

She looked at him closely, cigarette smoke curling between them. The tip of her tongue picked a shred of tobacco from the corner of her mouth. She said again that marriage was no great shakes. She added, as if to lend greater weight to this:

'I lay awake last night thinking I'd like this city to devour me.'

185

He did not comment, not knowing what she meant. But quite without wishing to he couldn't help think of this beautiful woman lying awake in her bedroom in the Albergo San Lorenzo. He imagined her staring into the darkness, the glow of her cigarette, the sound of her inhaling. She was looking for an affair, he supposed, and hoped she realized he wasn't the man for that.

'I wouldn't mind living the balance of my life here. I like it better every year.'

'Yes, it's a remarkable city.'

'There's a place called the Palazzo Ricasoli where you can hire apartments. I'd settle there.'

'I see.'

'I could tell you a secret about the Palazzo Ricasoli.'

'Mrs Faraday —'

'I spent a week there once.'

He drank some coffee in order to avoid speaking. He sighed without making a sound.

'With a guy I met at the Pitti Donna. A countryman of yours. He came from somewhere called Horsham.'

'I've never been to Horsham.'

'Oh, my God, I'm embarrassing you!'

'No, not at all.'

'Gosh, I'm sorry! I really am! Please say it's all right.'

'I assure you, Mrs Faraday, I'm not easily shocked.'

'I'm an awful shady lady embarrassing a nice Englishman! Please say you forgive me.'

'There is absolutely nothing to forgive.'

'It was a flop, if you want to know.' She paused. 'Say, what do you plan to write in your guidebook about Florence?'

'Banalities mostly.'

'Oh, come on!'

He shrugged.

'I'll tell you a nicer kind of secret. You have the cleverest face I've seen in years!'

Still he did not respond. She stubbed her cigarette out and immediately lit another. She took a map out of her handbag and unfolded it. She said:

'Can you show me where Santo Spirito is?'

He pointed out the church and directed her to it, warning her against the motorists' signs which pursued a roundabout one-way route.

'You're very kind.' She smiled at him, lavishly exposing her dazzling, even teeth as if offering a reward for his help. 'You're a kind person,' she said. 'I can tell.'

He walked around the perimeter of the vast Cascine Park, past the fun-fair and the zoo and the race-track. It was pleasant in the February sunshine, the first green of spring colouring the twiggy hedges, birches delicate by the river. Lovers sprawled on the seats or in motor-cars, children carried balloons. Stalls sold meat and nuts, and Coca-Cola and 7-Up. Runners in training-suits jogged along the bicycle track. *Ho fame* a fat young man had scrawled on a piece of cardboard propped up in front of him, and slept while he waited for charity.

Rosie, when she'd been his friend, had said he wrote about Italian cities so that he could always be a stranger. Well, it was true, he thought in the Cascine Park, and in order to rid himself of a contemplation of his failed relationship with Rosie he allowed the beauty of Mrs Faraday to become vivid in his mind. Her beauty would have delighted him if her lipstick-stained cigarettes and her silly, repetitious chattering didn't endlessly disfigure it. Her husband was a good man, she had explained, but a good man was not always what a woman wanted. And it had come to seem all of a piece that her daughter had lived for only a week, and all of a piece also that no other children had been born, since her marriage was not worthy of children. It was the Annunciations in Santo Spirito she wanted to see, she had explained, because she loved Annunciations.

'Would it be wrong of me to invite you to dinner?' She rose from a sofa in the hall of the Albergo San Lorenzo as soon as she saw him, making no effort to disguise the fact that she'd been waiting for him. 'I'd really appreciate it if you'd accept.'

He wanted to reply that he would prefer to be left alone. He wanted to state firmly, once and for all, that he had never met her in the past, that she had no claims on him.

187

'You choose somewhere,' she commanded, with the arrogance of the beautiful.

In the restaurant she ate pasta without ceasing to talk, explaining to him that her boutique had been bought for her by her husband to keep her occupied and happy. It hadn't worked, she said, implying that although her fashion shop had kept her busy it hadn't brought her contentment. Her face, drained of all expression, was lovelier than he had so far seen it, so sad and fragile that it seemed not to belong to the voice that rattled on.

He looked away. The restaurant was decorated with modern paintings and was not completely full. A squat, elderly man sat on his own, conversing occasionally with waiters. A German couple spoke in whispers. Two men and a woman, talking rapidly in Italian, deplored the death of the schoolgirl, Gabriella.

'It must have been extraordinary for the Virgin Mary,' Mrs Faraday was saying. 'One moment she's reading a book and the next there's a figure with wings swooping in on her.' That only made sense, she suggested, when you thought of it as the Virgin's dream. The angel was not really there, the Virgin herself was not really reading in such plush surroundings. 'Later I guess she dreamed another angel came,' Mrs Faraday continued, 'to warn her of her death.'

He didn't listen. The waiter brought them grilled salmon and salad. Mrs Faraday lit a cigarette. She said:

'The guy I shacked up with in the Palazzo Ricasoli was no better than a gigolo. I guess I don't know why I did that.'

He did not reply. She stubbed her cigarette out, appearing at last to notice that food had been placed in front of her. She asked him about the painters of the Florentine Renaissance, and the city's aristocrats and patrons. She asked him why Savonarola had been burnt and he said Savonarola had made people feel afraid. She was silent for a moment, then leaned forward and put a hand on his arm.

'Tell me more about yourself. Please.'

Her voice, eagerly insistent, irritated him more than before. He told her superficial things, about the other Italian cities for which he'd written guidebooks, about the hill towns of Tuscany, and the Cinque Terre. Because of his reticence she said when he ceased to speak:

'I don't entirely make you out.' She added that he was nicer to talk to than anyone she could think of. She might be drunk; it was impossible to say.

'My husband's never heard of the Medicis nor any stuff like this. He's never even heard of Masaccio, you appreciate that?'

'Yes, you've made it clear the kind of man your husband is.'

'I've ruined it, haven't I, telling you about the Palazzo Ricasoli?'

'Ruined what, Mrs Faraday?'

'Oh, I don't know.'

They sat for some time longer, finishing the wine and having coffee. Once she reached across the table and put her hand on one of his. She repeated what she had said before, that he was kind.

'It's late,' he said.

'I know, honey, I know. And you get up early.'

He paid the bill, although she protested that it was she who had invited him. She would insist on their having dinner together again so that she might have her turn. She took his arm on the street.

'Will you come with me to Maiano one day?'

'Maiano?'

'It isn't far. They say it's lovely to walk at Maiano.'

'I'm really rather occupied, you know.'

'Oh, God, I'm bothering you! I'm being a nuisance! Forget Maiano. I'm sorry.'

'I'm just trying to say, Mrs Faraday, that I don't think I can be much use to you.'

He was aware, to his embarrassment, that she was holding his hand. Her arm was entwined with his and the palms of their hands had somehow come together. Her fingers, playing with his now, kept time with her flattery.

'You've got the politest voice I ever heard! Say you'll meet me just once again? Just once? Cocktails tomorrow? Please.'

'Look, Mrs Faraday —'

'Say Doney's at six. I'll promise to say nothing if you like. We'll listen to the music.'

Her palm was cool. A finger made a circular motion on one

189

of his. Rosie had said he limped through life. In the end Jeremy had been sorry for him. Both of them were right; others had said worse. He was a crippled object of pity.

'Well, all right.'

She thanked him in the Albergo San Lorenzo for listening to her, and for the dinner and the wine. 'Every year I hope to meet someone nice in Florence,' she said on the landing outside her bedroom, seeming to mean it. 'This is the first time it has happened.'

She leaned forward and kissed him on the cheek, then closed her door. In his looking-glass he examined the faint smear of lipstick and didn't wipe it off. He woke in the night and lay there thinking about her, wondering if her lipstick was still on his cheek.

Waiting in Doney's, he ordered a glass of chilled Orvieto wine. Someone on a tape, not Judy Garland, sang *Over the Rainbow*; later there was lightly played Strauss and some rhythms of the thirties. By seven o'clock Mrs Faraday had not arrived. He left at a quarter to eight.

The next day he wandered through the cloisters of Santa Maria Novella, thinking again about the beauty of Mrs Faraday. He had received no message from her, no note to explain or apologize for her absence in Doney's. Had she simply forgotten? Or had someone better materialized? Some younger man she again hadn't been able to resist, some guy who didn't know any more about Masaccio than her good husband did? She was a woman who was always falling in love, which was what she called it, confusing love with sensuality. Was she, he wondered, what people referred to as a nymphomaniac? Was that what made her unhappy?

He imagined her with some man she'd picked up. He imagined her, satisfied because of the man's attentions, tramping the halls of a gift market, noting which shade of green was to be the new season's excitement. She would be different after her love-making, preoccupied with her business, no time for silliness and Annunciations. Yet it still was odd that she hadn't left a message for him. She had not for a moment seemed as rude as that, or incapable of making up an excuse.

He left the cloisters and walked slowly across the piazza of Santa Maria Novella. In spite of what she'd said and the compliments she'd paid, had she guessed that he hadn't listened properly to her, that he'd been fascinated by her appearance but not by her? Or had she simply guessed the truth about him?

That evening she was not in the bar of the hotel. He looked in at Doney's, thinking he might have misunderstood about the day. He waited for a while, and then ate alone in the restaurant with the modern paintings.

'We pack the clothes, *signore*. Is the carabinieri which can promote the enquiries for *la signora. Mi dispiace, signore.*'

He nodded at the heavily moustached receptionist and made his way to the bar. If she was with some lover she would have surfaced again by now: it was hard to believe that she would so messily leave a hotel bill unpaid, especially since sooner or later she would have to return for her clothes. When she had so dramatically spoken of wishing Florence to devour her she surely hadn't meant something like this? He went back to the receptionist.

'Did Mrs Faraday have her passport?'

'*Sí, signore. La signora* have the passport.'

He couldn't sleep that night. Her smile and her brown, languorous eyes invaded the blur he attempted to induce. She crossed and re-crossed her legs. She lifted another glass. Her ringed fingers stubbed another cigarette. Her earrings lightly jangled.

In the morning he asked again at the reception desk. The hotel bill wasn't important, a different receptionist generously allowed. If someone had to leave Italy in a hurry, because maybe there was sickness, even a deathbed, then a hotel bill might be overlooked for just a little while.

'*La signora* will post to us a cheque from the United States. This the carabinieri say.'

'Yes, I should imagine so.'

He looked up in the telephone directory the flats she had

mentioned. The Palazzo Ricasoli was in Via Mantellate. He walked to it, up Borgo San Lorenzo and Via San Gallo. *'No,'* a porter in a glass kiosk said and directed him to the office. *'No,'* a pretty girl in the office said, shaking her head. She turned and asked another girl. *'No,'* this girl repeated.

He walked back through the city, to the American Consulate on the Lungarno Amerigo. He sat in the office of a tall, lean man called Humber, who listened with a detached air and then telephoned the police. After nearly twenty minutes he replaced the receiver. He was dressed entirely in brown, suit, shirt, tie, shoes, handkerchief. He was evenly tanned, another shade of the colour. He drawled when he spoke; he had an old-world manner.

'They suggest she's gone somewhere,' he said. 'On some kind of jaunt.' He paused in order to allow a flicker of amusement to develop in his lean features. 'They think maybe she ran up her hotel bill and skipped it.'

'She's a respectable proprietor of a fashion shop.'

'The carabinieri say the respectable are always surprising them.'

'Can you try to find out if she went back to the States? According to the hotel people, that was another theory of the carabinieri.'

Mr Humber shrugged. 'Since you have told your tale I must try, of course, sir. Would six-thirty be an agreeable hour for you to return?'

He sat outside the Piazza della Repubblica, eating tortellini and listening to the conversations. A deranged man had gone berserk in a school in Rome, taking children as hostages and killing a janitor; the mayor of Rome had intervened and the madman had given himself up. It was a terrible thing to have happened, the Italians were saying, as bad as the murder of Gabriella.

He paid for his tortellini and went away. He climbed up to the Belvedere, filling in time. Once he thought he saw her, but it was someone else in the same kind of red coat.

'She's not back home,' Mr Humber said with his old-world lack of concern. 'You've started something, sir. Faraday's flying out.'

*

In a room in a police station he explained that Mrs Faraday had simply been a fellow guest at the Albergo San Lorenzo. They had had dinner one evening, and Mrs Faraday had not appeared to be dispirited. She knew other people who had come from America, for the same trade exhibitions. He had seen her with them in a restaurant.

'These people, sir, return already to the United States. They answer the American police at this time.'

He was five hours in the room at the police station and the next day he was summoned there again and asked the same questions. On his way out on this occasion he noticed a man who he thought might be her husband, a big blond-haired man, too worried even to glance at him. He was certain he had never met him, or even seen him before, as he'd been certain he'd never met Mrs Faraday before she'd come up to him in the hotel.

The police did not again seek to question him. His passport, which they had held for fifty-six hours, was returned to him. By the end of that week the newspaper references to a missing American woman ceased. He did not see Mr Faraday again.

'The Italian view,' said Mr Humber almost a month later, 'is that she went off on a sexual excursion and found it so much to her liking that she stayed where she was.'

'I thought the Italian view was that she skipped the hotel. Or that someone had fallen ill.'

'They revised their thinking somewhat. In the light of various matters.'

'What matters?'

'From what you said, Mrs Faraday was a gallivanting lady. Our Italian friends find some significance in that.' Mr Humber silently drummed the surface of his desk. 'You don't agree, sir?'

He shook his head. 'There was more to Mrs Faraday than that,' he said.

'Well, of course there was. The carabinieri are educated men, but they don't go in for subtleties, you know.'

'She's not a vulgar woman. From what I said to the police they may imagine she was. Of course she's in a vulgar business. They may have jumped too easily to conclusions.'

Mr Humber said he did not understand. 'Vulgar?' he repeated.

'Like me, she deals in surface dross.'

'You're into fashion yourself, sir?'

'No, I'm not. I write tourist guides.'

'Well, that's most interesting.'

Mr Humber flicked at the surface of his desk with a fore-finger. It was clear that he wished his visitor would go. He turned a sheet of paper over.

'I remind sightseers that pictures like Pietro Perugino's *Agony in the Garden* are worth a second glance. I send them to the Boboli Gardens. That kind of thing.'

Mr Humber's bland face twitched with simulated interest. Tourists were a nuisance to him. They lost their passports, they locked their ignition keys into their hired cars, they were stolen from and made a fuss. The city lived off them, but resented them as well. These thoughts were for a moment openly reflected in Mr Humber's pale brown eyes and then were gone. Flicking at his desk again, he said:

'I'm puzzled about one detail in all this. May I ask you, please?'

'Yes, of course.'

'Were you, you know, ah, seeing Mrs Faraday?'

'Was I having an affair, you mean? No, I wasn't.'

'She was a beautiful woman. By all accounts, by yours, I mean, sir, she'd been most friendly.'

'Yes, she was friendly.'

She was naive for an American, and she was careless. She wasn't fearful of strangers and foolishly she let her riches show. Vulnerability was an enticement.

'I did not mean to pry, sir,' Mr Humber apologized. 'It's simply that Mr Faraday's detectives arrived a while ago and the more they can be told the better.'

'They haven't approached me.'

'No doubt they conclude you cannot help them. Mr Faraday himself has returned to the States: a ransom note would be more likely made to him there.'

'So Mr Faraday doesn't believe his wife went off on a sexual excursion?'

'No one can ignore the facts, sir. There is indiscriminate kidnapping in Italy.'

'Italians would have known her husband owned a paper mill?'

'I guess it's surprising what can be ferreted out.' Mr Humber examined the neat tips of his fingers. He re-arranged tranquillity in his face. No matter how the facts he spoke of changed there was not going to be panic in the American Consulate. 'There has been no demand, sir, but we have to bear in mind that kidnap attempts do often nowadays go wrong. In Italy as elsewhere.'

'Does Mr Faraday think it has gone wrong?'

'Faraday is naturally confused. And, of course, troubled.'

'Of course.' He nodded to emphasize his agreement. Her husband was the kind who would be troubled and confused, even though unhappiness had developed in the marriage. Clearly she'd given up on the marriage; more than anything, it was desperation that made her forthright. Without it, she might have been a different woman – and in that case, of course, there would not have been this passing relationship between them: her tiresomeness had cultivated that. 'Tell me more about yourself,' her voice echoed huskily, hungry for friendship. He had told her nothing – nothing of the shattered, destroyed relationships, and the regret and shame; nothing of the pathetic hope in hired rooms, or the anguish turning into bitterness. She had been given beauty, and he a lameness that people laughed at when they knew. Would her tiresomeness have dropped from her at once, like the shedding of a garment she had thought to be attractive, if he'd told her in the restaurant with the modern paintings? Would she, too, have angrily said he'd led her up the garden path?

'There is our own investigation also,' Mr Humber said, 'besides that of Faraday's detectives. Faraday, I assure you, has spared no expense; the carabinieri file is by no means closed. With such a concentration we'll find what there is to find, sir.'

'I'm sure you'll do your best, Mr Humber.'

'Yes, *sir*.'

He rose and Mr Humber rose also, holding out a brown, lean hand. He was glad they had met, Mr Humber said, even in such unhappy circumstances. Diplomacy was like oil in Mr Humber. It eased his movements and his words; his detachment floated in it, perfectly in place.

'Goodbye, Mr Humber.'

Ignoring the lift, he walked down the stairs of the Consulate. He knew that she was dead. He imagined her lying naked in a wood, her even teeth ugly in a rictus, her white flesh as lifeless as the virgin modesty of the schoolgirl in the park. She hadn't been like a nymphomaniac, or even a sophisticated woman, when she'd kissed his cheek good-night. Like a schoolgirl herself, she'd still been blind to the icy coldness that answered her naivety. Inept and academic, words he had written about the city which had claimed her slipped through his mind. *In the church of Santa Croce you walk on tombs, searching for Giotto's* Life of St Francis. *In Savonarola's own piazza the grey stone features do not forgive the tumbling hair of pretty police girls or the tourists' easy ways.* Injustice and harsh ambition had made her city what it was, the violence of greed for centuries had been its bloodstream; beneath its tinsel skin there was an iron heart. *The Florentines, like true provincials, put work and money first. In the Piazza Signoria the pigeons breakfast off the excrement of the hackney horses: in Florence nothing is wasted.*

He left the American Consulate and slowly walked along the quay. The sun was hot, the traffic noisy. He crossed the street and looked down into the green water of the Arno, wondering if the dark shroud of Mrs Faraday's life had floated away through a night. In the galleries of the Uffizi he would move from Annunciation to Annunciation, Simone Martini's, Baldovinetti's, Lorenzo di Credi's, and all the others. He would catch a glimpse of her red coat in Santa Trinità, but the face would again be someone else's. She would call out from a gelateria, but the voice would be an echo in his memory.

He turned away from the river and at the same slow pace walked into the heart of the city. He sat outside a café in the Piazza della Repubblica, imagining her thoughts as she had lain in bed on that last night, smoking her cigarettes in the darkness. She had arrived at the happiest moment of love, when nothing was yet destroyed, when anticipation was a richness in itself. She'd thought about their walk in Maiano, how she'd bring the subject up again, how this time he'd say he'd be delighted. She'd thought about their being together in an apartment in the Palazzo Ricasoli, how this time it would be different. Already she had made up her mind: she would not ever return to the town where her husband owned a paper mill. 'I have never loved anyone like this,' she whispered in the darkness.

In his hotel bedroom he shaved and had a bath and put on a suit that had just been pressed. In a way that had become a ceremony for him since the evening he had first waited for her there, he went at six o'clock to Doney's. He watched the Americans drinking cocktails, knowing it was safe to be there because she would not suddenly arrive. He listened to the music she'd said she liked, and mourned her as a lover might.

Retired People

FRANK TUOHY

THEY HAD RETIRED early, many years ago, and had been fortunate enough to discover the perfect retreat. Blundell's End was scarcely more than a country cottage, but its situation had charmed them from the beginning. You crossed a bridge over a little stream which was bordered with king-cups, yellow flag irises or meadowsweet according to the season. A few yards further on, their garden began. Of course nowadays, without help of any kind, it had fallen into a state of neglect, but they loved it still. And the house itself, with its stone walls and casement windows and little rooms leading into one another – well, it too was still all they wanted. Time passed; Christmases, New Years, Midsummers slid gently by. Such a peaceful place, they said; we are so fortunate.

From time to time their peace was threatened. For some years huge trucks had groaned and roared at night along the main road which lay about a quarter of a mile up the hill. More recently, a milking machine had been installed in a local farm, and the cowman used to play his wireless to the cows in the early morning. Both of them accepted these developments without complaint.

At first, though, it was she who had been worried about him, because she had always thought him less adept than herself at coping with change.

The noise is undoubtedly a nuisance, he told her, but it's like the sparrows and starlings in springtime. They've been nesting under the roof every year but, at the beginning, do you remember, we found the din they made almost insupportable.

She laughed and admitted he was right.

Originally they had been Londoners: they had chosen to retire to this part of the country long before anyone else had considered doing such a thing. An early retirement had been recommended because of the state of her health.

Nowadays they had attained serenity, they thought, but in fact they protected each other. Each of them had decided that, if anything went wrong, it should not be discussed with the other.

Thus it came as a terrible shock when, one quiet Sunday evening in autumn, she suddenly broke into a flood of tears.

He watched her, without making a move. She had always been nervous – highly strung, they had used to call it – and for some years had undergone treatment. All that, however, belonged to past history. There had never been any recurrence of her trouble since they had come to live at Blundell's End.

Her tears were soon over. She faced him again and managed a small, ghostly smile.

He was about to speak, but he decided against it. Once more they were silent, sitting side by side in the half-darkness.

Two minutes later, she was on her feet, shouting: Oh no, he can't, he can't. It's too terrible. He can't do that to her. Stop him. Stop him.

Her husband was standing beside her. My poor love, he said, my poor, poor love.

She gripped his hand. I am so sorry, I've tried so hard not to worry you. It's all in my mind, I know, just like those times long ago. It'll pass away, I must be overtired. That was what we always used to say, wasn't it?

You mustn't worry, love. You mustn't worry.

She sat down again and, with some hesitation, began to talk. She told him that it had all begun two months ago, with doors banging and distant voices. Now the voices had grown to be quite clear, though still indistinct at times. No, she had no idea who was speaking. Blundell's End had its secrets: they seemed to have been living here as long as they could remember, but that was nothing compared to the life of a house like this.

It seems so dreadful, after all these lovely peaceful years we have had here. And now I have to inflict this on you.

You're not inflicting anything, love.

I feel wretched about it.

Don't do that, love, he said. I can hear them too.

She was immediately suspicious: was he just trying to humour her? To jolly her along, as he had always tried to do in the old days?

I really do hear them, he said.

That terrible scene that took place in the kitchen?

Yes, I heard it.

And the time she locked him out in the rain?

Yes, my love, that too.

They don't – she hesitated, and this time she managed a proper smile – they don't sound at all the sort of people one would have wanted to know, do they? Her language, it's just as bad as his.

Think of all the people who used to live here in the old days. We were, perhaps, unusual to think of coming to live here.

Once started, she could not stop talking. Different circles, that was what we always used to say, wasn't it? Well, whoever they are, I can't help myself – I feel sorry for them. That dreadful unhappiness, going on and on.

He rose, and walked up and down. She watched him, still a fine figure of a man, though somehow blurred by vagueness and indecision. Until now, of course, there had been little to be decisive about.

He said: I really think quite the most sensible thing for us to do is to continue as though nothing at all had happened. Pretend they don't exist – indeed, it is entirely possible that they don't. Or if they do, it must be – well – on a different level.

She did not take this in: for her the presences had become quite real. But the poor children, how damaging it must be for them! They don't cry, but they're always excited. They never get to bed early, I hear them at all hours.

Now, as he watched her, he reflected that their isolation had affected her far more than it had himself. It was quite obvious that she had already become deeply involved in these other lives, if that was what they were.

He wondered: Can she even remember our own children? Poor William, the brave young soldier killed in Africa in that wretched sideshow set up by the politicians. And Amelia, who ran off to Canada with her dreadful Irishman. It's years and years, he thought, since we had a letter from Amelia.

Curiously enough, soon after they had brought the matter into the open, as it were (though she still was not entirely sure of him, suspecting that his infinite kindness and concern might choose to express itself in this fashion), the intruders were no longer heard.

She herself felt quite certain that they would return. He kept wondering why they had turned up in the first place. He concluded that he and she were being punished, made the victims of their own egocentricity, of their passionate love of the house and the garden. Yet who could blame them? This love was undiminished on these afternoons in autumn and early winter, when the wind dropped suddenly and the thin light glowed over the bare woodlands and the tawny, surrounding hills.

If – if it had got too bad, for some reason, would you want to, well, leave?

Oh no. The idea distressed her deeply. We can never leave here, can we? Blundell's End is our only home. We've cherished it, all these years.

She was remembering summer mornings when she'd go out into the garden in her night-dress, while mist was still rising from the water-meadows, and she would find something interesting in one of the flower-beds – a first blossom on one of her favourite plants, a beetle or a caterpillar – and call up to him. He would come to the window covered in shaving lather and wave to her with his cut-throat razor, and then she'd race back into the kitchen because the coffee was boiling over.

No, we can never leave, she said. Besides, where on earth would we go?

You're quite right, love. Whatever happens, we must make

up our minds to sit it out; it may be frightening, but they cannot possibly harm us in any way. This may only be a temporary invasion, infestation, call it what you will. I've heard of that happening. At one time I used to read a lot about these things, in that journal they published – I wonder if it's still going? I forget its name. Of course, it's very possible that we've heard the last of them.

But his smile showed that he had failed to convince himself and the return, when it happened, was sufficiently dreadful to make him realize that all the time he had been whistling in the dark. They were doomed, and he knew it.

On Christmas Eve the sound of church bells reached Blundell's End across the intervening water-meadows. For them, each year the bells sounded a little farther away. There was no question of attending church on Christmas Day; throughout the years, though, the church bells had seemed to underline their peaceful survival and continuance.

Suddenly this year everything was terrifying. What had they done, he kept asking himself, to deserve this? What sin of omission, committed in all the years that had left them undisturbed in their sanctuary?

Cautiously, he watched her face, long and sad now: a version in *grisaille* of its former distinction, it was like an image you would see reflected in an infinite series of mirrors.

He knew she was listening all the time. They had become an obsession with her, those unhappy children, scuffling in corners or scattering upstairs to secret colloquies. Later that night, doors slammed and windows rattled; even the stone walls seemed to tremble. Whenever quiet returned, an atmosphere of extraordinary grief and loss seemed to seep through everywhere, like a gas heavier than air.

Upstairs they lay side by side, beyond fear now, remote and shrinkingly detached, with their noses in the air: rather as a knight and his lady fair might lie on a medieval tomb. Meanwhile disaster resounded again in the rooms beneath them. They heard a table upset, small objects rollicking away with a life of their own across the stone floors.

I can't stand it any more, she whispered.

Love, it will pass away.

He was wrong. If the sounds became quieter, denser, it was only because they were body blows.

Oh God, she whispered, he struck her, I'm sure he did.

There is nothing we can do.

After that, silence followed, lots of it, the heavy silky-thick silence of a cold winter's night. She may even have drifted off into a light sleep, because when she awoke she was aware at once that the situation had undergone complete change.

For a moment or two, she could not believe it. Horror at the closeness of the intruders was succeeded by wave upon wave of anguish and repulsion. It was only too evident what was happening. They were close by and they were declaring peace, patching it up after their quarrel in perhaps the only way possible to them, by making love.

It was Christmas night. She could still hear the bells pealing across the meadows from the village. The bells went on and on, and so did everything else. Nearby in the darkness actions were being performed which she would never have believed possible, of which she had never had the slightest conception. And the noise: how, she wondered, could at any time anyone of her own sex ever have abandoned herself so utterly, again and again, to the extremities of passion?

All the time her husband, her own 'verray parfit gentil knyght', was stretched out beside her, listening to it all. For him, she knew too well, it must have been a revelation. After tonight, what form of existence could lie ahead for either of them? Could they ever look each other in the face again? Would it go on, this monstrous imposition, disgusting yet somehow thrilling, haunting her, night after night?

Mercifully, Christmas night had no successors. Boxing Day passed, and the New Year, and soon they were into February and March, and their lives remained undisturbed. Doors suddenly flew open, chests of drawers cracked and stretched themselves, occasionally a squirrel sounded enormous and clumsy when it hurried across the roof. One day, a whole succession of noises which gave them concern turned out to be the starlings coming back to nest under the eaves.

Meanwhile her mind kept going back, revising, learning, past Christmas night into areas of the past which had been fenced off for a very long time. She began to surmise what Amelia might have felt, all those years and years ago, when she categorically refused to listen to the advice of her very own mother, and ran away with that dreadful man. For some reason the spring, arriving late this year, produced in her a poignant sense of solitude and loss.

In May, her husband called her down to the bridge over the boundary stream. Timidly and hesitantly, she made her way down through the garden, gazing around her half-blinded by the sunlight.

Just look at all the stinging nettles! Nettles everywhere. Where can they have come from? I haven't been down here for such a long, long time.

She had joined him and now they were both staring up at the thing he had wanted her to see. She gasped.

Does it mean – does it mean that there will be others?

I'm afraid that's just what it does mean, love.

They gazed back towards Blundell's End, quite at its best in the spring sunshine.

Sadly and very tenderly he put his arm round her and said: I expect it'll be very soon. We'll just have to be brave, shan't we? It's the only possible thing.

She, however, walked up through the garden with a glint in her eye, and trod with a lighter tread.

Behind them, the white-painted notice they had been examining creaked and swung in the spring wind. Of course, it read once again: Desirable Property Freehold Vacant Possession.

Cottage Rubbings

DAI VAUGHAN

*There is something boxy about horses, in spite of their orotund
thoraxes and their necks narrow as lancet windows. Perhaps it
is their faces, that flat hardness; or perhaps it is the clatter they
make, as today, on the way here, when two of them appeared
from nowhere and clip-clopped woodenly, hollowly, around our
parked car, their ochre and grey-raspberry flanks rippling close
against the rainy windows. Albermarle, who has experience of
horses, and for whom they exude no menace, took charge of the
situation and . . . But no. I should say only that I arrived after
a long journey, fatigued; dumped my rucksack on this table.*

A SWEET, PINK smell at first identified as damp plaster but the
following day to be recognized as whitewash. Whitewash flaking.
The cottage is whitewashed inside. Beams are painted with some
black matter which has never, however, deterred worm. And
now we have discussed the worm in the table-legs, the little
mole-casts of sawdust beneath: now that things are to be evacuated. The larder door left open to flies − no food in it − and
within, the fridge gaping baby-blue, somehow obscene − not
meant to be seen like that − the entrails of a splayed ox. On
the table a blue bucket of dried flowers and leaves, a per-
petualized autumn; also two ashtrays nestling. All as if forgotten

at a railway station. Lost property. A few stones remain on the mantelpiece; but most – last year's haul and earlier years' – are in a cardboard Ajax box on the lower shelf of the trolley. On its upper shelf are some felt-tips in a fruit bowl (as always, evidence of children's passage) and a dumpy ceramic table-lamp in a green of simulated bronze patina ringed with Celtic curlicues. Did this, though never consciously noticed, add its modicum to that compound general recollection which, without recourse to any detail in particular, I must have sustained during absences since it met me with the force of a recognition whenever I returned? If not, then, as my recollection was ostensibly without detail, how am I to know which details had contributed and which not?

The whitewash smell reminding me of somewhere. Tan-y-fron? Deep-grooved grain of the table-top with visible, rusty, countersunk screw-heads. Four high-backed oak dining-chairs with raffia seats. An oddity: the table is raised 1½″ on little cylindrical extensions to its legs like pre-war ice-cream wrapped in paper. Diamond-paned leaded windows, deeply recessed with window-seats and sill surrounds: small, triptych windows, one each side of the room, facing. Red tile and red brick fireplace, flush with the wall; ubiquitous 1930s grate in brick-red stove enamel, wooden fender, gilt mesh fireguard (though I have never known a fire lit there). Newish card-table of green baize folded behind the trolley where it conceals a bagatelle board, also green. Behind the Ajax box, a jig-saw puzzle of Garden Birds testifying to children's boredom staved off, circular, lamplit evenings, rainy days, rural preoccupations. The door with T-hinges and hook-latch, more appropriate to gates and allotment sheds, contrasts with the fitted carpet – jade green browned by decades of muddy wellies. Two easy chairs – one deep, cubic and uncomfortable, pushed into a corner, the other more upright, covered and valenced in stout field-grey cloth and with a red, yellow-flecked cushion, in which I doze to the Chinese chimes – flat circles of shell hanging, seven rows of seven, alternating apple-green and nacreous white, hung from the beam over the electrical radiator where – unlike any others, which either clank assertively or remain resentfully silent – they twist gently and microscopically to provide a music of such utter delicacy that only the fortissimi are audible. (This is no conceit. Often I see the rims kiss and hear nothing.) The green almost matches, in depth if not in tone, that of the curtains – a green not found in nature, unless within 'nature' one includes, the mineral (copper sulphate, perhaps, or beryl). In the hypnotic, breathbated hush of seeking to attune the ear to these evanescent registers, mere inferences of eye and harmony, I realize that this is the sound which has in the past accompanied moments of snatched relaxation, of suspension of life's hostilities, of the peace once called blessed, and that I am now, at last, though for the last time, free to listen for as long as I wish.

Tan-y-fron, I think, was whitewashed only on the outside. Done from a pail each spring; one of those white-enamelled slop-pails with a removable lid with a hole in the middle. A less eccentric place than this, of course: no tea-cosy thatch, more four-square and Congregational in its symmetry (except for the cegyn fach, which was neither small nor a kitchen but a cavernous lean-to where the wood-pigeon, inaccessible and incurable, escaped our childhood attentions by dying). Of course, basebed slate. Water was obtained from taps in the lanes, and you went with zinc buckets. When it was winter, you also took paper and dry sticks, as it was necessary to light fires around the standpipes before the water would flow.

I have often toyed with the fantasy of having this place to myself; and now, since Albermarle is staying with her mother in the adjoining one . . . The bath has accumulated dead woodlice. There is no water in the bend of the WC. But the cistern is full; and the taps, after a few coughs, flow. Now, writing this, seated at the head of this solid table, I curl my left leg under me – a childhood habit which was also a habit of my grandfather's – and recount how, immediately on arrival into the pink, sweet ambience, I dumped my baggage on to this table, this table, and sank into the chair by the chimes and awaited, patiently, the subsidence of that other music: that throbbing beat which has eaten into my substance like centaur's blood, trampling a wide circle, emphatic, inescapable, phrases ending where they began and beginning again; and against this the endless spin of detail never enough to keep sanity, metaphysical if necessary, no holds barred, clearing the conduits which will silt up as soon as I stop. Old stone building bricks; rubber lego; a polar bear of some material hard yet furry . . . Big black beetles creak their way across the carpet, impenetrable as obsidian yet returning no light.

It's a curious perspective, the voice of an eighty-year-old woman – just fleeting comments – set against old photographs of her as a little girl, these being alternated with images – but present-day images – of places she knew at that far time: a programme about the Queen Mother watched on Albermarle's mother's big, shiny, overwhelming set. The fascination of royalty lies in the teasing suggestion of the internality of those whose lives are presented as, by definition, pure externality, so that even the internal is, by mere fact of its presentation, instantly externalized. Paradoxically, the most 'natural' footage was some old newsreel which congratulated itself on having caught the King and Queen in a relaxed moment, feeding ducks; but what came across as natural, at this remove, was their *effort* to behave naturally, which contrasted with the effortless *un*naturalness of their normal self-projection: a gap opened only accidentally, by the warping and drying of representational conventions. All the same, it's strange to think a thing should mean something so different now from what it meant then whilst, even so, arriving ultimately at the same outcome.

The flat, stratified oak tree, shaped to the corner of the path, year-by-year spreading laterally across the lawn without gaining much in height, its mottled leaves clotted, as always since sap-linghood, with glutinous black flies. The lawn now gone almost entirely to clover and plantain; the yew a stilled mammoth panting with ancient over-exertion in the odour of its musk, its green velvet pelt be-jewelled with convolvulus; sumach seedlings in the vegetable plot; and only the rhubarb, of vegetables, clinging to its domestically-approved morphology, the remainder having advanced unnoticed to forbidden adult states forgotten as a curse hidden in a nursery rhyme. (Returning along shale-sided lanes, the swifts weaving traceries intricate as the Book of Kells over the hats, the buckled hats, of my godly, wicked aunties . . .)

The sleeping bags are warm from the airing cupboard. Sweet caramel-smell of scorch. 'My' bedroom, which I chose on my first visit as unerringly as I chose my room (turn right at the top of the staircase) on the first visit to Tan-y-fron, arriving at night to be woken next morning by a primordial sound, never before heard, the howl of castrated wolves, in fact the crow of the cockerel re-echoing from Dinas Lochtyn – spongy underfoot and locally reputed to be an extinct volcano ('Don't listen to your Grandpa, he'll fill you full of stories'.) A slip of wine-and-plum Axminster, frayed out of the oblong, on a bare floor whose edges were once painted cream around some now vanished carpet; a plethora of coat-hangers and some antiseptic shampoo; a canvas 'director's' chair; an old Belling perforated-cylinder electrical heater – small but still efficient, though the flex has worn to expose the wiring – and a small empty linen-basket, mud-green, on which is balanced precariously – for its top undulates – a globular-turned, lightweight but top-heavy table-lamp painted gloss pink with a posy of roses. The window opens on to moths and stars.

The glow from the smoky glass chimney of the paraffin lamp was furry and gentle as the flight of bats when, at evening, my cousin and I sat across the table from each other camouflage-painting the shoe-boxes in which we kept our toy soldiers. (He, being a little older than I, called them his 'troops'.) Nothing seemed to come into the village from outside, although it must have done: the paraffin, for example, and my Auntie's brandy. And the milk, which came by pony and trap from Nant-y-bach. There was little sign of warfare on the walk to school except for the tank traps and the occasional parachute caught in a tree. (It was generally believed that parachutes were filled with poison gas, and that parachutists had to be careful not to get caught underneath them as they landed.) At school we were taught to count in 'trots' – in clusters of three: perhaps some secretive salute to the Trinity submerged in the passion of Dissent, perhaps some vestige of neolithic numeracy: ugh, der, tr, too-many-to-count . . . We drank tea from basins. It may be, it now occurs to me, that they had simply forgotten to take cups to the cottage; but I accepted it without question as a Welsh custom.

We children were allowed sugar in our tea; but my Auntie, on account of the rationing, used fruit jam.

On the floor is a piece of hairy string. On the trolley with the Ajax box is a book of British Mesozoic Fossils with a shiny black cover, slightly curled, on which skeleton fish swim through the night of their own extinction. I sit before a committee of vacant chairs, an unlaid banquet, two dusty ashtrays. In another ashtray – Bauvillain Frères, Specialistes pour Cafés & Hotels, Brest – are a couple of toy soldiers with which Tommi and I played in the long grass some seven years ago and which, being left behind on that trip, were never subsequently restored to a place in his universe. Yet in front of me is a jug of freshly picked flowers. This is as it should be: welcome as if by magic, fire lit by goblins in exchange for a bowl of curds, windows aglow through the rain from afar, towels dry and waiting, table set impeccably by unseen hands . . . It is not a question of my wishing to be pampered. Indeed, before leaving home I left an almost identical jug of deadnettle, bluebell and viburnum upon the table for those who would follow – hoovered, warmed the bed-linen. But it is in the mute replies of this dwelling – every detail of it if need be, and with complete neutrality – that I must find, or from them construct, a self who putatively pre-existed, recently yet beyond call, that music which pulses, sleep and waking, through every conduit and capillary of my nervous system: the self of the memory which met me on our arrival.

Once before when we thought it was the end – thought there would be, as is now finally the case, no more times here – we went around fervently – Albermarle, Tommi and myself – making 'cottage rubbings' of all the interesting surfaces we could find; Tommi, I remember, whistling 'Tipperary' through his milk-teeth. No doubt, at five, he was too young to understand our reasons. Later, when one room was lost in the renovation of the adjoining cottage, a dispossessed chest of drawers was shipped up to London. The rubbings were still there, in the top left-hand drawer, along with the geological hammer. Handle of hickory . . .

For some reason which I was unable to fathom – assuredly it was not Nazism – most of the boys' playground adopted the

German insignia, by tacit protocol chalked on the front of the cap and the upper surfaces of the cuffs as we ran, arms out-splayed, banking steeply, machine-gunning with a flutter of thumbs, meaaaoooow-!-!-!-!-! . . . I suspect it was a pure impulse of enemyness: the very contrary, if so, of any blind obedience. At all events, only two of us – myself and a stout boy unknown to me, perhaps also 'English' – boasted the RAF markings. This did not mean, however, that we were immediately set upon by flocks of Heinkels and Messerschmitts. I was rarely molested as I coasted through the massed swastikas. Except for three friends who flew everywhere in formation, being an aeroplane was a solitary pursuit.

I can see, through this window, that the white paint is flaking from the window of the downstairs toilet (which still has hanging in it a shiny black oilskin, which has been there for as long as I can remember, and another gathering of coathangers one of which reads, '207 Baker St NW1 – LEVESON – Welbeck 5451 – 2 lines' and, on the windowsill, a jar labelled 'glycerine for leaves' which is the colour of Campari) to reveal the old-fashioned garden green, the green of lawnmowers, beneath; and rust is breaking through the paint of the electric radiator. Such things appear to the casual visitor – like the woodworm in the beams or the raised arm of the toy soldier clutching his primed grenade – only as arrested moments of threat and deterioration, adding to the charm, rather than as insidious processes to be halted. Yes, it is unrealistic. But, as I say, I am not someone who takes pleasure in seeing the products of his own labours flexing their muscles at him. I enjoy other people's gardens: a balance of wild and tame sustained, to all appearances, by supernatural fiat or by some localized grace of nature; process, or at least its effort, being effaced in the succession of instants each apparently eter-nal. I have never aspired to possession of a wife whom I might raise by the scruff of her neck at parties, shaking her till her jewellery jangled like a string of goods waggons in a siding, and announcing, 'See, gentlemen, what I have made of this un-promising material.'

A fishing float (a bottle-green orb), a terracotta jar which has once been painted whitish green but is now mottled with flakage, and a piece of pale grey driftwood, soft to the touch, which has the tantalizing look of having been shaped for some purpose – something concerned with milk or sparrows, or with railway safety – though it has clearly not. A railway used to run through the valley a mile or so away. You'd occasionally hear, over the cataracting of wind in the white poplars, the reassurance of its plaintive hoot. It doesn't seem so long ago, though it must be all of ten years. Is ten years a long or a short time? The rails and the sleepers have gone; but there are still a few iron nuts to be found among the granite chippings, ugly on the feet, where swallowtail butterflies tremble in the heat-haze. There is one of the nuts – square, rusty, utilitarian – in the Ajax box with the fossils. My position at this table is exactly the position – window to my right, wall at my back – which was 'mine' when I was six. There, however, there was a nail to the right of the window which caught my head every time my Auntie hit me: with the result that the hair above my right ear, being rarely washed, was most of the time matted with dried blood.

There were two chapels, two pubs and a shop. (There was also a church, but that stood on the fringes of the village like a ne'er-do-well relative on the fringes of a funeral . . .) Capel Cranog: a spick and span, buff-and-black-painted building standing at an angle to the road and approached by a driveway which slanted up the slope of the mountain. Unlike the Baptists, we did not have a balcony; but we had severity of proportion. We had severity of instruction, too: a grey crag of a man on his centrally-sited dais like Ahab addressing his dreadful adversary, cleaving keel of righteousness, figurehead towering above the seas of infamy which sat mutely in their black coats sucking their mint imperials and waiting for the next hymn (Rhaglen Goffa 1940 – they seem to have issued a new selection each year – the Joseph Parry hymnal, slim, orange-bound, with a pearly photograph of the mustachioed master). Not that I was able to follow his drift. My Welsh wasn't up to that. And in all my time of going there – twice a Sunday for fifteen months, with Sunday school on top – I heard him utter only one sentence of English: when, having gathered up his hearers in a mighty swell of ora-tory, he paused precipitously, savouring the hush in which, as it seemed, the very galaxy hesitated in its gyration, then unleashed upon the multitude the full passion of his vibrato: 'I eat the meat . . . and leave . . . the bones!' Perhaps it's in the Bible; but I've never found it.

Whenever I catch a glimpse of myself in a shop window – which I do as infrequently as possible – I see a pot-bellied dwarf with lank hair and a lumpy nose made of plasticine. But in the mirror of the upstairs bathroom here – perhaps because of the light, or perhaps because it is an elegant narrow oval of which one's upper trunk and head occupy only the lower three fifths – I look like someone who should have a dun cloak flung over one shoulder and be painted by Velasquez. I had always defined love as an act of commitment: but now I suspect that this was, if not wrong, too romantic and political in emphasis. Love is – or at any rate, the love of a place is – the way a rock feels when a wave has broken over it and has not yet dried in the hot sun with that swift, radial erasure which is the converse of the spread of a stain: in other words, it is a modality of time's articulation. (The arts keep this up their sleeve, and play it shamelessly. That Garance should disappear into the crowds was a *pre*condition of the prior consummation of Debureau's longing.) In its negative aspect, this is to say that we are all the dupes of immediacy. There is nothing like the proximity of elderly people, and of their suffering, to make us doubt the value of all we do. Yet I have been granted this week of reflection: a gift as arbitrary as the gift of life itself: a week in which to erase by grace of immediacy that stamp of the circuitous, the implacable, the re-petitive, the murderous which is the music in my brain. From the stair-head you look through the half-open bedroom door, across the dark of the inner bedroom, and see sunlight streaming across the boards like a flotilla of dusty dhows and catching the rain-faded, sweat-faded back of the director's chair. Returning to the living room, one smells the milky ooze of the sliced stems of flowers.

It had been a strange day. What I mean is that the day had had a strange atmosphere, though I can't recall by what signals I registered this. In memory there is simply a greyness, as if the world were coated with fine ash. What I recall is that a boy was

213

approaching me down the slope of a lane – an older boy, perhaps eleven or twelve, whom I did not know – and that he said . . . And I realize now, for the first time, that I do not know exactly what he said. 'Dunkirk has fallen'? 'Dunkirk has been evacuated'? 'The British Expeditionary Force . . .'? Hardly. In any case, he probably said it in Welsh. What's more, I'd no idea what he was talking about – we never saw newspapers, and the only wireless set I encountered, powered by a battery of batteries bigger in itself than most modern radios, was in the farmhouse across the fields, in whose kitchen neighbours crowded for such a special broadcast as a speech by the King – and the boy continued past me with irritation, his news wasted. But the point was that the events of that day were of sufficient importance to lead that boy to assume a community of concern with an infant whose very existence he would normally have ignored. The day survives in my consciousness as an oppressive atmosphere and as the image of a boy in grey clothes and slack socks approaching down a lane and inexplicably, speaking to me; and in the one word: 'Dunkirk'.

I sat in that chair – just where it stood awkwardly placed in no relation to the room – relaxing my defences, allowing the fury to flood me so that the elfin music might spirit it away. 'Hyper-tension', it is called in the medical columns on the magical principle that to name is to cure. But true shamanism requires more than that. In the kitchen are another two frayed and iron-on-patched strips of Axminster – secret plans, I was once told, of Persian gardens, lovingly rendered by women for whom their geometries still evoked the scents of blossom, freighted by camel through the gateways of successive mirages, translated into slotted pianola rolls for reproduction in an English manufactory and now awaiting digital storage in liquid crystal for however many generations it may take until that future when their message shall be deciphered and until which time we must be content with a truth only refracted and indirect, even arguably fortuitous, adventitious – on a cement floor the colour of red sandstone: a colour undiminished by wear.

The inner bedroom, to the right of the landing, has two single bedsteads set at right angles making passage to the outer (my) bedroom difficult. I am reminded of the big, saggy bed on the landing at Tan-y-fron where the girl-cousins nested on their summer migrations, pale-limbed in the windowless dusk. There is also the bottom half of a splendidly bourgeois tallboy with a lock on every drawer, keyholes embellished in rococo brass; fossil record of a distrust of the lower orders whom one was obliged to employ as house-servants. One of the beds has a Heal's patent 'Eitherside' reversible spring mattress – a weighty thing of teak and steel.

The squeak and crunch of slate-pencil on slate wood-framed, ruled one side for writing and squared the other for sums. There were three 'standards' in our, the lowest, class. I was placed in the middle block of desks, the older children being against the left-hand wall and the younger against the right. Some lessons, such as the Bible story from the battered red book and the fairy story from the battered blue book with which every day began, were taken in common; but for special tuition a standard would troop out to the front and form a horseshoe, boys on the right and girls on the left, open towards Teacher. In such a formation I was first handed my reading book, with its chapters devoted to the Ll, the Dd, the Rh. The teacher said to me, 'Do you speak Welsh?' I said, 'No', and she said 'Don't worry – it's easier than English.' And that was that. What she'd actually meant was that Welsh, being phonetic in its spelling, was easier to sight-read; but I didn't realize this until some twenty years later, and was left at the time with the impression that I was going to get little help from the authorities. What made these gruelling special sessions tolerable was Teacher's habit of leaving the room, without warning, for extended periods. The class was, naturally, expected to remain quiet until her return; but on one such occasion the sound of muted giggles opposite drew my attention to the fact that the boy at the end of the horseshoe, next-but-one to myself, had unbuttoned his flies and was, with a baffling air of self-possession, his reading book still held studiously before him, allowing his penis to hang exposed. This happened several times, and I had already begun to take it for granted as part of the unfathomable course of things when, one day, my reverie was again broken by a voice whispering, 'Look, Gwilym – here it is . . .' and I saw that the prettiest girl in the class, the one with the lemon sherbet curls, the one who had least need to court popularity but by the same token least cause to fear disfavour, had lifted her skirt and was pulling aside the leg of her knickers to display her cock (yes, we used the same for both sexes, without discrimination) to the gaze of her admirer and of us all.

To the left of the landing, the big bedroom, approached down a couple of steps, has an air of greater antiquity than the rest of the cottage. Two large beds and the top half of the tallboy (which is propped on two baulks of wood to redress the tilt of the floor) leave it looking empty. The ceiling is low and the joists squeak. The one window is tiny, and heavy timbers outcrop in positions which leave the roof-structure a puzzle. To the right of the door an alcove, board-topped to form a doorless cupboard, contains yet another clutch of coathangers. Somewhere on the floor is an upright lamp of disproportionately small base and shade – too tall for a table lamp, yet too small for a standard. Beside the tallboy a red, conical fire-extinguisher rests like an amphora in an iron cradle; and on top of the tallboy is a little pivotal mirror, set on a three-drawer jewel box, whose tired quicksilver pictures a world already darkened by the sulphurs of perdition. ('O God, let me grow up singing, like my Auntie Martha.' The well-attested punishment of prayers' answering!) It is a room of unforgiving childbirths and slow, envy-soiled, litigatory deaths: a place of bigotry and of judgments passed without waver. Somehow the fact that you have to step down into it sets it apart from the other rooms; and I seldom go in.

I accompanied Albermarle on a visit to old Mrs Matravers, whose arm is in plaster. She claims to have fractured it falling down her own stairs at night; but she is known to ride pillion on her eleven-year-old grandson's motorcycle, so rumours abound as to the true cause. She ushered us into a room which, though indisputably a room by virtue of its size, had nonetheless the proportions of a hall, so that you half expected a platform at one end of it. It was decorated in wallpaper once modernistic – no two walls alike – with a formica billiard table in the centre, a deep-freeze in one corner and, around the walls, a number of easy chairs in some of which rifles had been discarded. Voices murmured elsewhere. On the deep-freeze and on a china cabinet lolled Spanish dolls, in the form of flamenco dancers, each a good three feet tall and trailing an overflow of flounces in fluorescent turquoise, tangerine and amber. (Mrs Matravers introduced these as part of her daughter's collection; but the bizarre conjunction provoked a suspicion that they had been bagged, in some erotic dream-shoot, with the very firearms which lay insouciantly cast on these couches.) It was strange, and somehow moving, to meet this woman so representative of people met when one was too young to know how people might be supposed to behave. As she poured us drinks in thimblefuls, I was sure she was about to say, 'Don't clink the glasses too loud. The Reverend's in the front parlour.'

Rhaglen Goffa, 1940: 'Aberystwyth', 'Moliant', 'Hen Lyfyr Mawr y Bywyd' in four-part tonic-sol-fa notation . . . No, not a miracle of remembering; I've still got it at home on my book-shelves: earliest of my relics, nearest to some lost, true source unimaginable. I do, of course, possess mementos from earlier in my childhood; but those are things my *parents* chose to keep for me. The worn, orange hymnal is the earliest object preserved at my own decision, the sole object to survive out of exile as if miraculously fallen intact into another universe – though which was the exile and which the home is something I have not to this day resolved. Yet in a sense it is untrue to say the booklet has survived. It takes on a persona, as one among my present possessions, which was not its persona as an object of use. It gives off no odour. It is not opened in unison with a hundred others; it is not carried in winter-mittened hands. And if it bears somewhere on its semi-gloss pages fingerprints which, though miniature, would be forensically identifiable as my own, I cannot detect them. Perhaps I should not have kept it. All the same, though, its materiality challenges – no, perhaps anchors – the dream-tissue of my memories which, without its vouchsafing, might have evaporated altogether: a childhood the prelude to an adulthood which never happened, left meaningless, tantalizing, yet mine.

The difference between then and now, there and here, is that I can now take verbal rubbings (not newsreels – no – which would reduce the world to a common level of banality, recording only the *fact* of a thing's having once been; and certainly not mementos, cutting off the fingers of the dead to recover their rings) – verbal rubbings. Moreover, since I have no money and no position, this is indeed *all* I have between me and the perils of the world. I should like to get a large piece of paper and do a rubbing of this entire tabletop (perhaps, in some other room where there might be space for it, to frame it and hang it on the wall behind). But rubbings of texture, of course, give no indication of colour – the surface stains, scribbles in crayon by children long grown out of it ... Writing, likewise, is blind to much.

The announcement of a disagreeable lesson provoked mock groans, as is customary and was tolerated; but pleasurable anticipation was expressed in a sound which I was never to hear in any other of my many schools: a rapid repetition of the consonants k-t-k-t-k-t-k-t which, when performed out of phase by forty-odd children, produces an effect similar to that of Ligeti's concerto for metronomes. When one standard was summoned to the horseshoe, the others were either given work or granted silent recreation – or, should they have offended by uttering sounds other than the ritually permitted groans or k-t-k-t-k-t, made to sit still with hands on heads, hands behind backs, arms folded, hands on desks or whatever. Individual punishment took the form of a sharp slap to the side of the head, this being particularly associated with shortcomings in 'composition', which was something the top standard did. It's a wonder to me now that no child ever had its ear-drums burst. Perhaps they did, and just didn't dare mention it.) There were, it is true, some so rough and unruly as to resist this treatment, such as little Aaron Rhys, whom Teacher had to lift physically off the ground to stop him scampering for the door, then hold at arm's-length to avoid the furious kicks he was aiming at her belly with his cruel iron shoddings, screaming 'Cachi!' and 'Pish!' at the top of his voice, whilst the rest of us sternly contained our glee; but they were few. Materials for recreation comprised nine uncoloured wooden cubes – except that I was one short – and a lump of plasticine usually too cold to be malleable. Was the plasticine in a square tin box? I think it was. Was there a window in my vision; and if there was, could anything be seen out of it? I don't know. But here is my memory: I am gazing out of the window, during a recreation period, at the branches of some trees, my hands smelling of plasticine, as some poor child is beaten around the head for his attempts at composition, and it occurs to me quite suddenly that the time will come when I shall look back on this and it will no longer matter. Presumably I did not phrase it in these words – if, indeed, I phrased it at all. It was more in the nature of a shift in the temporal perspective: an awareness of the contingency of the present: an involuntary insight which I have never been able subsequently to reproduce. The startling clarity of my recollection of it – questions of windows and plasticine aside – derives from the fact that its appeal, its appeal for help, was lodged explicitly with my future adult self; and it is this same fact which, conversely, enables me now to look back upon that six-year-old and say, 'I am still with you. I will not let them hurt you. Trust me.'

Persist. Kneel before the carpet as if praying. On a central area, the colour of sandy earth, stretch before you like desks in a classroom five files of ciphers, the outer two containing eight ciphers each, and the inner three eleven, so that the area narrows to a sort of apse at the far end. The ciphers are identical in shape: a highly indented shape approximating to the square in outer perimeter – in which description the deepest indentations would be said to be in saltire – but perhaps better described as a squared-off hourglass crossed at the neck by a band branching into three at either end. This band, in fact, assumes in most cases a certain prominence, as if it – though not its lateral branchings – were laid *across* the remainder of the cipher, and is marked by a sharper emphasis of alternating colour, the remainder of each cipher being subdivided by colour, squarely and diagonally, into what might be considered eight areas – though four of these comprise merely the lateral branches of the superimposed bands. The colours employed are lilac, soil brown, blush pink and indigo; and each subdivided area is in general, though not without exception, limited to one colour. In addition, each cipher is lightly edged: for the most part in a darker brown, but in just

219

two cases – the bottom centre and right – with the pink. The wools used in the manufacture do not, however, appear to have been of constant dye even within what one designates a single hue; and the matter is complicated by the fact that wear has been uneven. Now: between these files of ciphers lie single ribbons of alternating colour, as if twisted like rope of contrasting strands, wider and more continuous versions of the 'bands' already mentioned, horizontally separating the ciphers which vertically are almost continuous. At the right and left edges there are two such ribbons, the outer being of brown striped diagonally with indigo and the inner, in common with the others, with pink. I have, it must be understood, even now, described only the scheme and not its deviations. But the border is more difficult to write about, since the model of 'scheme' and 'deviations' is less easily applicable.

To idle in a doorway watching the rain fall outside. Tan-y-fron, Tommi's childhood here, the Queen Mother's childhood for that matter . . . A house is only a tent, when all's said and done. Roll up your garden and spread it elsewhere. After dark, there is sometimes a sound outside as if someone were walking around the cottage and chafing it with his shoulder – chafing continuously and circuitously against the rough stone walls. Yet even more strange is that this does not scare me. I seem to have an unshakable conviction that the spirit – if such it is – is benign, and see it, when I see it at all, as the bottle-green mammoth of the yew protecting one whom it has, in imponderable mercy, elected for safekeeping. (What fancifulness is this?)

Perhaps I had just discovered that stamping one's feet could make them warm. Certainly it was a bitter day, and the dry snow was skeeting across the asphalt – or was there just earth, compacted and stony? – to form driftlets against my clogs as I stood under the shelter (possibly a place for bicycles, though I don't recall that any of the children was rich enough to own a bicycle except the headmaster's son) looking forward to lunchtime when we would be served our bowls of cawl in the top class's classroom, whose benches were raked and where there was a map of the world, or perhaps a big globe, and which was flanked with high cupboards on top of which stuffed sea-birds moulted with neglect. Sometimes a fleeting smell, I'm not sure of what, will bring back to me that room, its colours muted by chalk-dust and history. (In summer we took bottles of pop, but I had to ask a bigger boy to push down the marble which sealed it, because my thumb wasn't strong enough and I was frightened of getting it stuck in the bottleneck if I pushed too hard . . .) Dunkirk, the epiphany with the plasticine, the little girl's genital generosity: it's natural I should remember these things; but why, when every cell of my body has replaced itself six times over since, then, should my mind hold so resolutely to a moment lasting – what, ten seconds? – when I stood preoccupied in an icy playground: a moment of which almost no details of substance remain? I was there. I was there, and doing something which is perhaps un-finished yet. Had some idea just occurred to me? Was I pon-dering the privilege of being still under seven and therefore allowed to frequent both playgrounds – the girls' and the boys'? Was it in fact the last playtime of the day (dusk seems to be falling, and the classroom lamps to be lit), and was I wondering whether it would be treacle pudding, mixed fruit pudding or jam roly-poly after the two-and-a-half mile trudge home?

In the passage between the staircase and the downstairs loo – which is also the frontier between this cottage and the other – stand two enormously stout wicker baskets, perhaps made for the portage of spoil from mine workings or of Seville oranges to the marmalade vats, which now store the logs for Albermarle's mother's fire. In the very centre of the white window-recess of the inner bedroom is a tiny fragment, sea-scoured, of eye-blue glass . . .

The past has the clarity of memories. It is clear, paradoxically, precisely because it is vague: because it cannot contradict us with any confidence. It is the present, in the inexhaustibility of its detail, which eludes me. Roll out the garden in your new home and you will find, after all, it is nothing but a rug. There is no immortality that way. How long must it have taken God to invent it all?

I returned, splendidly, for the night of the City fire, those famous panning shots from the golden dome of St Paul's: returned to a world where landmines fell like thistledown and

221

nobody was going to smack me for things I had not done and my repertoire of nervy tics could be eradicated within a few years; returned to a world of Kings and Queens with nothing for remembrance but a Congregational hymn-book in a language I was already beginning to forget and the fading image of a little girl with freckles asking me what was the English for barrage balloon. Perhaps if I had kept the language ... Now there's a thought! Perhaps that moment of tantalizing consciousness in the playground is lost because it was framed in lost words? Perhaps Welsh does not distinguish between 'cup' and 'basin', just as German, let's say, does not distinguish between a chair and a stool. But at the age of fifty one is not expected to be worrying about such nonsense. Just a convalescence; recharge the batteries; unwind ... Yet what does it all mean? It's a childhood, after all. It's supposed to add up to something. (You've got your sums wrong. Do them again.) Something you could lay voice over, even today, like the Queen Mum: 'Yes, that was the dressing-up box ...' You're not supposed to raise a diffident arm, fearful of a thump around the ear-hole, and say, 'Please, Miss, I still don't understand. I still don't understand what the preacher meant when he said he ate the meat and left the bones, Miss. I was late starting, Miss. Didn't speak the language ...' And it's too late to catch up now. Besides, that I may have let slip the one magical tongue in which the truth of myself might have been spoken is an idea to be taken seriously only in fairy-tales.

If I say that I wish to describe this cottage, do I mean, by 'describe', simply 'to record', or, more problematically, 'to evoke'? And if the latter, to evoke for oneself or, more problematically, for others? Suppose, for example, that that which might best evoke for others did not have the force of an accurate description for myself? For royalty, of course, the problem does not arise. How could a royal personage confess to mystery: to values potentially in contradiction to that union of appearance and reality which defines their role as symbols of what is unquestionable in the nation's self-knowledge – potentially, in a word, seditious – when the sole function of royalty is to affirm at least the possibility, if not themselves as the actuality, of such unproblematical knowledge? A paradigm of selfhood as pure exteriority: therefore, by implication, as purely defined by consensus, by the status quo. For the rest of us, there are no such assurances. Whatever the past may have been, at least its tense is indisputable. But what of the present? I sit here writing, 'I sit here,' but meaning, 'I sat here half an hour ago' – which was when I actually noticed the thing I am describing – or even, 'a night's sleep ago'. And when I come to revise what I have written, or to type it, I shall not change the tense. What would be the purpose? The past begins instantaneously, before the sentence has even reached its main verb. Yet the past is nothing but broken toys.

Let us say, making a story of it (for cottages, like boats, may be accorded femininity, and for the same reasons), that he has loved her for many years but has never had her to himself. Now, at last, he is able to spend a week alone with her; but he knows, too, that this is the last time he will ever see her. There is little they can talk about under the circumstances, since conversation requires a perspective (or one might say a vista) which is denied to them, and they are too old for the continuous, meaningless verbal caresses of youth. He sees, moreover, that his image of her has not kept pace with her ageing – suspecting also that the same may be true, for her, of him – and that their mutual language of sign and gesture, of sigh and stance, built up over a long period of casual (or supposedly casual) encounters in other people's homes and in other people's company, being in essence a language for the articulation of the minutest degrees of their separation and of consequent sadness (all hues and shadings, that is to say, of melancholy, fortitude and regret), is ill-adapted to their use united. Yet he can admit all this to himself because there is still magic: the magic of possibilities not yet bonded into actuality. And, as he can in any case never look more than three days ahead, this contents him.

The table has gone. The dining chairs stand at random attention, ignoring one another. The music has departed unnoticed, which is a blessing – salved away by the ministrations of the ghostly green mammoth, or more likely fallen through the mesh of a code which, though defying our decipherment, is none-

223

theless too coarse to render and preserve it. (Imperfection has its uses!)

Thus the boy-king was restored to his realm – a dominion, though awesome as a prophecy, which he hugged around him for comfort. He was overjoyed to discover that the desolation of his spirit was now manifest, physically, in the destruction of brickwork, of stonework, the rupturing of highways, the severance of pipes and conduits, a vermicelli of communication cables. How else, indeed, would he have recognized the kingdom as his own? But no: to be truthful, he did not see these things. At dawn, with the taking down of the blackout shutters of heavy plywood sawn to measure by his father just before the outbreak, he saw from his high window only the ruddiness of the sky as it murmured in the distance like the murmuring of his defective heart. And from his high window, with his father's marine telescope, he scanned that vista – that vista of glistening grey roofs and of power station stacks and of gasometers, in which there was not a school with room for him – searching inquisitively for each night's new gaps and obliterations.

And when the sentry-boxes, like abandoned dining chairs, were scattered from the forecourt of the Queen's palace, the soldiers within them continued to face, with exact and disciplined vacancy, straight ahead of them. Only then was it discovered that the sentries, like their boxes, were made of lead.

The Bottom Line and the Sharp End

FAY WELDON

'I'LL GET MY pennies together,' said Avril the night-club singer to Helen the hairdresser. 'I'll come in next week and you can work your usual miracles.'

Helen thought the time for miracles was almost past. Both Avril's pennies and Avril's hair were getting thin. But she merely said, 'I'll do my best,' and ran her practised fingers through Avril's wiry curls without flinching.

Avril was scraggy, haggard and pitifully brave. Helen was solid and worthy and could afford to be gracious. Avril had been Helen's very first client, thirty years before, when she, Helen, had finally finished her apprenticeship. In those days Avril had worn expensive, daring green shoes with satin bows, all the better to flirt in. Helen had worn cheap navy shoes with sensible heels, all the better to work in. Helen envied Avril. Today Avril's shoes, with their scuffed high heels, were still green, but somehow vulgar and pitiable, and the legs above them were knotted with veins. And Helen's shoes were still navy, but expensive and comfortable, and had sensible medium heels. And Helen owned the salon, and had a husband, and grown-up children, and money in the bank, and a dog, a cat and a garden, and Avril had nothing. Nothing. Childless, unmarried, and without property or money in the bank.

Now Helen pitied Avril, instead of envying her, but somehow couldn't get Avril to understand that this switch had occurred.

With the decades, the salon had drifted elegantly up-market, and now had a pleasing atmosphere of hushed brocaded luxury. Here, now, the wives of the educated wealthy came weekly, and the shampooers were well-spoken and careful not to wet the backs of blouses, and decaffeinated coffee was provided free, and low-calorie wholewheat sandwiches for a reasonable charge, and this month's glossy magazines in sufficient quantity – and still Avril would walk in, unabashed, and greet Helen with an embarrassing cry of 'Darling!' as if she were her dearest friend, in her impossibly husky and actressy voice. And she'd bring wafting in with her, so that the other clients stirred uneasily in their well-padded seats, what Helen could only think of as the aura of the street; and what is more, of a street in rapid decline – once perhaps Shaftesbury Avenue, and tolerable, with associated West End Theatre and champagne cocktails – but now of some Soho alley, complete with live sex shows and heroin pushers.

Sometimes Avril would vanish for a year or so and Helen would hope she had gone for good, and then there she'd be again, crying, 'Do something, darling, work your usual miracles. My life's all to hell!' and Helen would pick up the strands of brown, or red, or yellow or whatever they currently were, and bleach them right down and re-colour them, and soothe them and coax them into something presentable and fashionable.

This time Avril had been away all of two years. And now here she was back again, and the 'do something' had sounded really desperate, as she'd torn at crisp dry henna-and-grey curls with ringed finger-claws, and Helen had been affected, surprisingly, with real sorrow and real concern. Perhaps you didn't have to like people to feel for them? Perhaps if they were merely around for long enough you developed a fellow feeling for them?

She remembered how once – way, way back – when Avril's hair had been long and smooth and shiny, the rings had had diamonds and rubies in them. Then, at the time of her auburn pony-tail there'd been engagement rings and remembrance rings; and later, once or twice – at the time Avril's hair was back-

combed into blonde curls – a wedding ring, Helen could remember. But nowadays the only rings she wore were the kind
anyone could buy at a jewellery stall in the market on Saturdays
– they came from India or Ethiopia or somewhere ethnic, and
the silver was base and the stones were glass. 'Cheap and
cheerful,' Avril would cackle, from under the dryer, waving
them round happily for all to see, as the other clients looked
away, tactfully. They didn't wear much jewellery, and if they did
it was either real or Harrods make-believe, and certainly *quiet*.

Avril came in for the latest, desperate miracle on Friday
evening. She had the last appointment, and of course wanted a
bleach, a perm, a cut and a set. Helen agreed to work late. It was
her policy to oblige clients – even clients such as Avril – wherever possible, and however much at her own expense. It was, in
the end, good for business. Just as, in the end, steadiness, for-
bearance, endurance, always succeeded whether at work, in marriage, in the establishment of a home, the bringing up of children.
You made the most of what you had. You were not greedy; you
played safe; and you won.

Helen rang up her husband Gregory to tell him she would be
working late.

'I'll take a chicken pie from the freezer,' he said, 'and there's a
nature programme on TV I want to see. And perhaps I'll do a
little DIY around the house.'

'Well, don't try mending the electric kettle,' she said, and he
agreed not to. Still she did not hang up.

'Is there something the matter?' he said, and waited patiently.
He was wonderfully patient.

'Don't you think,' she said presently, 'don't you think
somehow life's awfully sad?'

'In what way?' he asked, when he'd given some time to considering the question.

'Just growing older,' she said, vaguely, already fearing she
sounded silly. 'And what's it all for?'

There was a further silence at the other end of the line.

'Who's the client?' he asked.

'Avril le Ray.'

'Oh, her. She always upsets you.'

'She's so tragic, Gregory!'

'She brought it on herself,' said Gregory. 'Now I must go and take the pie out of the freezer. It's always better to heat them when they're thawed out a little, isn't that so?'

'Yes,' she said, and they said goodbye, and hung up.

Avril was ten minutes late for her appointment. She'd been crying. Her mouth was slack and sullen. Melted blue eyeshadow made runnels down her cheeks. She insisted on sitting in the corner where one of the old-style mirrors still remained from before the last renovation. Avril claimed it threw back a kinder reflection and probably did, but Avril sitting in front of it meant that Helen was obliged to work with her elbow up against the wall. The neck of Avril's blouse was soiled with a mixture of make-up, sweat and dirt. And she smelt unwashed, but Helen, to her surprise, found the smell not unpleasant. Her Nan had smelt like that, she remembered, long ago and once upon a time, when she'd put little Helen to bed in a big, damp feather bed. Was that where the generations got you? Did they merely progress from chaos to order, dirt to cleanliness? Was that what it was all about?

'Remember when I had long hair?' said Avril. 'So long that I could sit on it! I played Lady Godiva in the town pageant. I was in love with this boy and he said if I wanted to prove I loved him, I would sit on the horse naked. So I did. Listen, I was sixteen, he was seventeen, what did we know? My mother wouldn't speak to me for months. We lived in the big house, had servants and everything. What a disgrace! She was right about one thing, I failed my exams.'

'What about the boy?' asked Helen. Whole-head-root-bleaches, the kind Avril wanted, were old-fashioned, but were less finickity than the more usual bleached streaks. Helen could get on quite quickly at this stage.

'He was my one true love,' said Avril. 'We'd never done anything but hold hands and talk about running away to get married. Only after I played Godiva he never wanted to run any further than behind the bicycle shed. You know what men are like.'

'But it was his idea!'

Avril shrugged. 'He was only young. He didn't know what he'd feel like later, after I'd gone public, as it were. How could he have? So I went with him behind the bicycle sheds. It was glorious. I'll never forget it. The sun seemed to stop in the sky. You know?'

'Yes,' said Helen, who didn't. She'd only ever been with Gregory and someone else whose name she preferred to forget, at a party, a sorry, drunken episode which had left her with NSU – non-specific urethritis – with that special brand of unlikely punishment reserved by fate for the virtuous who sin only once, and either get pregnant or a social disease. And she'd only ever made love to Gregory at night, so how could she know about the sun stopping? But at least it was love: warm, fond and affectionate, not whatever it was that ravaged and raddled Avril.

'Anyway, then he broke it to me formally that he and me were through. He'd met Miss Original Pure and planned to marry her when he had his degree. I thought I'd die from misery. But I didn't, did I? I lived to tell the tale!

'I do look a sight, don't I,' Avril said, staring at her plastery hair, but her mind was on the past. 'It was funny. I stood in front of that full-length mirror, at the age of sixteen, and tried to decide whether to do Godiva naked or in a flesh-coloured bodystocking. I knew even then it was what they call a major life decision. Naked, and the future would go one way: bodystocking, another. I chose naked. Afterwards I cried and cried, I don't know why. I've always cried a lot.

'Then of course I couldn't get into college because I'd failed my exams so I went to drama school. I got no help from home, they'd given me up, and I couldn't live on my grant, no one could. So I did a centre spread in *Mayfair*, perfectly decent, just bra-less, only the photographer took a lot of other shots I knew nothing about and they were published too, and got circulated everywhere, including in my home town. I tried to sue but it was no use. No one takes you seriously once you take your clothes off. I didn't know – well, I guess I was trying to take advantage of him, too, in a way, so I can't complain. And I can tell you this, if the sun stopped behind the bicycle shed, that photographer made the whole galaxy go the other way. Know what I mean?'

'Oh yes,' said Helen, testing a lock of Avril's hair: the bleach was taking a long time to take. She wondered whether to ring Gregory and remind him not to try to mend the kettle, or whether the reminding would merely make him the more determined to do it.

'Do I look as if I've been crying?' asked Avril, peering more closely into the mirror. 'Because I have been. This guy I've been living with: he's a junkie trying to kick the habit. He's really managed well with me. He was getting quite, well, you know, affectionate – that's always a good sign. He used to be a teacher, really clever, until he got the habit. Young guy: bright eyes, wonderful skin – didn't often smile, but when he did . . . Notice the past tense? When I got home from work this morning he'd vanished and so had my rent money. It gets you here in your heart. You can't help it. You tell yourself it was only to be expected, but it hurts, Christ it hurts. I shouldn't have told him I loved him, should I? Should I, Helen?'

'I don't know,' said Helen. She told Gregory she loved him quite often and there seemed no sanction against it. But perhaps the word, as used by her, and by Avril, had a different meaning. She rather hoped so.

'So you only love people who hurt you?' she asked, cautiously.

'That is love, isn't it,' said Avril. 'That's how you know you love them, because they can hurt you. Otherwise, who cares? How am I going to live without him? Just lying in a bed beside him – he was so thin, but so hot. He was so alive! It was life burning him up, killing him. Just life. Too strong.' Tears rolled down Avril's cheeks.

'She looks eighty,' thought Helen, 'but she can only be my age.'

'Anyway,' said Avril, 'I want a new me at the end of this session. Pick yourself up and start all over, that's my motto. Remember when you cut off all my long hair? That was after the *Mayfair* business; I didn't want anyone to recognize me, but of course they did. You can't cut off your breasts, can you? I got picked out of the end-of-the-year show by a director: very classy he was, National and all that, and he and I got friendly, and I got the lead but I wasn't ripe for it, and the rest of the cast made a fuss and that was the end of me; three weeks later, bye-bye National. He had a wife living in the country somewhere, and it got in the papers because he was so famous, and none of his friends would hire me, they all sided with the wife, and I got a part in the Whitehall Revue and did French maids for five years. Good wages, nice little flat, men all over the place; wonderful dinners, diamonds – you wouldn't believe it, like in a novel, but it wasn't me. I don't know what is me, come to think of it. Perhaps no one ever does. I wanted to get married and have kids and settle down but men just laughed when I suggested it. I had a blonde, back-combed bob in those days. Remember?'

Helen did. That was in the days when you used so much hair spray on a finished head it felt like a bird's nest to the touch.

'Then I had a real break. I could always sing, you know, and by that time I really did know something about theatre. I got the lead in a Kurt Weill opera. Real classy stuff. You did my hair black and I had a bee-hive. How we could have gone round like that! And I fell in love with the stage manager. God, he was wonderful. Strong and silent and public school and he really went for me, and we married, and I've never been happier in my life. But he was ambitious to get into films, and was offered a job in Hollywood and I just walked out of the part and went along. That didn't do me any good in the profession, I can tell you. And I kept getting pregnant but he didn't want us tied down so I'd have terminations, and then he went off with the studio boss's daughter. She was into yoga, and they had three kids straight off. He complained I could never sit still. But I can, can't I? You should know, shouldn't you, Helen?'

'About as still as anyone else,' said Helen, and took Avril over to the basin and washed the bleach off. She hoped she hadn't overdone it: the hair was very fine and in poor condition and the bleach was strong.

'I left them to it; I just came back home; I didn't hang around asking for money. I never do that. Once things are over, they're over – I didn't have any children: why should he pay? We gave each other pleasure, didn't we? Fair exchange, while it lasted.

Everything finishes, that's the bottom line. But I never liked bee-hives, did you?'

'No. Very stiff and artificial.'

'I wept and wept, but it was good times while it lasted!'

Avril examined a lock of hair.

'Look here,' said Avril, 'that bleach simply hasn't taken. You'll have to put some more on and mix it stronger.'

'It's risky!' said Helen.

'So's everything!' said Avril. 'I'm just sick of being hennaed frizz: I want to be a smooth blonde again.'

Helen felt weary of the salon and her bank account and her marriage and everything she valued: and of her tidy hair and sensible shoes and the way she never took risks and how her youth had passed and all she'd ever known had been in front of her eyes, and fear had kept her from turning her head or seeing what she would rather not see. She re-mixed the bleach, and made it strong. Avril would be as brassy a blonde as she wished, and Helen's good wishes would go with her.

'Well, of course,' said Avril, cheerfully, 'after that it was all down hill. Could I get another acting part? No! Too old for *ingénue*, too young for character and a reputation as a stripper, so Hedda Gabler was out. And frankly I don't suppose I was ever that good. Met this really nice straight guy, an engineer, but he wanted a family and I guess my body got tired of trying, because I never fell for a baby with him, and he made some nice girl pregnant and they got married and lived happily ever after. I went to the wedding. But how was it, I ask myself, that she could get pregnant and still stay a nice girl, and I was just somehow a slut from the beginning?'

'So late,' thought Helen, 'and the perm not even begun. Gregory will have gone to bed without me – will he notice? Will he care?'

'So now I sing in nightclubs; I'm a good singer, you know. All I need is the breaks and I'd really be someone . . . I do the whole gamut – from the raunchy to the nostalgic, a touch of Bogart, a touch of Bacall. Those were the days, when love was love. And I tell you, Helen, it still is, and the only thing I regret is that it can't go on for ever – love, sex. The first touch of a man's hand, the feel of his lips, the press of his tongue, the way the mind goes soft and the body goes weak, the opening up, the joining in. I still feel love, and I still say love, though it's not what men want, not from me. Perhaps it comes too easily, always did. Do you think that's what the matter is?'

When Helen took Avril to the washbasin and washed the second lot of bleach away, a good deal of Avril's hair came away with it. Helen felt her hands grow cold, and her head fill with black: she all but fainted. Then she wept. Nothing like this had ever happened before, in all her professional career. She trembled so much that Avril had to rinse off what was left of the bleach from what was left of her hair, herself.

'Well,' said Avril, when it was done, and large areas of her reddened scalp all too apparent, 'that's the bottom line and the sharp end. Nothing lasts, not even hair. My fault. I made you do it. Thirty years of hating me, and you finally got your revenge!'

'I never hated you,' said Helen, her face puffy and her eyes swollen. She felt, on the other side of the shock and horror, agreeably purged, sensuous, like her Nan's little girl again.

'Well, you ought to have,' said Avril. 'The way I always stirred things up in here. I just loved the look on your face!'

When both women had recovered a little, Avril said, 'I wonder what my future is, as a bald night club singer? I suppose I could wear a wig till it grows again, but I don't think I will – it might be rather good. After the Godiva look, the Doris Day look, the Elizabeth Taylor look, then the Twiggy look – the frizz-out, the pile-up and the freak-out – none of which did me any good at all – just plain bald might work wonders for a girl's career.'

A month later Avril de Ray was billed in Mayfair, not Soho, on really quite tasteful posters, and Helen, bravely, took Gregory around to listen to her sing. They went cautiously down into the plump and sensuous darkness, where Avril's coarse and melancholy voice filled out the lonely corners nicely, and a pink spotlight made her look not glamorous – for truly she was bald, and how can the bald be glamorous? – but important, as if her sufferings and her experience might be of considerable interest to others, and the customers certainly paid attention, were silent when she sang, and clapped when she'd finished, which was more than usually happened in such places.

'How you doing, Kiddo?' asked Avril of Helen, after the last set, going past on the arm of a glowing-eyed Arab with a hooked nose, waving a truly jewelled ring, properly set in proper gold. 'Remember what I told you about the bottom line and the sharp end? Nothing lasts, so you'd better have as much as you can, while you can. And in the end, there's only you and only them, and not what they think of you, but what you think of them.'

Authors' Biographies

J. G. BALLARD was born in Shanghai, China, of English parents in 1930, and lived there until he was fifteen. After the attack on Pearl Harbor he was interned by the Japanese in a civilian prison camp. He moved to England in 1946, and after leaving school he read medicine at King's College, Cambridge. Thereafter he worked variously as a copy-writer, a Covent Garden porter and, after a spell in Canada with the RAF, an editor of technical and scientific journals. His first short story appeared in 1956, and in 1962 he published *The Drowned World*, which won him instant critical acclaim and had a dramatic effect on the state of science fiction. His other books include *The Terminal Beach*, *The Voices of Time*, *Crash*, *The Unlimited Dream Company*, *Hello America* and *Empire of the Sun*, which was shortlisted for the 1984 Booker Prize.

GEORGE MACKAY BROWN was born in Stromness, Orkney in 1921. He went to school there, and later attended Newbattle Abbey College when the poet Edwin Muir was warden. After Newbattle he read English at Edinburgh University, where he later did some postgraduate work on Gerard Manley Hopkins. Several of his stories have been televised, and some of his books published in the USA, Sweden and Norway. The composer Peter Maxwell Davies has put music to several of his texts. Davies's opera *The Martyrdom of Saint Magnus* is based on the novel *Magnus*, and the children's opera *The Two Fiddlers* on the short story of the same name.

Short stories: *A Calendar of Love* (1967); *A Time to Keep* (1969); *Hawkfall* (1974); *The Sun's Net* (1976); *Andrina* (1984).

Novels: *Greenvoe* (1972); *Magnus* (1973); *Time in a Red Coat* (1985).

Poetry: *Winterfold* (1976); *Selected Poems* (1977); *Voyages* (1984).

Plays: *A Spell for Green Corn* (1970); *Three Plays* (1984).

Essays: *An Orkney Tapestry* (Gollancz 1969); *Letters from Ham-navoe* (Gordon Wright Publishing 1975); *Under Brinkies Brae* (Gordon Wright Publishing 1977).

Children's books: *The Two Fiddlers* (1974); *Pictures in the Cave* (1977); *Six Lives of Fankle the Cat* (1980).

Except where otherwise indicated all these books are published by The Hogarth Press/ Chatto & Windus.

CHRISTOPHER BURNS is married, with two sons, and lives in Cumbria. His novel *Snakewrist* was published by Cape earlier this year. His short stories have appeared in the *London Magazine*, the *London Review of Books* and *Interzone* as well as British and American anthologies.

BARBARA CARTLAND, the romantic novelist, is also an historian, playwright, lecturer, political speaker and television personality. She has written over 400 books and more than 390 million copies have been sold throughout the world. She has had many historical works published, and written four autobiographies as well as biographies of her mother and her brother, Ronald Cartland, the first Member of Parliament to be killed in the Second World War. In 1976, by writing 21 books, she broke the world record and has continued for the following eight years with 24, 20, 23, 24, 24, 25, 22 and 26. In *The Guinness Book of Records* she is listed as the world's top-selling author.

UPAMANYU CHATTERJEE was born in Patna, Bihar, in 1959, and led a completely conventional school and college life in Delhi. He taught English for a year at St Stephen's College, Delhi, and joined the Indian administrative service in 1983. His interests include Indian history and walking (meaning the taking of long walks). He has published a few stories in the *London Magazine* and in *Debonair* (India), and has written a novel.

ÉILÍS NÍ DHUIBHNE was born in Dublin in 1954. She went to school and university there, studying Old and Middle and modern English, Old Irish and folklore. She did postgraduate work on Chaucer's use of tradition, and received an M.Phil. in 1976. In 1982 a Ph.D. in Irish folklore was conferred on her. She has worked as a teacher, civil servant, folklore collector, and assistant keeper in the National Library of Ireland. She is married to Professor Bo Almqvist and they have two children. She writes short stories (six have been published in the *Irish Press*), and poems and is currently working on a novel.

DOUGLAS DUNN grew up in Inchinnan, Renfrewshire, where he was born in 1942. After attending local schools, he was educated at the Scottish School of Librarianship and the University of Hull. He lived in Hull for seventeen years and now lives in Scotland. *Secret Villages*, his first collection of stories, appeared in 1985. He has also published seven collections of verse with Faber and Faber, the most recent being *Elegies* (1985), which won the Whitbread Book of the Year Award, and *Selected Poems* (1986).

MARIAN ELDRIDGE, born in 1936, grew up on a farm in Victoria, Australia. She was educated by correspondence, then at Kyneton High School and Melbourne University. She has worked as a secondary school teacher, copy editor and seed collector. She is married with four children and lives in Canberra where she teaches adult education, writes book reviews for the *Canberra Times*, works as Community Literature Co-ordinator for the ACT Arts Council, and writes short stories. They have been published in numerous Australian journals, newspapers and anthologies as well as overseas. Her collection, *Walking the Dog and Other Stories* (University of Queensland Press) came out in 1984.

ALICE THOMAS ELLIS was born in Liverpool before the war and educated at Bangor Grammar School and Liverpool School of Art. She has written five novels, all published in hardcover by Duckworth and in paperback by Penguin. Her latest novel, *Unexplained Laughter*, won the *Yorkshire Post* Novel of the Year Prize (1985). She writes a regular column, 'Home Life' in the *Spectator*, and a book of her articles was published under that title by Duckworth in 1986. Under her real name (Anna Haycraft) she has also written two cookery books. She is married to Colin Haycraft, chairman and managing director of Duckworth, of which she is a director and the fiction editor; they have five children.

DESMOND HOGAN is thirty-five. He has published three novels and two collections of stories. His first collection, *The Diamonds at the Bottom of the Sea*, won the John Llewellyn Rhys Memorial Prize, 1980; his last novel, *A Curious Street*, was recently issued by Picador and will be published in French shortly. In 1985 he received an *Irish Post* Community Award. Apart from having written fiction and plays he has also done introductions to a few Kate O'Brien novels for Virago. He left Ireland in 1977 and has lived in London since; having moved a lot in London, he now lives in Lewisham. A new novel, *A New Shirt*, has recently been published (Hamish Hamilton) while a reissue of his first and very early novel, *The Ikon Maker*, is expected from Pulsifer Press.

CHRISTOPHER HOPE was born in Johannesburg, South Africa in 1944. He has lived in London since 1975. In 1974 he received a Cholmondeley Award for poetry. His books of fiction have been awarded the David Higham Prize, the International PEN Silver Pen Award and the Whitbread Prize.

Novels: *A Separate Development* (Routledge & Kegan Paul 1981); *Kruger's Alp* (Heinemann 1984); *The Hottentot Room* (Heinemann 1986).
Poetry: *Cape Drives* (London Magazine Editions 1974); *In the Country of the Black Pig* (London Magazine Editions 1981); *Englishmen* (Heinemann 1985).
Short stories: *Private Parts and Other Tales* (Routledge & Kegan Paul 1982).
Children's books: *The King, The Cat and the Fiddle* (Ernest Benn 1983); *The Dragon Wore Pink* (A. & C. Black 1985).

FRANCIS KING was born in Switzerland in 1923. He passed his childhood in India, before being sent 'home' to be educated at Shrewsbury School and Balliol College, Oxford, to both of which he won Classical Scholarships. He joined the British Council, serving in Italy, Greece, Finland and Japan. Since 1964 he was written full-time. He is drama critic of the *Sunday Telegraph*. He has won the

Somerset Maugham Prize, the Katherine Mansfield Short Story Prize and the *Yorkshire Post* Prize. This year, he was unanimously elected International President of PEN. He has served as Chairman of the Society of Authors. His last published work was a reissue in hardback of his novel, set in Japan, *The Custom House*.

Novels include: *The Needle* (Hutchinson 1975, Penguin 1986); *Act of Darkness* (Hutchinson 1983, Penguin 1984); *Voices in an Empty Room* (Hutchinson 1984, Penguin 1985).

Short story collections include: *The Japanese Umbrella* (Longmans 1964); *The Brighton Belle* (Longmans 1968); *Indirect Method* (Hutchinson 1980); and *One is a Wanderer* (Hutchinson 1985).

Critical biography: *E M Forster and His World* (Thames and Hudson 1978).

DEBORAH MOGGACH was born in 1948, one of four girls in a writing family – her father Richard Hough is the author of over sixty books and her mother Charlotte is a children's author and illustrator. She read English at Bristol University but only started writing fiction while living for two years in Pakistan. Her first novel, *You Must be Sisters* (1978), was followed by *Close to Home*, *A Quiet Drink*, *Hot Water Man* and *Porky*. Her most recent novel *To Have and To Hold*, has been dramatized into an eight-part TV serial, which was shown in autumn 1986. She also writes for newspapers and magazines, and is currently working on a situation comedy series for BBC TV. She lives in Camden Town, London, with her two children.

JOHN MURRAY was born in industrial West Cumbria in 1950. After Workington Grammar School he studied Sanskrit and Old Iranian at University College, Oxford. In 1971 he won the Boden Sanskrit Prize. After graduating he worked on Ayurvedic manuscripts at the Wellcome Institute in London. He began writing seriously in 1974 but it was ten years before his first novel was accepted. He has taught in Tech colleges and worked in chocolate and furniture factories and an off-licence. He edits a fiction magazine, *Panurge*, in Cleator Moor, Cumbria where he lives. His wife is a social work training officer.

Short stories have appeared in the *London Review of Books*, the *London Magazine*, the *Literary Review*, the *Fiction Magazine*, the *Irish Press* and *Stand*.

Novels: *Samarkand* (Aidan Ellis 1985), broadcast on Radio 3, August 1985; *Kin* (Aidan Ellis 1986).

PHILIP OAKES was born in the North Staffordshire Potteries in 1928. He has been an agency reporter, a film critic (for the *Standard* and the *Sunday Telegraph*) and for fifteen years worked for the *Sunday Times* as arts editor, columnist and feature writer until he resigned in 1981. His short stories have been included in many anthologies. He has written film and TV scripts and is a regular broadcaster.

Novels: *Exactly What We Want* (Michael Joseph 1962); *The Godbrothers* (Deutsch 1971); *Experiment at Proto* (Deutsch 1973); *A Cast of Thousands* (Gollancz 1976).

Poetry: *Unlucky Jonah* (Reading University Press 1955); *In the Affirmative* (Deutsch 1968); *Married/Singular* (Deutsch 1973); *Selected Poems* (Deutsch 1982).

Autobiography: *From Middle England* (Deutsch 1981); *Dwellers All In Time and Space* (Deutsch 1982); *At the Jazz Band Ball* (Deutsch 1983).

RUTH RENDELL has, since her first novel *From Doon With Death* was published in 1964, won many awards, including the Crime Writers' Association Gold Dagger for 1976's best crime novel with *A Demon in My View* and the Arts Council National Book Award – Genre Fiction for *Lake of Darkness* in 1980. In 1984 Ruth Rendell won her second Edgar from the Mystery Writers of America for best short story with *The New Girl Friend*, and in 1985 received the Silver Dagger for *The Tree of Hands*. Her books have been translated into fifteen languages and are also published to great acclaim in the United States. Ruth Rendell is married and lives in a sixteenth-century farmhouse in Suffolk.

WILLIAM TREVOR was born in Mitchelstown, Co. Cork in 1928 and spent his childhood in provincial Ireland. He attended a number of Irish schools and later Trinity College, Dublin. He is a member of the Irish Academy of Letters. Among his books are *The Old Boys* (1964; Hawthornden Prize); *The Ballroom of Romance* (1972); *Angels at the Ritz* (1975; The Royal Society of Literature Award); *The Children of Dynmouth* (1976; Whitbread Award); *Lovers of their Time* (1978); *Fools of Fortune* (1983; Whitbread Award); *The News from Ireland* (1986). In 1976 William Trevor received the Allied

Irish Bank's Prize and in 1977 was awarded the CBE. He is married and has two sons.

FRANK TUOHY was born in 1925, educated at Stowe School and Cambridge. He has worked abroad for many years and is at present living in Japan. He has written three novels, three collections of short stories and a biography of W. B. Yeats. His novel *The Ice Saints* won the James Tait Black Memorial Prize and the Geoffrey Faber Memorial Prize. His collection of stories *Live Bait* won the William Heinemann Award.

Stories: *The Collected Stories* (1983).
Novels: *The Animal Game* (1957); *The Warm Nights of January* (1960); *The Ice Saints* (1964).
All published by Macmillan.

DAI VAUGHAN has worked since 1963 as a documentary film editor, most recently on the series *Diary of a Masai Village* (BBC 2) and *About Time* (Channel 4).

Short stories have appeared in various periodicals and collections, including *Bananas*, *Iron*, *Stand*, *London Magazine*, *Panurge* and *Firebird 2* (Penguin).
Essays on film have appeared in *Sight and Sound*, *Screen* and elsewhere.
Critical monograph: *Television Documentary Usage* (BFI, 1976).
Biography: *Portrait of an Invisible Man: the working life of Stewart McAllister, film editor* (BFI, 1983).

FAY WELDON was born in England and taken as a small baby by her parents to New Zealand where she spent her childhood. Her father was a doctor, her mother came from a family of writers. After their divorce she returned with her mother to Britain and did her BA at St Andrew's University. In her twenties she went through a series of 'odd jobs and hard times' before going into advertising and thereafter becoming a professional writer. She is married and lives in Somerset with the two youngest of her four sons. She has written extensively for film and television, as well as having had ten novels published. Novels include *Praxis* (1989); *Puffball* (1980); *The Life and Loves of a She-Devil* (shortlisted for the Booker Prize in 1983); and *The Shrapnel Academy* earlier this year.

Acknowledgements

'Answers to a Questionnaire', copyright © J. G. Ballard 1985, was first published in *Ambit* 100 and is reproduced by permission of the author care of Margaret Hanbury, 27 Walcot Square, London SE11 4UB

'The Last Island Boy', copyright © George Mackay Brown 1985, was first published in the *Scotsman* 24 December 1985 and is reprinted by permission of the author

'Dealing in Fictions', copyright © Christopher Burns 1985, was first published in the *London Magazine* August/September 1985 and is reprinted by permission of the author

'A Present for Christmas', copyright © Barbara Cartland 1985, was first published in *Punch* 23 October 1985 and is reprinted by permission of the author care of Rupert Crew Ltd, King's Mews, London WC1N 2JA

'The Assassination of Indira Gandhi', copyright © Upamanyu Chatterjee 1985, was first published in the *London Magazine* June 1985 and is reprinted by permission of the author

'Fulfilment', copyright © Éilís Ní Dhuibhne 1985, was first published in *Panurge* Summer 1985 and is reprinted by permission of the author care of Curtis Brown, 162–168 Regent Street, London W1R 5TB

'Needlework', copyright © Douglas Dunn 1985, was first published in the *New Yorker* 19 August 1985 and is reprinted by permission of the author care of A. D. Peters & Co Ltd, 10 Buckingham Street, London WC2N 6BU

'Primavera', copyright © Marian Eldridge 1985, was first published in *Southerly* (Australia) 1/1985 and is reprinted by permission of the author

'Away in a Niche', copyright © Alice Thomas Ellis 1985, was first published in the *Spectator* 21/28 December 1985 and is reprinted by permission of the author care of Duckworth, The Old Piano Factory, 43 Gloucester Crescent, London NW1 7DY

'Martyrs', copyright © Desmond Hogan 1985, was first published in the *Irish Times* 7 August 1985 and is reprinted by permission of the author care of Deborah Rogers Ltd, 49 Blenheim Crescent, London W11 2EF

ACKNOWLEDGEMENTS

'Carnation Butterfly', copyright © Christopher Hope 1985, was first published in the *London Magazine* April/May 1985 and is reprinted by permission of the author

'Credit', copyright © Francis King 1985, was first published in the *Listener* 1 August 1985 and is reprinted by permission of the author care of A. M. Heath, 40–42 William IV Street, London WC2N 4DD

'Smile', copyright © Deborah Moggach 1985, was first published in *Cosmopolitan* January 1985 and is reprinted by permission of the author care of Curtis Brown, 162–168 Regent Street, London W1R 5TB

'Master of Ceremonies', copyright © John Murray 1985, was first published in *Stand* Autumn 1985 and is reprinted by permission of the author care of Curtis Brown, 162–168 Regent Street, London W1R 5TB

'Cruising at Fifty', copyright © Philip Oakes 1985, was first published in *Woman's Own* 20 July 1985 and is reprinted by permission of the author care of Elaine Greene Ltd, 31 Newington Green, London N16 9PU

'Fen Hall', copyright © Ruth Rendell 1985, was first published in *Good Housekeeping* October 1985 and is reprinted by permission of the author care of A. D. Peters & Co Ltd, 10 Buckingham Street, London WC2N 6BU

'Cocktails at Doney's', copyright © William Trevor 1985, was first published in the *New Yorker* 8 April 1985 and is reprinted by permission of the author care of A. D. Peters & Co Ltd, 10 Buckingham Street, London WC2N 6BU

'Retired People', copyright © Frank Tuohy, was first published in the *London Magazine* November 1985, and is reprinted by permission of the author care of A. D. Peters & Co Ltd, 10 Buckingham Street, London WC2N 6BU

'Cottage Rubbings', copyright © Dai Vaughan 1985, was first published in *Stand* Summer 1985 and is reprinted by permission of the author

'The Bottom Line and The Sharp End', copyright © Fay Weldon 1985, was published in *Cosmopolitan* January 1985 and is reprinted by permission of the author care of Anthony Sheil Associates Ltd, 43 Doughty Street, London WC1N 2LF

The editors are grateful to the editors of the publications in which the stories first appeared for permission to reproduce them in this compilation.